T0096759

Family
Inheritance

by

Terri Ann Leidich

BQB

Alpharetta, Georgia

Family Inheritance
© 2014 Terri Ann Leidich. All rights reserved.

No part of this book may be reproduced in any form or by any means, electronic, mechanical, digital, photocopying, or recording, except for the inclusion in a review, without permission in writing from the publisher.

This is a work of fiction. All of the characters, names, incidents, organizations, and dialogue in this novel are either the products of the author's imagination or are used fictitiously.

Published in the United States by BQB Publishing
(Boutique of Quality Books Publishing Company)
www.bqbpublishing.com

Printed in the United States of America

978-1-939371-46-1 (h)
978-1-939371-38-6 (p)
978-1-939371-39-3 (e)

Library of Congress Control Number: 2014936930

Book design by Robin Krauss, www.bookformatters.com
Cover design by David Grauel, davegrauel.com

To
my husband Glenn,
who supports my dreams,
and
my daughter Lori,
who is my biggest fan.

Other Books by Terri Ann Leidich

From a Grieving Mother's Heart

For a Grieving Heart

Chapter 1

Northern Minnesota

July 6, 1990

The old farmhouse creaked in the night air, and the wind howled through the badly caulked windows. Nausea, shortness of breath, and stomach pain were assaulting Anna Teresa Miller's body as she lay in her bed in the darkened bedroom. She figured she was dying, but she didn't care. Her life had never been very good, so how could death be worse? The doctor had warned her that diabetes could kill her, that it would attack her kidneys and her other vital organs, but what did it matter?

As her mind fought to stay alert, thoughts rambled in and out, scrambled together, leaving her unsure of what was happening and what was just a memory. In one moment, she was three years old standing beside her mother in the ramshackle barn where cows were herded in each night and milked. Anna's stomach rumbled and hunger pains gripped her thin body, but she knew she wouldn't get supper until all the chores were done. Even at her young age, she had chores.

Suddenly, she was fourteen and her mother had dropped her off at Walter's family's farm to work for them. Her father had died, and her mother could no longer care for her.

As the memories floated in and out, she fought to remember where she was now and what year it was. For a brief moment, she knew it was 1990 and she was still in the farmhouse she had moved to as a teenager.

Then she was sixteen, pregnant, and being forced to marry Walter, a reluctant groom at best.

Her mind relived the pain of losing that baby and three more after that. She was certain then that she wasn't supposed to be a mother and had convinced herself that she didn't want to be.

By that time, the farm could no longer support them, so Walter would pick up odd jobs, leaving most of the farm chores to her. Life with Walter had been hard—oppressive poverty, backbreaking work, and abuse. Then Helene, Alice, and Suzanne had been born, adding to her workload and escalating Walter's laziness, drinking, and anger—at her, at life, at the kids, and at the fact that he'd never had a son.

When she'd first become pregnant, Walter's mother, who sometimes tried to be good to Anna, told her that having children meant she wouldn't be lonely when she grew old. Now, as she lay dying alone in the creaking house that had been her prison and her home for over forty-five years, a cynical chuckle passed through her lips and a tear slid down her cheek.

Her mind once again slipped into the past to a day when her daughters, with their dirty faces, tangled hair, and soiled clothing, sat on the rough wooden floor, cutting out pictures from old magazines and catalogs as slight drafts of wind shivered through the poorly insulated walls and ruffled the pages. Chatter occasionally erupted in an otherwise silent and serious atmosphere.

"I'm going to marry a rich man and live in a big, beautiful house," ten-year-old Helene had exclaimed as she carefully arranged the figures of a handsome man and a beautiful woman among pictures of luxurious homes.

"I'm going to have lots of kids and be a really good mom," Alice proclaimed with the determination of an eight-year-old.

Seven-year-old Suzanne's voice was serious as she declared, "I'm going to work in a big office and be the boss of people."

That day, Anna had felt anger, fatigue, and defeat at her girls' wild imaginations and their ideas that life could be better. Anna knew it wouldn't be.

Overwhelmed by the constant work that the farm, the old house, her three girls, and Walter required of her, Anna's life had no room for dreams or play.

That particular day, and many before and after, Anna had felt as though the world rested on her shoulders. She had often been bitter that nobody seemed to know how hard she worked or what a burden the old house and those three girls were on her. It certainly wasn't the life she had wanted, but her mother had reminded her often enough by saying, "You made your bed, you lie in it." So Anna had done just that.

Anna's eyelids fluttered, and a shiver ran through her body as the same memory took hold again. A noise had erupted in the kitchen when the back door slammed open against the wall. Fear crossed the faces of her young daughters as a drunken voice bellowed, "Where are you, Anna? I'm hungry. Get in here and fix me something to eat!" The sound of a fist pounding against the kitchen table resonated into the living room as Anna scurried toward the raging man who now stood in the kitchen doorway, swaying unsteadily on his feet.

The memories stopped running through her mind like old motion pictures, and everything was starting to go dark. It had done that several times during the night. Her conscious mind knew she should call an ambulance, but she wasn't ready yet. Maybe she would just die in bed because it didn't really matter to her where she died. She was tired of living.

Anna's kids didn't know about her health problems because Helene had stopped talking to her years ago, and Suzanne had just slipped out of her life. Alice tried, but Anna didn't know how to talk to her middle daughter. In fact, she never did know how to talk to any of them. She had tried to raise them better than her mother had raised her, but her kids hadn't responded the way she had expected them to.

Walter had been a mean, abusive man his entire life, and Anna knew she had never loved him. For much of his life, she hadn't even liked him. Yet, when he died, she missed his presence. He was all she had ever known.

As darkness covered her eyes, momentary panic overwhelmed her because the shadows were so thick. *Is this what it will be like forever?*

"No, Anna, there is light waiting for you, but you're not done yet," a voice whispered in the darkness.

Quickly opening her eyes, she scanned the room. At the end of her bed, she saw a shadow. "Who's there?" Her weak voice tried to reach the specter.

A cold breeze echoed throughout the dusty, dingy room. The figure became clearer as Anna grappled with her fading consciousness. *It's a man, an old man, gray and unshaven.* It took a moment, but her weary mind grasped a vision of her husband looking like that just before his death. Scared at the thought of seeing him again, her voice quivered into the empty room, "Walter? Is that you, Walter?"

The apparition inched closer. Anna's hands shook as she grappled to pull the sheet up over her face. "No, please, Walter. Go away," she pleaded. "Don't hurt me. Please don't hurt me anymore."

The specter seemed to stop moving, hovering there, and the voice became a whisper. "I can't hurt you anymore, Anna." Anna slowly pulled the sheet down and watched with wide, fearful eyes as darkness surrounded the vision; it began to fade. Pain-filled words echoed, "Don't come yet. I don't want you to suffer this pain. Set your life right, Anna."

"I don't understand," she whimpered.

The voice grew louder. "I didn't do right by you, Anna. We didn't do right by them. You have to do right by them. You can't come yet, Anna. You can't come yet." The words were so tortured that Anna quickly pulled the covers up over herself again, cowering lower in the bed, shivering with fear.

The sounds were farther away now, echoes in the quiet room. "Set your life straight, Anna. Do right by them . . . do right by them." The voice faded, and Anna could feel in the air that the ghost had disappeared.

The room was eerily quiet except for her own labored breathing. "I don't know what you mean. I don't understand . . ." she cried.

Memories of her life and her daughters once again floated through the darkness like a movie—visions of her children as babies, then toddlers, teenagers, and then young women. Tears slid down her cheeks as she called their names into the empty room.

With her last bit of consciousness, she reached for the pad and pen on the bedside table that had three telephone numbers neatly printed on it, and scribbled a message. Picking up the bedside phone and summoning the last of her strength, she dialed 911. After mumbling her address into the receiver, Anna closed her eyes and the world went black.

Chapter 2

Atlanta, Georgia

A beautiful April morning peeked in through the windows as Helene sat on the king-sized four-poster bed. Picking at the decorative pillow she held in her lap, she watched Bill's reflection in the mirror in the adjoining bathroom. She could smell the lemon scent of his shaving cream as he maneuvered the razor over his face. She gazed in fascination as he guided the sharp edge over his chin and down his cheek. She pulled at the embroidery of a brightly colored flower as he made stroke after careful stroke with confidence. Mesmerized, Helene watched in silent fury, yet part of her was still drawn in, even after twenty years of marriage, by the man's self-assurance.

Caught up with the reflection of his handsome face, almost-black hair, and blue eyes, she refused to deal with the reality of her life because it was much easier to keep pretending that things were different. Helene's voice stuck in her throat. There were so many questions she wanted to ask. *Why do you cheat and lie? Who is she this time? Why do I put up with it?* Even with those questions blasting in her mind, she took a deep breath and spoke in even tones that belied the tension building at her temples. "Will you be home for dinner?"

Bill didn't glance in her direction as the lies flowed smoothly through his lips. "No, I've got to work late on a case that's going to court next week. I'll probably work most of the night."

Helene furiously grabbed the tassel on the corner of the pillow. *How did you get so good at lying?* As she listened to his words, she remembered the smell of the familiar perfume that had assaulted her nose, and the ever-so-light smudge of red lipstick on the collar of his shirt that she had taken to the cleaners yesterday. Her heart pinched in agony as the man at the cleaners smiled and winked at her, teasing her that she might want to change the color of her lipstick—red, he had said, was hard to remove.

Bill moved away from the mirror and continued talking about his heavy workload. Helene's demeanor didn't change as she quietly maimed the pillow with her pulls and tugs. *Shut up, Bill, shut up,* she wanted to scream. *Don't you know I've known about all of them throughout the years? I've given them names. Can you beat that? I name your mistresses!* The turmoil inside of her was at a full boil today, but she held it in tightly, not letting it erupt or even seep through her calm exterior. A divorce would be much more traumatic and expensive than replacing decorative pillows.

She gazed at Bill through the mirror and said, "I'll leave you something to eat in the fridge." He walked out of the bathroom, straightening his shirt. Her hands clenched firmly around the small pillow in front of her as she pasted a smile on her face. She raised her lips to accept his quick kiss.

Helene sat motionless for several moments after he left the room while the scent of his cologne gently lingered. In the quiet bedroom, her hands finally stopped their assault on the defenseless pillow as she willfully silenced her tormented mind.

After showering and preparing for her day, Helene stood in front of the mahogany dresser, leaning close to the mirror, and examined her appearance. Her large, blue eyes stared back at her, and she frowned at the wrinkles decorating her face. Her blonde, shoulder-length hair accented her fair skin. Her white blouse and shorts shone bright in the morning light. Anyone else peering at Helene through that mirror would see an attractive woman of forty-two, but Helene saw none of those things. Disgusted, she pinched less than an inch of flab around her middle.

The wedding picture on the edge of the bureau caught her eye, and Helene was drawn to the happiness in the faces of the young couple staring back at her. Gingerly, she picked up the photograph in its crystal frame, held it close against her heart, walked back to the bed, and sat down as her memory took her back over two decades.

Helene had hated her childhood—the poverty, the abuse, the cruelness of the kids in school making fun of the way she dressed, the way her family lived, and her father's constant drunkenness. The minute Helene graduated from high school she'd left the farm and eventually Minnesota, and she never looked back. She had known that college was out of the question, but that limitation hadn't stopped her dreams and her determination to live a life without poverty and fear. With the help of one of her teachers, she had applied for a job behind the ticket counter with a major airline at the Minneapolis-St. Paul airport, and to her amazement, she had been hired.

The day after graduation, Helene had loaded the few possessions she owned into the backseat of a classmate's 1966 white Ford Mustang. With her sights set on the future, Helene refused to turn around to look at her sisters standing on the gravel driveway waving and crying. Helene knew her mother and father weren't watching her drive away—they couldn't care less—and she had shared the same sentiment.

Learning had come easily for Helene in her job with the airline, and so had interacting with people. She liked watching them, imagining what their lives were like, and where they were going. As she booked tickets for destinations all over the world, she dreamed of moving someplace warm, someplace far away from the state that held few good memories for her. After a year with the airline, Helene had learned about a position at the airport in Atlanta, Georgia. Immediately, she had known she wanted to move there.

When news of her transfer came through, she felt as though she was living a dream, and the move to Georgia happened quickly and easily.

Helene had immediately fallen in love with Georgia and felt that she was a Georgian by choice instead of birth. Life was simple but good as Helene planned her future. She'd often think back to the catalog pages of her youth and the world her imagination had designed—a world filled with love and beautiful surroundings. Even in the midst of a childhood filled with pain and lack, she knew a better life was possible, and her determination to have that life kept her on the path to that destination. In the beginning, her apartment was bare, but she window-shopped and planned exactly what she wanted it to look like, and week by week, she was making that dream come true.

Helene hadn't dated much in high school. She kept to herself and people seemed to know not to cross the invisible but solid wall she had erected around her. When she moved to Georgia, her heart expanded and she was more open to the world and experiences, and men started asking her out. But she refused the majority of offers. Even though she was far away from home and lived on her own, it hadn't changed her mind about relationships or marriage. She would never let herself end up like her mother, so marriage was the furthest thing from her mind. Until she met Bill Foster.

It had been an ordinary day at the ticket counter, with lines of travelers going all over the world. She'd just finished checking in an elderly woman, who was flying to California to see her grandchildren, and placed the suitcases on the conveyer belt behind her. When she stepped back to help the next person in line, she was met with the bluest eyes she had ever seen. Helene had never believed in love at first sight until that moment. It had been hard to breathe and concentrate as she helped Bill with his ticket to Boston, told him his departure gate, and put his suitcase onto the conveyor belt.

Helene assumed she would never see him again, but when she went on her break fifteen minutes later, Bill was waiting for her. She walked with him to his departure gate, and they talked non-stop, as though they had so much to say and not much time to say it. She learned that he was twenty-six and in his last year of law school. When he graduated, he would join his father's firm in downtown Atlanta. His family roots were firmly planted in Georgia. He'd told her that she was the most beautiful woman he had ever seen. He took her phone number, called her every evening while he was in Boston, and they went on their first date when he returned. Helene had fallen deeply in love.

She had been so nervous the first time she met Bill's parents because they lived a totally different lifestyle than the one she had grown up in. They were both professionals, lived in a nice house, drove nice cars, and belonged to a country club. While they were not demonstrative people, they had made her feel welcome and a part of their family.

One year later, she and Bill had married in a big church, and it had been the wedding of her dreams. Bill's family paid for everything she could possibly imagine, both in her wedding and in her life. She didn't send her family an invitation or even let them know she was getting married. When Bill and his mother asked questions about them, she simply said she wasn't close to her family, and they hadn't pressed her on the subject.

After their honeymoon in Cancun, Mexico, Helene left her job at the airport and spent her days and years creating a beautiful home and what she thought was a happy relationship. When she became pregnant in their first year of marriage, Helene wasn't sure how she felt about it. Children had never really been a part of the world she had wanted to create, but the moment she had held Thomas in her arms, Helene once more fell deeply in love.

In the beginning, Bill had doted on Thomas and been a loving, attentive husband. But when Thomas was a toddler, Bill stayed away from home more and more often, blaming it on a heavy workload. Then she'd found the lipstick on his shirt. The first time she told herself there was a reason. But when she could no longer ignore the signs of infidelity, she had dropped to her knees and sobbed. From that point on, Thomas had become her world, and she accepted the fact that her relationship wasn't perfect, but Bill and Thomas were all she had.

Her mind coming back to the present, she put the picture back on the dresser and quickly glanced at herself in the mirror again. Then she left the bedroom and walked down the back stairs that led to the large kitchen, with its marble countertops and hanging racks of copper pots and pans. She smiled as she heard the oldies station playing, "Shake, Rattle, and Roll."

Soft laughter spilled from her lips as she stopped at the bottom of the stairs to watch Lily, her housekeeper and cook, shake her hips, dance to the music, and sing along to the song. Lily was a contradiction in motion in her freshly ironed flower-printed dress, her golden-brown skin glowing, and neat braids of hair wrapped around the back of her head.

When Lily spotted Helene, she danced over to her, grabbed her hand, and twirled her around. Helene tried to pull her hand away and resist the playfulness, but soon Lily had her dancing. When the song ended, Lily patted her hair and said with a smile, "You're just in time for a cup a tea and a fresh muffin."

Laughing, Helene sat down at the cheery, little breakfast nook in the large kitchen. Lily was the closest Helene had ever come to having a loving, caring mother. She often gladly relaxed into the security of Lily's love.

Over the steaming cup of tea, Lily eyed Helene carefully as she stated, "I'm making Mr. Bill's favorite chicken for dinner tonight. Thought maybe just the two of you could have a nice, quiet dinner, and Mr. Thomas and I could rent a movie. Haven't sat down and talked with that young one in a while—seems to always be off doing something or going somewhere." Lily paused for a moment. "Thought a rest would do him good. And you and Mr. Bill need more quiet time."

"Nice thought, but Bill's working late again. Thomas should be home for dinner, though."

Just as Helene was ready to bite into her muffin, the phone rang and Lily answered it. She listened for a few seconds, then handed the phone to Helene. "It's Mr. Thomas's school. They want to talk about Thomas's excessive absences."

A lump darted into Helene's throat. *What excessive absences? He goes to school every day.*

"This is Mrs. Foster."

"Hello, Mrs. Foster, this is Vivian Middleton from Thomas's school. We're very concerned about Thomas missing so much school. He has brought in all of his absence slips signed by you, but we wanted to make sure it was you who signed them."

Helene's thoughts were spinning. *What is she talking about? What absences? What permission slips?*

"Mrs. Foster?"

"Oh, yes . . . I signed them. He seems to be catching every bug this season." *I just lied. Why am I lying for my son?* Yet, she knew why. Something had to be wrong and she wasn't about to make it worse.

"Well, as long as you know about the absences."

"Yes, I do. Everything is fine," Helene assured her. "He's in school today, isn't he?" She closed her eyes, waiting for the answer.

"Yes, he is, Mrs. Foster, but we're very concerned about his grades. Thomas's numerous absences have put him behind. Something needs to be done."

Helene's thoughts were trying to catch up with what she was hearing. How much school had Thomas missed and why didn't she know he was missing school? Thomas had always loved school and had been a good student. *What's happening with my son? And why didn't I know about it?*

"Let me talk with Thomas when he gets home today. We'll come up with a plan and I'll get back to you."

"Thank you, Mrs. Foster."

After Helene hung up the phone, she slumped against the wall, worry and concern flooding her mind. She thought of calling Bill, but he'd probably just get angry at Thomas, and she didn't want to deal with that. She could talk with Thomas, but would he tell her the truth? And when had he started lying to her? Something was wrong, and she had to find out what it was.

She spent most of the day curled up on her bed or sitting quietly in the sunroom, barely responding to Lily's attempts at conversation. Memories of Thomas as a little boy kept dancing through her mind. They had been so close. He had excelled in school, and their times together had been playful and fun. When had it all changed? What had gone wrong? When in the world had he started skipping school? And why? As much as she tried to deny the fact that her son's behavior was far from normal and acceptable, she knew better.

As afternoon turned to evening, Helene walked into the kitchen where Lily was making a cake. Thomas wasn't home yet. At five-thirty, she called Thomas's best friend Chuck to see if Thomas had stopped by after school but Chuck hadn't seen Thomas since their last class together, which was just after lunch.

"What if something has happened?" she asked Lily. "What if he's been in a car accident, and he's lying somewhere breathing his last breath and calling for his mother? What if—"

"Now whoa there," Lily interrupted. "Don't you think you're going a little fast in your worrying? Yes'm, all those things do happen in this world of ours, and we gotta be aware of them, but not everything that happens is bad."

At seven o'clock, without saying a word, Lily set two places at the counter that separated the large kitchen from the adjoining family area with its leather sofas and big stone fireplace. She filled the plates and motioned for Helene to sit down on one of the comfortable bar stools that edged up to the counter where they often had tea or shared a snack in the middle of the day. Helene reluctantly sat down, picked up the fork, and began to nibble at her food.

Lily pulled out the stool next to her, sat down, and placed her hand over

Helene's with a look that told Helene how much Lily cared about her, Bill, and Thomas. "It will be fine."

"I've got to make it fine, Lily. I just have to!"

It wasn't until after sunset that a car pulled into the driveway. Lights flashed across the kitchen windows and disappeared into the garage. They both seemed to be holding their breath as footsteps approached the back door and the knob turned.

Thomas entered with a crooked grin on his face. His eyes were bloodshot. "Hi, guys" was all he said as he moved through the kitchen toward the stairs at the back of the house.

"Thomas, are you okay? Where were you? Why are you so late?" The questions flew from Helene's lips as her heart beat wildly in her chest.

"I'm fine, Mom." His walk was unsteady, and his few words were slurred.

"Thomas, wait a minute. I want to talk to you. Your school called today about your being absent a lot and me apparently signing the slips." Helene stood firmly with her right hand on her hip.

"Can we talk about this later, Mom? I've got studying to do." His hand reached out for the wall to steady himself.

A part of Helene's mind noticed his lack of balance, but she ignored it. "Where were you tonight?" her voice sharpened as she slowly walked toward the stairs.

Thomas was halfway up the staircase. He stopped with his back still toward her, clutching the banister to steady himself, but he didn't say a word.

"Thomas, please answer me." Helene's voice was louder now. She stood at the bottom of the staircase, her brow furrowed with worry.

Thomas took a few steps forward, widening the space between them. "I just needed some space," he said without turning to look at her. "Everything's just crowding in on me. You understand, don't you?" His shoulders slumped and his voice softened. "Mom, I thought you'd understand."

Helene's mind refused to acknowledge his slurred speech and the implications of his unsteady gait. Running her fingertips over her forehead, her words were firm as she spoke. "You absolutely can't miss any more school. And you've got to catch up with your homework. This has got to stop. Do you understand me?"

He still hadn't turned to look at her.

"Yes, ma'am." He took another step up the stairway and then paused. "Can I be excused now?"

"No, Thomas, we've got to talk about this." As Helene moved up the stairs, her nose picked up the smell of alcohol, and reality finally marched in. *What in the world?* Fear gripped Helene as long-ago memories of alcohol assaulted her mind, yet she quickly dismissed them because they were a part of another life, another time. Pulling down the blinders of love, Helene once more let denial envelop her in its firm grasp. Feelings of overwhelm cemented her to where she stood. "Just don't miss any more school, okay? Promise me?" she pleaded.

Chapter 3

Northern Minnesota

The houses in the government-subsidized neighborhood were tiny square boxes situated on small square lots, and the streets were overrun with children in varying degrees of dress. Many of them wore soiled clothes that had seen better days. Alice Hudson trudged up the walk to her cracker-box house, seemingly oblivious to her surroundings. She had lived in the development so long that familiarity blurred it into the background of her consciousness.

When she first moved here, Alice had planted flowers, washed her windows, hung pretty, fresh curtains, and even tried to dig up soil for a garden in the backyard. She had been full of hope and dreams back then. Dreams of a happy family and a nice, neat little house with a white picket fence. Now, the windows were dirty, the curtains were gone, the garden had been overtaken by weeds, and her dreams were tiny little specks in the back of her mind. The reality of life had weighed her down into acceptance. She just tried to get through each day, dealing with as little as possible.

Alice huffed, and sweat dripped from her tightly permed hair down her face as she dragged her five-foot-four-inch frame up the few steps to the front door. The elastic band on her XXXL pants squeezed into her stomach as she bent over to place her grocery bags on the stoop, then she leaned against the doorjamb for a moment to catch her breath. Her youngest child, Sam, was out there somewhere in that throng of kids. He would have come home from school an hour or so ago, raced in to grab some Kool-Aid, and then back out to play.

"Boy, it's hot today," she complained to herself as she mopped the back of her neck with her hand. The temperature was sixty degrees, very warm for an April day in northern Minnesota, but with her massive frame, even a pleasant day felt hot to Alice.

Opening the door and stooping once more for the grocery bags, Alice slowly pulled herself inside, and as she scanned her surroundings, exhaustion completely took over her body and soul. The breakfast dishes were still on the counter. The table was cluttered with empty cereal boxes, a loaf of bread, the peanut butter jar, and five empty beer bottles. Alice hadn't felt like cleaning up before going over to Thelma's to have coffee and watch soap operas, and since she had been gone, her husband, Jake, had added his collection of beer bottles to the mess.

She plopped the grocery bags on the counter, moved dirty dishes off to one side with a sweep of her hand, and walked toward the living room to find Jake. Her foot caught on the edge of the curled linoleum as she stepped out of the kitchen and almost fell. She had long ago stopped asking Jake to fix anything in the house, because it just made him mad, and Jake was mean when he was mad. Alice and the kids had learned to pick up their feet so they wouldn't trip on the jagged edge.

As she headed into the small living room, with its outdated and worn furniture, Alice wasn't sure why she pretended to search for Jake. She knew she would find him passed out on the couch in front of the television. He hadn't gone out to try to find a job again today, she was certain of it. He had made excuses about his back hurting for the past two years. Why would today be any different? Besides, the welfare coming in every month kept food on the table, and he always figured out ways to make sure there was money for beer, so why work? Alice had accepted that things would never be different. As her mother often said, "You made your bed, lie in it."

And there he was, sleeping on the couch. She moved as quietly as she could, not wanting to wake him. If he woke up, he would scream about the dirty house and the dishes not being done. He would grab a beer or two, demand dinner, call her fat and lazy, then head out of the house to play poker with the boys. It was better to let sleeping dogs lie.

As Alice walked down the hallway, she kicked a pile of dirty clothes out of her way. The kids were running out of clean clothes to wear. *I'll wash tomorrow.* Slowly, she made her way to her bedroom and closed the door. Then she lay down on the sagging mattress, placed her arm over her eyes, and gave way to the peaceful oblivion of sleep.

It seemed like a matter of minutes before she felt someone pushing on her arm. "Mom . . . are you awake? I'm hungry. You gonna make dinner?" Her eight-year-old son, Sam, was tugging at her elbow. "Dad says to tell ya to get your lazy lard outta bed. He's hungry and wants something to eat before he goes to play poker."

Alice groaned and slowly pulled herself awake. Her dream was so nice. She had been thin, lived in a clean house, her children resembled the ones in the magazines, and her husband . . . oh, her husband . . . he was clean and smelled like Dial soap. But best of all, he treated her special. The dream had been so warm and comforting that it was hard to come back to reality. Alice didn't want reality. She wanted them all to leave her alone.

"Mom, come on. Dad's getting mad, and I'm hungry." Sam's hands were now gently pushing on her shoulder as his voice rose.

Alice's eyes came fully open. She gazed at Sam, with his red scraggly hair and freckled face. He was the oddball of the family. When Sam was born, Jake had been sure that he wasn't his. In fact, he had really raised a scene at the hospital, refusing to talk to her for two days and calling her a slut and a pig. Then his mother had come to see the baby and told Jake that his grandfather had been born with red hair. Jake had calmed down, but he had never apologized. Jake didn't apologize. He didn't seem to think he ever did anything to apologize for.

Sluggishly sitting up, Alice ran her stubby fingers through her hair, tugged at her wrinkled shirt, and straightened the elastic waist on her polyester slacks. She felt disgruntled and dirty, disgusted with life, and madder than hell. She was not sure why she felt so mad. Maybe it was because they had interrupted her dream, her only chance at peace and happiness.

"Mom, for heaven's sake," her daughter, Sarah, screamed from the kitchen, "you left the groceries on the counter, and the ice cream melted onto the floor. Now guess who gets to clean up that mess! This whole place disgusts me!"

"Sarah, quit your bellyaching," Jake bellowed from the living room. "Your lazy slob of a mother can barely drag her carcass around. Just clean up the mess, and somebody make me my damn dinner so I can get the hell out of here."

Tears flooded Alice's eyes, and her shoulders slumped. "Mom, are you crying?" Sam peered up at her as they walked toward the kitchen. A lump formed in Alice's throat. She placed her hand on his shoulder and gave him a small hug.

"Damn it, Alice," Jake bellowed as she walked into the kitchen. "You look like something that just walked out of a garbage dump. Don't you ever comb your hair?"

Alice glared at him. *Look who's talking, you unshaven jerk. Why should I clean up when you're such a filthy pig? Why should I take care of myself when nobody ever takes care of me?*

Quietly going to the cupboard, Alice pulled out three packages of macaroni and cheese. She started cooking the macaroni, sliced in some frozen hot dogs, and pulled a can of corn off the shelf. Pouring the corn into a pan, she turned to set the table. "Sarah, wash off some silverware, will ya?"

"I've got homework to do." Sarah finished cleaning the melted ice cream off the counter and floor. Throwing the rag in the sink, she muttered, "Do it yourself." Then she stalked out of the room.

With a quiet sigh, Alice washed the silverware. This was not the life she had dreamed of when she was a girl. She had always believed that growing up held some magic to it and that somehow she would have a different life than her mother had. Now she knew how wrong she was. Her life was just like her mother's. As she scrubbed the dried food from the silverware and watched the crumbs slip into the drain, she sent the last of her childhood dreams right along with them.

When the timer went off for the macaroni, Alice mixed milk, margarine, and cheese into the hot, drained pasta and stirred it around. Then she set the pot with the macaroni on the table next to the pan with the cooked corn, tossed a spoon into each, and yelled, "Supper's ready."

Everyone rushed into the kitchen. Jake flopped himself into his chair, the spot he deemed for the "head of the household." Sam and Sarah slumped into their customary spots, and Alice heaved herself into her chair. Jake scooped the macaroni onto his plate, slopped a spoon of corn down next to it, and started shoveling the meal into his mouth.

They ate their meal in silence, except for Sam, who chatted excitedly. "We played this neat game after school today. Teddy's dad showed us. You kick this ball around, but it's not a kickball. Teddy said the game is called soccer!" He took a sip of water, then continued. "I got an A on a test today. And it was a 'specially hard test too. Mrs. Williams gave me two stars on it, and they were red stars. That means I did real good."

No one responded to Sam. Instead, Jake regarded the food on Alice's plate. She had taken very little. "Thank God you're cutting down. You look like an overgrown hippo. It's about time you did something about that bulk you carry around."

Sam lowered his head and finished eating without saying another word. Alice silently nibbled at her food. The glare in Jake's eyes was intense, and out of the corner of her eye Alice noticed Sarah carefully watching the interaction between her parents, her eyes shooting angry darts at Alice. Sadness encompassed Alice as she felt her husband's anger and her daughter's hatred. *Why do they both hate me? What have I done? Am I that awful that my own husband and daughter find me disgusting?* A headache grew at her temples.

When dinner was over, the house was quiet. Jake had gone to play poker, Sarah was at Karen's, and Sam was outside playing. Cloaked in sadness and despair, Alice moved slowly down the hallway toward her bedroom. The small, crowded room had a sagging double bed and two dressers that were chipped and badly in need of paint. Clothes were scattered on the floor all around the room and piled onto every available surface. Alice didn't even notice her surroundings as she closed the door, locking it behind her.

In a daze, she stepped into the small walk-in closet, pushed through clothes that were hanging on both sides until she came to a pile of old clothes in the back corner. She pawed through the pile much like a dog digging in the ground searching for whatever might be buried underneath. At the bottom, she found what she was foraging for—a box of chocolate candy bars. Twelve delicious chocolate nut bars that she had bought just days earlier. She'd hidden them away for when she needed them. Tonight, she did.

Alice sat down on the bed with the precious box on her lap. She carefully unwrapped a bar of chocolate, then lifted it to her mouth and shoved it in. Her movements became jerky and sporadic, and her eyes glazed as she ate one candy bar after another.

She was a woman possessed.

Her mind didn't seem to be present as she stuffed the chocolate into her mouth, barely having room to chew the first one before another bar followed. All too soon, the twelve bars were gone, and Alice lay back on the bed. Calmness invaded her. As she settled back to enjoy her sugar high, she sighed, grateful that she didn't have to think about her pain or deal with Jake, Sarah, or Sam. The chocolate took care of that.

Except, her euphoria didn't last long. Ten minutes later, Alice was disgusted with herself. She surveyed the wreckage from the candy bars. Wrappers were strewn everywhere, and chocolate smudges decorated her fingers. She tried to wipe the chocolate smears off her hands, but the more she rubbed them, the bigger the mess became. She stopped and sat silently on the bed. The headache she always experienced after her binges was starting at the nape of her neck. Somehow it was disturbingly comforting.

Alice grabbed a piece of dirty clothing from the floor and angrily wiped at the chocolate smudges. An internal struggle was beginning to build inside of her. The part that needed comforting railed against the part that knew she was ultimately hurting herself. Alice felt caught in the middle of the battle that was raging between her mind and her desperate need for nurturing.

Feeling exhausted, she lay back on the sagging mattress. Gathering a bulge of stomach fat between her hands, she whispered into the empty room, "I won't do this again. I'm going to start losing weight. I'm going to start cleaning my house, and I'm going to be a better mother. I am. I swear I am."

With purpose, Alice climbed out of bed and cleaned up the mess from the candy bars. As she headed into the kitchen to make good on her promise to herself, the phone rang. She huffed as she answered.

"That you, Alice?"

"Yes, Mom, it's me." Her mother always asked the same question each time she called. *Who the heck else is gonna answer my phone, Queen Elizabeth?* Alice thought as she lowered herself in the chair near the phone.

"I'm feeling poorly today, Alice."

Alice closed her eyes and leaned her head back against the wall. *This will be another long call. Mom is in one of her whining moods again.* Knowing that her mother expected her to just be quiet and listen, Alice sunk into the reality of her life, acquiescing to the silent demand.

When Alice didn't say anything, her mother continued. "Well, did you hear what I said? Doesn't anybody care how I am? I could die right up here in this old farmhouse, and you wouldn't care at all." She let out a long, purposeful sigh. "A woman raises three daughters, and then they all go off to leave her to be lonely and die alone. Some gratitude after all I did for all of you. And you're the worst. Seems you could come out and see me more than once a week."

As the voice droned on and on, Alice sunk farther into the chair, rolled her eyes, and closed off her mind. She knew she didn't have to really listen because it was the same old words she had been hearing for years now. She could probably recite them before Mom even spoke them.

Several minutes passed before her mother ran out of anything to say and returned to her original statement. "I'm feeling poorly today. Chest seems to be aching some. I'm gonna die, you know that? I'm gonna die, and I'll probably be alone in this old farmhouse when I do."

"You're just tired. You'll be okay. Why don't you get some rest? I'll come to see you tomorrow, I promise."

"You sure?"

"I'm sure." Alice sighed. "I'm tired now, Mom. I'll talk to you tomorrow." As Alice hung up the phone feeling exhausted from listening to her mother, she scanned the dirty kitchen, then slowly walked back to the bedroom, locked the door, and headed to yet another well-hidden stash of chocolate.

The streetlight shining through the window cast shadows on the ceiling in Alice's bedroom. After lying awake for hours, her eyes were accustomed to the semi-darkness. She hadn't been able to sleep tonight. Everything in her life was in chaos. Even her children were out of control. One of the neighbors had accused Sam of stealing money from her pocketbook. Sarah hadn't come in until after midnight, and it was a school night.

Alice felt scared and helpless. The candy bars helped her feel better, but it never lasted long. Plus, she was getting worried about her headaches and the blurriness in her eyes. Yet, without her chocolate she didn't think she could put up with Jake, the kids, and the house. Especially Jake.

A sob started in her belly as her mind wandered to the large bottle of aspirin in the bathroom and what it would feel like to peacefully sleep forever. Then the front door opened, and Alice heard Jake drunkenly stagger through the house. She glanced at the clock. It was three a.m.

Bile churned in her stomach, and a lump lodged in her throat. Her fear-filled eyes glared into the darkened room as she heard him bump into something, swear, then kick whatever he'd bumped out of the way. Alice quickly turned on her side, away from the door, and scooted down lower in the bed, trying to become invisible. She didn't want to face him. She didn't want to deal with him. If she pretended to be asleep, maybe, just maybe, he'd leave her alone tonight. Sometimes he did if he thought she was sleeping. Maybe tonight she would be lucky.

She listened as he made his way down the hall. He stopped briefly, twisted a doorknob, slapped his hand hard on a door, swore, and continued his stumbling toward their bedroom. *Did he try the closet door again? Is he so drunk he doesn't know where his own bedroom is?* Her breath seemed to stick into her throat as Jake staggered into the room.

Even from a distance, Alice could smell alcohol and could tell from the sound of his movements that he was worse off than usual. Her fingers curled tightly around her pillow, pulling it closer to her, trying to shield herself from what she knew was coming. Tonight he sounded like an angry drunk. There were times when he came home a happy drunk, and he was *almost* kind to her. Then there were nights like tonight when he was mean and angry.

She unconsciously curled into a fetal position. A large hand roughly grabbed her shoulder. "Alice! Hey, fatso! Wake up! I've got a hard-on and need your body." Alice cringed. Deep inside, she felt another piece of herself die.

It hurt when he was nasty to her. It hurt when she was just a release for him. She longed for tenderness, for caring. She continued to pretend she was sleeping. She couldn't take this, not tonight. His hand briskly slapped the back of her head and his voice became louder. "Damn it, Alice. I said wake up."

Light blared into her eyes as he flipped on the wall switch. He forcefully turned her toward him. She sensed that he wouldn't give up. She knew it was one of those nights, and she might as well just endure it. *It will soon be over. Please, God, let it soon be over.*

There was no gentleness in Jake tonight, no concern for her or if her body was ready to receive his. He climbed on top of her. When she started to protest that he was hurting her, he slapped her, telling her to shut up. Alice closed her eyes, gritted her teeth in pain as another chunk of her soul was torn from her.

Jake grunted and groaned as he spurted into her, heaving into the air in angry, gasping thrusts. Then he rolled off her and almost instantly slipped into a drunken sleep. Alice lay in the well-lit room feeling bruised and broken. She wondered how many more pieces of her heart and soul she could lose before she would just be a hollow shell.

Chapter 4

Dallas, Texas

Suzanne stood facing the floor-to-ceiling windows that covered one wall of her large office and gazed out at the Dallas skyline. One sigh followed another as she picked at her fingernails, making a mess out of her latest manicure. She hated this part of her job. *Why do I have to discipline?* She exhaled another deep sigh. Why couldn't everyone just do what they were told? *Especially Jeff. Why do I keep listening to his excuses?* She slammed her fist against her leg and quickly plopped into her chair. Why didn't she just fire him?

Leaning toward her intercom, Suzanne buzzed her secretary. "Melanie, send Jeff in now, would you please?" Sitting back in her chair, Suzanne braced herself for the confrontation.

Jeff Davidson casually walked into Suzanne's office, stood for a few minutes and took in the view, then slowly slid into one of the chairs facing her desk. "Now what, Suzanne?" He straightened his tie, sat up a bit taller, and stared directly at her. "Are you worried about my sales figures again? I've told you before that I've got several big sales just on the verge." As he smiled at her, Suzanne felt like she was looking at a cat that was about to pounce on its prey. "I've been working on them for some time. They'll come to fruition any day now."

Suzanne gazed directly into his eyes until the smile began to leave his face, then she leaned forward in her chair and slowly enunciated her every word for impact. "I don't want excuses, Mr. Davidson. I want results. If you can't get them, I'll hire someone who can."

Her eyes were cold and her face, bereft of warmth, could be molded out of steel. "I'll give you six more months, Mr. Davidson. But consider this a probationary period. You get your act together and those sales up, or you're history." Her voice lowered for emphasis and effect. "I've got documentation of all those days you didn't work. Days you thought you got away with. Expenses you thought you covered. Well, you didn't. I've got enough on you to not only boot you out of here, but to make sure you don't land another good job in this company or any other successful company in this industry. You've played around enough, Romeo. Now you're going to get your act together. Do you understand that?"

With anger glistening in his eyes, Jeff sat silently, watching her. For a moment his stillness and the expression in his eyes frightened Suzanne, but she refused to acknowledge it. Turning away from him, she simply said, "That will be all."

After Jeff left her office, Suzanne leaned back in her chair and sucked in a deep breath. She was exhausted from dealing with him. She had wanted to fire him a long time ago, but somehow he always charmed her into giving him another chance. Her body ached as her late nights were starting to tell on her, but she couldn't think about them. She couldn't remember enough of them to think about. *I'm not going to do that again. I'm not. I don't need it. I won't.*

Suzanne had made that pledge to herself many times before but never kept it. During the day was one thing. She could do that. During the day, she had work to occupy her. She had her own little kingdom to control, and control it she did. Everything, including her appearance, was precisely how she wanted it. Her dark brown hair was always pulled back from her face and wrapped in a tight coil at the back of her neck. The severely tailored navy-blue suit and white silk shirt did little to accentuate her figure. She used very little makeup and did little to even acknowledge her femininity. That part of her scared her. She didn't feel safe with it. At least, not when she was sober.

At work, she could focus her mind on other things, but at night, she was plagued by her past and by her father. As she thought about him now, her stomach coiled into a tight knot and sunk deep inside of her. Nausea nearly overcame her, and she quickly pushed her father's face and all the memories connected with him as far away as possible.

"That was pretty tough, wasn't it?"

Startled, Suzanne quickly turned toward the door to see her secretary, Melanie Dawson, standing there. "Yes, but I think I got my point across."

"He's such a worm." Melanie leaned against the doorjamb. "I just don't get it. Why do you put up with him?"

Suzanne shrugged. "I don't know."

"He's not that good, Suzanne." Melanie easily used Suzanne's first name and had for several years as their relationship had built into a friendship as well—at least as much of a friendship as Suzanne would allow herself to have with anyone.

"Maybe I see his potential," Suzanne replied.

"Potential, yes. But all the garbage that's piled on top of it makes it hard to see his potential or to even deal with him," Melanie said.

Suzanne sat back in her chair and studied the pretty, blue-eyed blonde. "Sometimes I think you should be the boss. You're a very smart cookie."

Melanie smiled. "For a dumb blonde." She pulled on one of the many curls that surrounded her face.

"Beauty does not take away from brains or your abilities." Suzanne grabbed the cup of cold coffee on her desk.

"So, why do you hide yours?" Melanie asked.

"What? My abilities?" Suzanne coughed, but she wasn't sure if it was in reaction to the cold coffee or Melanie's comment.

"No, your beauty."

Suzanne squirmed in her chair. "I don't have any. I'm a very plain person. Brains, yes, but that's it."

"Boy, I'd like to know who sold you that bill of goods."

"I know I've got that report that needs to go out today." Suzanne was suddenly all business.

"Stepped on tender ground, did I?" Melanie quietly asked.

"Really tender."

"Okay. But I care."

"I know." Suzanne smiled as Melanie turned to leave.

A male voice sounded from the outer office. "Hi. Anybody home?" Melanie grinned at recognition of the voice as Suzanne began searching her desk for something.

"We're in Suzanne's office, Richard," Melanie called and headed to her office to greet the man.

"Is it break time yet?" A man's head peeked around the door of Suzanne's office. "Have time for a cup of coffee? You've probably been working too hard."

Suzanne's heart beat a little faster. The dark-haired man entered the room. He was about five-ten with a stocky build.

"Sorry, Richard, but I can't get away now. We don't take breaks here. I've told you that. I'm such a slave driver. I keep Melanie anchored to her desk." Suzanne grinned, and the man smiled in return.

Richard casually leaned against the doorframe. "Well, ease up, girl. You work too hard, and Melanie could probably use a break."

The conversation was relaxed and pleasant. Richard would often stop by for small talk and occasionally ask her out for coffee, lunch, or a drink after work. Each time he did, she had an excuse why she couldn't go. He still occasionally asked, and actually, she was really glad he did, but she wasn't ready to accept his invitations. She didn't know if she ever would be, and she knew someday he would just quit asking.

Richard left after a little more light teasing, and Melanie came back into Suzanne's office and sat down. "I don't understand why you don't take him up on it. He's cute, nice, educated, has a great career, and is definitely interested. Besides, all work and no play and all that stuff."

"I've told you before, I just don't have time for dating." Suzanne leaned back in her chair.

"I know you well enough to know that you definitely are not into women, so what is it? Don't you get lonely?" Melanie's tone was light but careful. She seemed to sense she was pushing the boundaries of their relationship. Even though Suzanne considered Melanie a friend, the walls that surrounded Suzanne were very high and very thick. But today for some reason, Melanie pushed just a bit against those barriers, and Suzanne wondered if she could sense her hidden desire for someone to be brave enough to reach in and pull her out of her solitary world.

But she wasn't ready to reach out, even if Melanie was reaching in. Suzanne got busy with something on her desk so she did not have to look Melanie in the eye as the reality of her life settled into her thoughts. *Yes, I'm lonely! Sometimes so lonely that it consumes me with its darkness. But I don't have a choice. I can't get close—not to somebody nice.* Her thoughts created a tightness in her throat and a longing in her belly. She couldn't let anyone into her world. If she did, they'd find out—they'd know. *They'll know who I really am. How disgusting I am.* Panic grabbed at her chest. She had to do something to stop the thoughts, so she reached for the phone and the list of calls she needed to make. Melanie quietly left her office.

Chapter 5

Dallas, Texas

That evening, Suzanne paced the floors of her spacious condo as she ran her hands through her hair. *I'm not going out—not tonight.* She was surrounded by a calming, beautiful environment with soft blue walls, contemporary furniture, and sleek pictures in shades of black, white, and blue, but she didn't see any of it. Her internal demons were so dark and menacing that they often overshadowed the beauty she intentionally created in her rare moments of serenity.

Yes, I'm going out, damn it. She couldn't stand it. The walls were closing in, and she needed to get out, even her nightly drinks of scotch weren't helping keep away her demons tonight. She would go where there were people and music, somewhere dark and cozy. *I'll have just one drink—no more. I promise. Just one.* She ignored the fact that she had been making this promise to herself for over two decades and never kept it. Besides, it was the weekend. She hated weekends. They were so long— too long—devoid of any distractions. She punched the soft sofa as she passed by.

She was thirteen the first time she had snuck a drink of her father's whiskey. The alcohol soothed her and helped her cope. By the time she left home at the age of eighteen, alcohol was a part of her daily routine. She was the youngest of three girls, and the last to leave home. Her oldest sister, Helene, had left home as soon as she graduated, three years before, and Alice had graduated and gotten married right out of high school.

The sisters had been close when they were very young, but over the years they had grown further and further apart. At first, she had called Alice once a month and had even called Helene several times a year, but the conversations had been stilted, so Suzanne had quit calling. From the time she left home, she had made no effort to stay in touch with her mother or father. She had wanted to wipe them and her painful childhood completely out of her memory.

With the help of one of her high school teachers, Suzanne had found a receptionist job and a room at the YWCA in Duluth, Minnesota, and had left home early in the morning the day after graduation. She had taken the bus to Duluth and hadn't been home since that day, over twenty years ago.

Standing at the mirror, Suzanne took in her appearance. Melanie had said she was beautiful. She ran her hand over her cheek but didn't notice her delicate features, high cheekbones, and smooth, almost flawless skin. Instead, she saw a plain face with little or no attractiveness. Removing her glasses, she unpinned her hair and let its gentle curling ends fall past her shoulders, taking a moment to run her fingers through its silkiness. Maybe tonight she would wear it down and try some lipstick.

Abruptly turning away from the mirror, she resisted the urge to pull her hair tightly away from her face. Suzanne ran a brush through its thickness, then quickly headed out the door.

As soon as she was seated in her car, Suzanne turned on her favorite country music station and spent the thirty-minute drive from Dallas to Fort Worth singing along. The parking lot was crowded, but Suzanne found a spot, parked, and hurried inside.

As she paid her cover charge, Suzanne watched the man who was taking her money gaze over her from head to toe. She was so uncomfortable that she wanted to reach up and pull her hair back. Maybe it was a mistake to wear it down, to try to feel pretty. She didn't like the attention, especially this kind. Lowering her head, she hurried past him and into the anonymity of the crowded, noisy, Crazy Horse Saloon.

The twanging guitar sounds of the country band permeated into the dimly lit, smoke-filled rooms. The bars in Fort Worth were much different than the posh bars near her office and condo in Dallas, and Suzanne preferred the country hangouts that were filled with men in cowboy hats and boots. They felt more real to her and answered an ingrained need that she didn't understand, but one that demanded to be fed.

Her hands were shaking as she slid onto one of the wooden bar stools that were lined up along the long wooden bar and ordered a shot of whiskey. She had intended to sip it, but when the bartender set it in front of her, Suzanne picked up the glass and gulped down the contents. Warmth invaded her chest and stomach, working its way down her body. She ordered another drink, and then another. As she continued to drink, the warmth consumed her. Now she could finally relax.

She enjoyed country music, especially songs where women were special and loved. She would like that. But she wouldn't ever have it. She was tainted and damaged, and nobody wanted damaged goods.

Her eyes wandered to the adjacent room where a dance floor was packed with couples dancing to a slow tune, and her body began to sway to the music. An ache deep inside her chest reached out its ragged fingers and grabbed at her heart. She yearned to be held. It would be nice to feel the warmth of arms around her, kisses on her face and lips, gentle caresses whispered in her ears. She was heartbreakingly lonely. She ordered another drink.

The more she drank, the more her mind blurred and the less lonely she felt.

"Can I buy you a drink?" a deep voice from behind her interrupted her thoughts.

The alcohol haze in Suzanne took over as she turned and smiled. "Sure."

"Great. Are you alone?" A tall man was smiling down at her. His dark brown eyes twinkled at her, and he was dressed just the way she liked, in a western shirt, jeans, cowboy boots, and cowboy hat.

"I am." She felt brave. The alcohol did that for her. It helped her to not be so frightened by life. In this state, she could allow herself to be held and loved.

This man wasn't really good looking, but he seemed nice. What more could someone like her expect? Maybe he would hold her. The liquor blocked out her memory of all the other men who had bought her drinks and how often she ended up in bed with them. She never intended to, but a desperate need to be held and touched took over. The need gnawed away at her insides. It was a need that had to be filled at any price . . . any price at all.

As the evening progressed, Suzanne became vague about where she was, but she was dancing and being held, and it felt wonderful and calming. The arms around her smothered the lonely, aching need. That was all that mattered. His kisses started out gentle and Suzanne was pulled into the softness. She responded, and they grew more and more demanding. With little prodding or encouragement, she quietly followed as he took her hand and led her outside.

Suzanne stirred and felt a body next to her. In her confused mind, past and present blurred into one surrealistic cloud. She stretched her hand and touched the mound of covers next to her. *It's okay. It's Stephen, your husband, remember?*

Warmth spread through her. She loved Stephen. But pain and agony nipped at the heels of the warm glow as memories scorched their way into her hazy mind. Stephen had been trying to make love to her. She hadn't been drinking, and she had panicked, fought, screamed. He had not understood. She'd told him she needed a drink, that it would have helped her relax. She had needed to relax to do what he wanted. *Please, Stephen.* Stephen's face loomed large in her dream. He was sad, so very sad. And he was leaving, fading farther and farther away.

No, don't go. Don't go . . .

Early morning light filtered into the room. Suzanne ran her hand over her throbbing head, slowly awakening. Traces of her dream clung to the shadows of her mind, and she turned in bed, hoping it wasn't a dream. A man's body was curled away from her. She could see his shoulders and dark hair. It was not Stephen. Stephen's hair was blond, and a part of her mind kept trying to remind her that Stephen had left long ago after just a few short years of marriage. Yet, the longing in her heart made it feel like it was just yesterday.

It doesn't matter who it is.

She had met Stephen when she was twenty-two and, by that time, she had advanced to a sales position in her company. Drinking had been a way of life for her for years by then. When they were married for six months, Stephen's work had transferred them to Houston, Texas.

They had waited until they were married to have sex and, when they did, Suzanne realized there was really something wrong with her. She learned that if she was drinking she could have sex, but when she was sober, she couldn't. And Stephen refused to be intimate when she was drunk. Just before their third anniversary, they filed for divorce. By that time, they hadn't been intimate for close to two years, and their arguing had become constant. Finally, they were both so miserable with no solution in sight that they agreed to go their separate ways.

After her divorce, Suzanne had found a sales position in Dallas. Her life was very lonely in Dallas and her drinking had escalated. At first, she always carried around a small bottle in her purse and would often drink during the day when she was out making sales calls.

Then one day a client had called her boss and she had been questioned and warned that drinking during working hours wouldn't be tolerated. Suzanne's career was her lifeline, so from that point in time, any drinking she did was in the evenings or on weekends. She was now a Regional Sales Manager and had learned to keep her drinking and her private life to herself.

The mystery man stirred beside her. Suzanne groaned in agony. Shame flooded her body as she surveyed her nakedness, trying to forget any memories she had of how she had gotten here and what had happened last night.

Her clothes were scattered all around the room. Without even looking at the man in the bed, Suzanne grabbed her belongings and headed out of the bedroom. Pulling on her clothes, she walked toward the door and stepped outside. The morning light assaulted her as she gazed around the apartment complex's parking lot. She couldn't find her car, but she was used to that.

Her stomach contents pushed up into her throat as she rushed behind a nearby tree. Afterward, she limply clung to the coarse bark. Then wiping her mouth, she pulled her hair up and away from her face, walked several blocks until she found a phone booth, and called a taxi to take her to her car.

Chapter 6

Atlanta, Georgia

It was Tuesday and Helene typically played tennis on Tuesdays. This morning she had struggled with whether she should, but it had been a week since she had attempted to talk to Thomas and apparently it had helped. He was coming home after school each day and spending time with her and Lily, the way he had since he first started school. She convinced herself that Thomas was no longer missing school and that he must have just had a bad week or two.

As Helene drove her Mercedes into the wide circular driveway of the country club in an upscale suburb of Atlanta, her stomach tightened. It always did that. Even after all these years of clubhouses, cocktail parties, and fancy restaurants, her stomach still turned into knots when she interacted with the wealthy population in which she lived. Although she was an adult and sophisticated on the outside, on the inside Helene still felt like a little girl, with long dirty braids, dirty elbows, and clothes that were old, wrinkled, and often stained. Even though she was always appropriately dressed, she often felt like she was holding her breath, waiting for them to make fun of her, to tell her she didn't belong, yet she was never quite sure who "they" were.

The valet stepped out from the curb as she pulled up to the front of the country club. "Morning, Mrs. Foster." He smiled as he opened her door. "Nice to see you today."

"Thanks, Nick," Helene said with a smile, then headed inside.

Laura, Catherine, and Stephanie were waiting for her in the lounge, and although it was still morning, Stephanie had a mixed drink in front of her, and from her demeanor, Helene could tell that it wasn't her first.

She smiled as she walked up to the group of women, her "friends" she spent time with at the club. "I hope you haven't been waiting long. Lily insisted I sit down to have a muffin and fruit before I left."

"Really, Helene," Catherine sneered. "She's your servant. How can she insist you do anything? I just don't understand why you let the hired help interfere in your life the way you do."

They had had this conversation before, and Helene didn't want to get into it again. Some people couldn't understand that Lily was her friend, probably the only real friend she had. She could be herself with Lily. Here she couldn't. She knew there was a guise of friendship with these women, but beneath the surface their claws were long and sharp.

Her mind jumped to a reoccurring dream she had where she, Catherine, Stephanie, and Laura were ten years old. They were outside her old schoolhouse in Minnesota, and the three of them were jumping rope as Helene watched from the sidelines. Their frilly dresses bounced around them as the ribbons in their pigtails streamed and bobbed with each jump. Helene stood there with her long, straggly hair and an old hand-me-down dress that her mother had gotten from somewhere. As their young legs jumped to the rhythm of the rope, their sing-song voices filled the air. "Helene's daddy is a drunk. Helene is a big, old frump." Then the three faces turned toward her and continued their ditty. "Go away, 'cause we won't play, not today or any day." Helene tried to smile at the absurdity of her dream, but a shudder passed through her.

Coming back to the present, Helene observed the fake smiles on Catherine and Stephanie's faces and tuned in to today's conversation.

"This one isn't much different than all the other women Mark has had affairs with," Stephanie said in a bored, monotone voice. Then taking a long drag on her cigarette and exhaling, she stared off into space before adding, "It just means I'll get a month at a spa and the new Mercedes I've been eyeing."

Even though these conversations had become "normal" with this group, Helene was always surprised at the nonchalance in which the topic of infidelity was handled. *How can you talk about it so casually? Doesn't it rip you in two?*

She didn't talk about Bill to these women. In fact, she didn't talk about her life at all. Until recently she had accepted her life as it was because she knew life wasn't perfect, and hers was certainly a lot better than most. She wasn't about to rock the boat to which she was clinging. But she wasn't going to make Bill's infidelity or her worries a part of casual conversation with these women either.

After Stephanie finished her drink, they walked out to the tennis courts. Stephanie was already unsteady on her feet, and Helene wasn't sure how she would be able to play tennis today. She wondered the same thing week after week, but Stephanie always managed.

Tennis was hard for Helene. She felt as though she had to run harder, hit harder, and play harder than anyone else just to stay even. In fact, life felt that way. No matter how hard she played or tried, she still came in last, or third, or second place, but never first. Over the years, she had accepted that fact and settled for being in the game.

They just finished their second set when Nick called to her, "Hey, Mrs. Foster, I'm off in an hour. If you're still around the club, I'd love to play a set with you."

Helene smiled. "Thanks, Nick. But today's my day for errands and this is my last set. I'd love to take you up on it another day. Maybe next Tuesday."

"Sounds great." Nick smiled as he turned toward the clubhouse.

"I don't know why you bother with that lowlife," Catherine scowled.

Helene peered at her in surprise. "He's not a lowlife. He's a nice, hard-working young man who enjoys tennis."

A malicious grin crossed Stephanie's face. "Aw, Helene, Catherine's just miffed because she couldn't get him into bed the way she has most of the young men around here. Nick won't be bought off, and Catherine doesn't know how to handle the rejection." Catherine made an obscene gesture at Stephanie and sulked off to shower. Stephanie headed back to the lounge.

As Catherine and Stephanie went in opposite directions, Helene watched and wondered why she socialized with them. *Because you're familiar with the behavior,* a small voice from within Helene's mind suggested. *No, I'm not,* she silently argued, then she realized that Catherine and Stephanie reminded her of her father—drunk and surly.

It was funny how money could clean up even the ugliest habits.

As Helene watched the two women stagger away, she suddenly began to understand that the ugliness was still there.

"Why do we keep spending time with them?" Laura voiced Helene's silent questions.

Helene turned. At thirty-five, Laura was younger than the rest of them. She had short, dark hair, hazel eyes, and a young, athletic body. Helene knew she had two children in grade school and that her husband was the CEO of a company. She didn't know more than that. In fact, that was all she knew about any of them. They had been playing tennis together for five years now, had gone to each other's houses for parties, and talked on the phone from time to time. Even with all of that, she didn't know much about them, the real them, down underneath their skin. She didn't know what they thought, what made them tick, and what they really, really felt. Whenever the conversation started getting too deep, someone always changed it. Fear of closeness seemed to permeate the air in their worlds.

"Because it doesn't get dull with them around, I guess." Helene smiled.

"Helene . . ." Laura's voice became serious. "Do you have affairs?"

Helene fumbled around in her purse, pretending to search for her keys as she tried to figure out what to say, flustered by the personal question, the kind she typically avoided.

Laura looked uncomfortable. "I know that's a really personal question, Helene. I thought we were friends, and well, friends talk personal, don't they?"

Helene watched Laura for a few moments. *Oh, for heaven's sake, I'll just be honest.* "No, Laura, do you?"

Laura seemed to sense Helene's unwillingness to continue the conversation. "Helene, I'd really like to have you as a close friend. I have feelings, thoughts, and ideas I'd like to share with another woman, and in our circle that seems hard to come by. I'm so lonely." Sadness was etched on her face.

Helene stood there speechless. How could Laura be lonely? She had everything. She came from a family with money, she married a nice man with money, and they lived in a great house, had two great kids, and seemed to get along well. *I'm not lonely*, Helene assured herself. Yet from deep down inside a tiny voice whispered, *Yes, I am. Listen to me. Yes, I'm lonely.*

Inside, Helene was fleeing. This was too close, and she began to panic. "Sorry, Laura, not today. I've got tons of errands to do. Can we do it some other time?"

"Sure." Laura's voice was sad, but Helene tried to ignore it as she escaped to the comfort of her lonely, safe, controlled world.

"Helene, Helene, wake up." Bill gently shook her.

She opened one eye and peered at him, fresh from his shower. He leaned close to her. She caught the scent of freshly applied aftershave. "Time to get up, sleepy head."

Still wrapped in the fringes of soft, innocent sleep, Helene smiled. "Hi."

"Hi, yourself. Tough morning?"

"I can't seem to wake up. I know the alarm went off, and since you're all dressed, that must have been some time ago."

"About an hour." He smiled. "Why don't you just curl up and go back to sleep?"

"I've got an exercise class this morning," she groaned.

"You could probably miss one if you're tired."

Helene lay still for several minutes watching him. Last night, the movement of the bed had awoken her, and she'd become aware of a body slipping in beside her. She'd started to reach up and curl her arms around her husband's neck, but the strong smell of another woman stopped her. In the beginning, Bill would shower either before he came home or before he climbed into bed with her. Now he did neither.

Why was he always so nice the morning after his late-night escapade with another woman? And why did Helene want to make love to him anyway? A deep sigh escaped from her. It had been over two months since they'd made love. *Right now, I'd take sex, just raw, wild sex.*

She pulled herself from the bed and walked to the shower. *Maybe I'm just oversexed.* How was she to know? Maybe married couples really didn't make love very often. Maybe most husbands had affairs because most married women didn't like sex. *How would I know what couples do? From my parents?* Helene uttered a cruel laugh as she turned her face up to the flow of the water.

Bill was still sitting on the bed when Helene came out of the bathroom, wrapped in a towel, her hair damp and her face fresh and without makeup.

"Has Thomas been sick a lot lately?" His voice was sharp.

"No, why?" She ran her hand through her damp hair. *Now what?*

Bill watched her as he stood up from the bed. "His school just called. They said Thomas is absent again today. Apparently, he has been absent a lot."

"Why did they call you?" She stood in front of him, pulling the towel snugly around her. "What is this? They call one parent and if they don't get an answer they like, they call the second one?"

"Helene, settle down. They called here a few minutes ago and I answered the phone, but why did you lie?" He glanced down at her, then stepped back and sat on the bed.

"I talked with him. He needed some space, that's all. Pressures just build up. We all need some time and space once in a while." She walked toward the clothes she had laid out on her side of the bed and began to dress.

"That's the purpose of evenings and weekends. How is he ever going to learn responsibility if you keep lying for him?" Bill's voice started to get louder. "Helene, you're not helping that boy by babying him. He's going to turn into a useless bum if you don't make him accept some responsibilities. You're mothering him to death."

She glared at him with anger dancing in her eyes. "Well, at least I'm mothering. That's more than I can say for you about your fathering." Those words fueled the fire flaring beneath the surface. They didn't fight about things concerning themselves. Helene never mentioned her knowledge of his cheating, their lack of lovemaking, or her loneliness, but they often fought about Thomas. It was easy to divert their problems in their marriage to Thomas. They could defend or attack him. They could focus on him, but their own problems were too muddled and confusing. It was best that those were ignored.

They continued to fight, scream, and throw damaging words at each other until they were both exhausted and drained. Helene lay quietly on the bed, half-dressed, with her arm across her eyes, and Bill sat slumped in a chair, his hands covering his face. Neither of them had said a word for a long time. The wedge between them had grown even wider. Helene felt lonely and scared.

Slowly getting up from the bed, she walked over to Bill and put her hands on his shoulders. "I'm sorry. I never mean to scream at you."

"I know." He shook his head. "I know."

Helene rested her head against the top of his. "Please forgive me, Bill. Please, I'm really sorry. I'll try better with Thomas. Honest I will."

Bill stood up, pulling her arms away from around his neck. "I've got to get to work," he answered as he walked out the door.

Helene stood behind the chair and sobbed.

Bill didn't come home for dinner, and he didn't call. Even though his behavior wasn't unusual, Helene felt abandoned. Her mind raced, and she was sick to her stomach. Thomas was out again too. She had told him she didn't think he should go out, but he had gone anyway.

It was after midnight when Helene heard Thomas come in and go to his room. She walked down the hall and tapped on his door. He didn't answer. She heard him trip, fall, and giggle. Everything in her world was out of control, and she had no idea how to fix it.

Chapter 7

Atlanta, Georgia

A week had passed and nothing changed. Bill was distant, and Thomas ignored Helene and any attempts she made to talk with him.

Helene was just finishing up her breakfast when the phone rang.

"Mrs. Foster, this is Principal Griffin." His voice was brisk. "Could you be in my office in half an hour?"

Helene's heart started to race. "Well, yes, I suppose so. What's the problem?"

"I'd rather discuss it with both you and Mr. Foster when you get here."

"Okay, but half an hour isn't much time. Have you called my husband?"

"I've called him and he should be on his way. As I explained to your husband, it's imperative that you both get here as soon as possible. We have a situation that has to be handled now, and delaying could only make it worse. I'll expect you in about half an hour, and I really appreciate your cooperation on this." The phone conversation ended as abruptly as it began.

Helene sat still, staring into space for a moment. Then she grabbed her cars keys and headed to the garage.

Helene felt like a child as she sat in the secretary's office waiting to see Principal

Griffin. She had already waited fifteen minutes beyond their appointment time, and Bill still wasn't here. Anger boiled deep within her.

I can't count on him. I can never count on him when I really need him!

By the time Bill finally showed up and they were both ushered into the principal's office, Helene was so angry she couldn't even look at her husband. It was so much easier to be mad at Bill than to be scared about Thomas.

Principal Griffin was somber as he gazed at Helene then at Bill. "Mr. and Mrs. Foster, we have a real problem with Thomas."

Bill's frustration flooded to the surface as he leaned forward in his chair with his fists clenched. "What has he done now? Has he skipped class again? If he has, I'll take care of it this time. His mother babies that boy. She always has. It's time he grew up. It's time I stepped in."

Helene reeled toward him with eyes glaring as her hands flew into the air. "Big hero! Now you step in! Where were you all the years when Thomas was doing well? When he wanted his father at his baseball games, his science fairs, and all the other activities he used to participate in? Maybe if he had a father who was involved in his life, he wouldn't be in trouble now."

Principal Griffin took a deep breath, then said, "We're here to talk about the situation with Thomas." He strongly enunciated each word. "I said we've got a problem and I mean a serious problem. This is beyond skipping school. Thomas was intoxicated in one of his classes, and when we searched his locker, we found an opened pint of whiskey." He paused and leaned over. "I believe your son has a drinking problem."

Silence spread throughout the room as Bill appeared dumbfounded. Finally, in a weak voice, Helene asked, "Intoxicated? In the middle of the day?"

"What?" Bill roared at her. "You mean if it was night, it would be okay?"

Principal Griffin turned to Bill. "Mr. Foster, can we stick to the issue?" Then he turned back to Helene. "I'm recommending Thomas for alcohol counseling. This boy has a drinking problem. We've noticed indications of it before, but today it crossed the line. I don't know if alcohol is his problem or if he's using it to deal with his problems, but I'm going to give you the name of a counselor. I suggest you contact him right away." Lowering his voice for emphasis, he continued, "Thomas is suspended from school for two weeks for drinking on campus, and before he can re-enter, I want written verification from his therapist that Thomas has seen him at least twice and is set up in a steady counseling program."

Sitting back in his chair, Principal Griffin looked squarely at Bill and Helene. "I sincerely hope that the two of you will participate in this."

"Why wouldn't we participate?" Bill ran his hand through his hair, stood up, and began to pace behind the chair he had been sitting in.

Principal Griffin gazed at Bill for a few moments before responding. "Sometimes parents don't want to look at behaviors that may be contributing to a child's problems."

"Are you saying that we're the cause of Thomas's problems?" Bill stopped pacing.

"I'm simply saying that I hope you will both participate with Thomas in his counseling," Principal Griffin calmly reiterated.

Helene's voice quivered as she reached out her hand. "I'd like the name of that counselor, Mr. Griffin. I'll see to it that Thomas goes to see him."

A lump lodged in Helene's throat. Was he trying to say that the problems between the two of them had something to do with Thomas's behavior? *It can't be. I've been so careful to keep my thoughts and feelings away from him.* Her stomach churned as she remembered her childhood and the pain of listening to her parents fight, watching her father slap her mother and belittle her with his words. Thomas had never seen anything like that. But how much had he heard from behind closed doors?

Her son had an alcohol problem? It couldn't be. It just couldn't be. There must be another answer, another reason. There had to be. She would figure it out and fix it no matter what it took.

Thomas rode home with her. He was quiet. But when they were all inside the house, Bill exploded in anger. Thomas stomped up the stairs, slammed the door to his room, and didn't come out for the rest of the night. Helene and Bill spent the evening in silence.

The next day, Helene called the counselor. It was agreed he would meet with Thomas once later this week and then once next week. Then, she assured herself, Thomas would be back in school and everything would return to normal.

Everything will be okay. I know it will.

A few weeks went by and life settled down. Thomas had seen the counselor and was back to being himself now. He was getting up for school with no hassle, going to classes, coming right home after school, and spending time with her and Lily before doing his homework. Helene assured herself that it had just been the pressures he had been experiencing that had caused him to drink.

Tonight was a rare occasion with Bill home for dinner. Conversation between Helene and Bill was limited. They were like two strangers sitting across from each other, but they were not fighting. For right now, that was enough for Helene.

Thomas was at the library, studying to try to catch up with all the classwork he had missed. The meal they enjoyed was superb—chicken breasts stuffed with herbs and cheese, steamed vegetables fresh from the farmers' market, a salad of mixed greens with goat cheese, and strawberry pie for dessert. Lily seemed to be trying to fix things through good food. Tonight it felt like it had worked. Peace permeated the room and the house, and Helene began to relax.

After the meal, Bill and Helene went into the family room with its large, comfy chairs and sofa that she loved to sink in to. Music softly filled the room, and the gas fireplace was peaceful. Helene curled up on the sofa, and Bill was comfortably relaxed in one of the chairs. They were attempting to carry on a conversation like two people who really cared about what was going on in each other's life. They were beginning to make some headway, and Helene warmed to the idea. When the phone rang, they didn't pay much attention to it. Lily, who was cleaning up the kitchen before she left for home, answered it. Her steps were slow as she approached.

"Mr. Foster, it's for you. It's the police. It's about Mr. Thomas."

Helene's throat constricted.

Bill's face was white as he picked up the phone. As he listened, color returned to his skin and flushed his cheeks. Then he hung up, slamming the phone down. "Damn him!"

"What's wrong, Bill?"

"Thomas has been picked up for a DUI."

Helene collapsed back against the sofa as her stomach rolled toward her throat and nausea took over her body. Her mind circled and silently screamed as reality crashed headlong into the fantasy she had been trying to hold on to. She reached for Bill's hand as he walked back toward her. "Don't" was all he said as he heavily sat down and held his head in his hand.

After a few quiet minutes, Bill studied Helene with emotionless eyes. "We need to go deal with this."

After getting Thomas released into his custody, Bill had asked for a referral to a family therapist. The therapist, Raymond Welsh, had agreed to see them the next day. Now, they sat facing the middle-aged balding man. After several minutes of asking numerous questions and receiving reluctant replies and long moments of silence, Raymond sat back in his chair, surveyed them one more time, then asked, "Thomas, are you an alcoholic?"

Suddenly, Helene leaned toward the counselor, her eyes blazing. "How dare you? We didn't come here to have you insult our son!"

"Why did you come here, Mrs. Foster?" Raymond calmly turned toward her.

"Why?" She felt baffled that he would even ask such a question. "To get counseling so Thomas will stop drinking."

"And why do you think he drinks?" Raymond quietly asked.

Helene squirmed in her chair, and the fingers of her right hand harshly pushed her hair behind her ear. "He's stressed, that's all. It's not an addiction or anything."

"Do you drink when you're stressed?" Raymond asked Helene.

"Well, of course not," she responded indignantly.

"Then why does Thomas?" Raymond asked in a calm tone.

"I don't know." She crossed and uncrossed her legs as her eyes wandered toward the view outside the window.

Raymond remained quiet for a few minutes, then asked, "Did your father drink, Mrs. Foster?"

Helene sat straight in her chair and glared at him. "He doesn't have anything to do with this!"

"What about your mother? Did she drink?" Raymond's voice was even softer now.

"What do my parents have to do with this?" she yelled. "Leave them out of this." She stood up from her chair, her fists clenched at her sides, and her eyes wide with terror. "I won't talk about them. Do you hear me?"

Clearly startled by her response, Bill reached for her hand. "Shh, honey, it's okay. Calm down, it's okay." Helene looked at him blankly and quietly fell back into the chair.

"What about you, Mr. Foster, do you have a drinking problem?" Raymond asked.

"I have a drink from time to time, but I don't have a drinking problem," Bill answered.

"What problems do you have?" Raymond sat back in his chair.

"I don't know what you mean." Bill wiped the palms of his hands against his legs, suddenly looking very uncomfortable.

"Don't you?" Raymond gazed quietly at Bill, then turned to Thomas. "What about you, Thomas? Do you have a drinking problem?"

Surprise and fear covered Thomas's face as he scrutinized the therapist, seemingly trying to understand what he was asking. Thomas glanced at Helene, then crossed his arms over his chest and slumped into the chair.

Bill started to speak, but Raymond held up his hand for silence as it seemed Thomas was going to speak.

"Yes, sir . . . yes, I do," Thomas said shakily.

At Thomas's confession, Helene leaped from her chair. "We're paying money for this!" she screamed. "You're supposed to fix Thomas. We don't need this. We don't need you prying into our lives and into our pasts. We don't need you putting ideas into our son's head. He doesn't have a problem. He's not an alcoholic. Stop this. Just stop this! He can't be an alcoholic. He just can't be!" She sunk back into her chair, overcome with despair.

Bill and Thomas both turned toward her with shock on their faces.

"Why can't he be, Mrs. Foster?" Raymond asked. "Because your father was an alcoholic, and you can't stand the thought of failing with your child the way your father and mother failed with you?"

Helene violently shook her head. "No! It just can't be."

"Do you know anything about alcoholism, Mrs. Foster?" Raymond asked gently. Helene stared blankly at him, so he continued. "There are many theories about it. Some believe it's a disease, some an addiction, but whatever you believe, we know that it is generally cyclic and usually goes from generation to generation. You might not have carried down the drinking, but you've probably carried down some of the dysfunction."

Helene weakly shook her head in denial. "It's not my fault. It's not. If Bill would just be a better father."

"This isn't a blame game, Mrs. Foster." Raymond beckoned Bill into silence as he leaped to defend himself at Helene's words. "You all have responsibility in this, and Thomas has the most. He is responsible for his behavior, and it's time he starts knowing that. You have a lot of work ahead of you. All of you do, and you can do it. But it's up to you to let me know when you really want to start." He stood up. "That's all for today. Call me when you want another appointment."

Chapter 8

Atlanta, Georgia

The therapist's questions rolled around in Helene's mind as panic lodged in her chest. She couldn't find a way to admit to herself that her issues might have led to Thomas's problems. Throughout the years, she had shared very little of her childhood or family with Bill and Thomas. They knew she had grown up in Minnesota and had two sisters. Beyond that, if the subject came up, she would always change it, and they never seemed to notice, or if they did, nothing was ever said.

Heaviness settled on her like a weighted cloak, and her mind focused on the box that was buried up in the attic. No one was aware of its existence except her, and she hadn't thought about it in years. It was the one thing she had taken with her when she left home, and right now, it was all she could think about.

When they got home, they all retreated to separate parts of their huge house. Helene hesitantly walked to the stairs at the back of the house. Once on the second floor, she went to the end of the hall opposite their master bedroom and stood in front of the door to the attic. They seldom went up there; it was only used for storage of Christmas decorations, memorabilia, and items they had long forgotten.

Hesitantly moving up the steps, feeling both dread and anxiety, Helene was nervous about uncovering the past that she had kept contained inside a cardboard box for over twenty years. At the top of the stairs, she stopped and scanned the crowded attic, trying to remember where she had last seen the box containing memories she didn't want to be reminded of, yet but couldn't quite throw away.

Thanks to Lily's ability to keep every corner cleaned, the attic was surprisingly free of the normal dust and spiderwebs that usually accumulated around boxes that have been stored for a long time. It took Helene several moments, but back in a far corner buried behind holiday decorations that had long ago been replaced by new ones, Helene found what she was looking for. It was a simple cardboard box sealed with packing tape, unopened for close to two decades. It contained reminders of her past, ones that she thought she would never deal with again, but now the therapist's questions were stabbing at her mind.

Her hand shook slightly as she slowly sliced through the tape using a kitchen knife she'd brought up with her. Then, sitting back on her knees and inhaling a deep breath, she opened the box. From beneath layers of tissue paper, Helene carefully pulled out an old photo album that she had put together when Thomas was a baby and then had packed away and forgotten.

Holding the book in her hands, she closed her eyes and leaned against a stack of boxes behind her. She felt caught between the fear of stepping back into her past and the fear of what would happen if she didn't. Opening her eyes, she slowly turned from page to page, scanning the faces of her childhood as memories circled like ghosts.

She had forgotten what a tall, handsome man her father was in his youth. Her fingers touched the picture as her mind went back to the vision of the angry, drunken old man who had hurled threats at her that day she'd left so many years ago. Left, never to return. She remembered the man who had come to her high school graduation in a drunken stupor and who had so often hit her mother, herself, Alice, and Suzanne.

Turning the pages, Helene examined the faces of her sisters. For a brief moment, tenderness overcame her as she remembered them as small children. Parts of her missed them, or missed what she wished they could have together. Over the years, the three of them had occasionally connected via phone on birthdays or holidays, but they had never talked long because they didn't know what to say to each other, or if they even wanted to try. It had been close to ten years since the last phone call. When Helene heard other women talk about their families, the void that existed inside of her would grow. If things were different, she would enjoy a family she could be close to, but she didn't have that kind of family or that option. There was too much pain.

When they were still in grade school, the sisters were all close, but once Helene entered junior high, she'd tried to separate herself from her family, including her sisters, as much as she could. Alice became an embarrassment for Helene because she paid no attention to her appearance and had gotten fat at a very early age. Suzanne kept to herself, had very few friends, and ignored any attempts Helene had made toward friendship. Being close to her sisters was just a wish—a fantasy—that she had long ago discarded. Yet as she studied the pictures from years ago, a tear trickled down her cheek as yearning bloomed within her, as well as contempt and disgust that she still felt about her childhood and where she came from.

As she flipped through the pictures, Helene was surprised at how sad they all appeared to be as children. She knew their childhood had been hard because of their father's drinking and abuse, but she hadn't realized how deeply the sadness had apparently penetrated. She recalled Thomas's childhood, and children she would now see in restaurants or the supermarket. Their eyes typically glowed with excitement, life, and even mischievousness. But the girls in the picture were forlorn little waifs with long, scraggly hair and tattered clothes.

Was that really me?

Helene slammed the book closed. Painful sobs erupted as the scabbed-over wounds of long ago bled afresh. Clutching the album, she continued to weep. She longed for a sister or a mother to whom she could confide her fears and confusion over what was happening in her life. It felt like a runaway truck that was headed for a steep embankment over which it would tumble to its demise, and she didn't know how to stop it. She yearned for someone who knew her and really cared.

After long moments, Helene ran her hand over the front of the book and, ever so slowly, opened it again. In the front, there was a picture of her father and mother's wedding day. The expression on her father's handsome face was grim, and her mother was just a girl. Sadness surged through her as Helene turned the page and, picture by picture, watched the stars fade from her mother's eyes as age and life took their toll.

Toward the end of the album, her father's once tall, handsome form was dirty and unshaven, often stretched out on a ragged old sofa, a bottle of beer or whiskey in his hand. Even the Christmas pictures showed faces that were beleaguered, exhausted, and tired of life. The faces of Helene and her sisters seemed to be tired of life before it had even begun.

As she scanned the childhood pictures, Helene began to see them all in a new light as scared, lonely little girls. In the early pictures, Alice was a slender, pretty child. Around age twelve, her pictures showed a constant weight gain until, at her high school graduation, she was fat. Helene glanced at Suzanne's pictures and was drawn back again and again. She touched Suzanne's young face, grasping, trying to understand what she saw. As if a shadow had been removed, she picked up the picture and examined it closely; she was startled by the eyes. She had never noticed it before, but Suzanne's eyes were haunting, as if she knew a deep, dark secret. Helene was stabbed with heartache greater than she could handle, and she quickly placed Suzanne's picture deep within the book.

As she turned the pages, Helene's eyes refused to look at her own pictures. The edges of her mind saw them, but she wouldn't acknowledge them. It hurt too much. That scraggly, sad little girl couldn't be her. She couldn't claim her, it would make her too vulnerable, too open to what she really felt about herself. If she didn't look at the pictures of herself, maybe they would just go away. Maybe that hurt, lonely little girl would just cease to exist.

Hurriedly Helene closed the book. *This is not a part of me. I didn't come from that.*

She placed her head in her hands as fatigue washed over her. She sat still for a long time. Then she carefully packed the photo album back into the box, stored it in a far corner, and left the attic.

Once inside her bedroom, she closed the door, picked up the phone, and dialed Mr. Welsh's number. It rang once. Helene hung up and stared at the phone. Moments later she reached for it again. Her hands shook as she picked up the receiver. The dial tone screamed into the silence. Slowly Helene dialed—the phone rang three times and was answered by his secretary. Angrily, Helene slammed down the phone.

Reaching for a pillow from the bed, she hurled it across the room. The pillow hit the wall with a thud and sank to the floor as Helene lay back on the bed. Minutes passed as she stared blankly at the ceiling. Feeling totally depleted, Helene once again reached for the phone and dialed.

The secretary answered after a few rings. Helene mumbled her name.

"Just a moment, Mrs. Foster." The secretary put her on hold.

After a couple moments, Raymond said, "Mrs. Foster, what can I do for you?"

Anguish circled each word as she slowly replied. "Mr. Welsh, I'd like to come to see you by myself." She was quiet for a few moments, and Raymond didn't break the silence. "There are a lot of things I need to talk to someone about."

"Okay. When would you like to come?" His voice was gentle.

The appointment made, Helene lay down on the bed and fell into a tired sleep. She was startled awake as Bill pulled her close to him. He cradled her in his arms, and whispered, "I love you, Helene. I really do love you." Tears glistened in her eyes as sleep pulled her back into its comforting embrace.

After a few weeks, the family settled into a routine of life and sessions with Raymond Welsh. At times they danced around each other like they were stepping on eggshells, and at other moments small windows of communication and connection would open where they would each join in, as though they were gingerly putting their toes into a lake to test out the temperature of the water.

Helene, Bill, and Thomas were all trying to right the capsized boats that each of their lives had become, trying to figure out how to be comfortable in their lives once they were right-side up again. Taking steps forward and faltering several steps backward, they were dancing a dance of reconnection and recovery.

Chapter 9

Northern Minnesota

"Thelma, I was reading this woman's magazine that I picked up at the grocery store. It had an article about rape." Alice took a deep breath. "It says it's rape if a husband has sex when a wife doesn't want to." Again, she drew a deep breath. "What do you think?"

Alice and her best friend, Thelma, were sitting at Thelma's kitchen table enjoying their daily gossip sessions with a fresh brewed pot of coffee and bags of sweet treats from the Day Old Bakery.

Thelma just stared at Alice. "I think you'd better stop reading those magazines that put fancy ideas in your head. If a husband wants his wife, it's her duty. It's not rape. Get that rubbish outta your head."

"But he hits me," Alice bitterly spat out her protest.

"Sometimes men just can't control themselves. It's no big deal." Thelma seemed to dismiss Alice's words as easily as if she had just commented on the weather.

"But I'm just so tired of Jake hitting me and forcing his way into me. He'll do it every night for weeks at a time. Then he'll just leave me alone for a long time. It don't make sense. There's gotta be better. This can't be right. That article says it's not." Alice refused to let go of the subject. She needed someone to know what she was going through, someone to tell her she deserved better, and she hoped her best friend would understand.

But Thelma replied with obvious cynicism. "An article says it ain't right? That's just some writer talking. There ain't no better for you and me. You think some knight in shining armor's gonna come and rescue you? Or you think you can go off and get a job, work eight hours a day, and still take care of your family by yourself? You've got a man, don't ya? Just put up with what you gotta put up with and get on with life. Life's not meant to be a fairytale, Alice. If you'd quit dreaming and reading those magazines, you'd be better off."

Defeat swallowed Alice. "Does Al still hit you?"

Thelma lowered her head. "Yeah, once in a while, but not so often anymore. I quit asking for it. If I keep my mouth shut, I'm okay."

"But it's not right. It just can't be right. Not all men hit their wives, they just don't."

"And who says? Some fancy writer? Your father hit your mother. My father hit my mother. Al hits me. Jake hits you. What's that tell you, Alice? Who do you know that's got it different?"

"I betcha my sister Helene don't get hit by that lawyer husband of hers."

"So, you think you're gonna get a lawyer husband, Alice? Just quit your moaning and be glad of what you've got." Thelma got up and walked toward the television. "Besides, I don't wanna talk no more. *As the World Turns* is coming on and I haven't missed one of these for years. Did you know that . . ." and she went on to talk about the characters in the soap opera as though she knew them personally.

Alice was silent. *What's wrong with me? It just don't feel okay no more to be hit or have Jake's kind of sex.* She felt like a balloon full of feelings that was getting ready to pop and spill its contents all over everything around her.

"Where the hell have you been?" Jake raged at her as she came in the door.

"At Thelma's."

"Damn it, Alice. I'm hungry, and I expect you to be here when I want something to eat. A man deserves to have his meals made for him and his house clean."

Alice didn't think before she spoke. "Maybe a working man does."

Jake turned on her with dark, evil eyes. "What did you say?"

Alice realized she had made a mistake. "Nothing, Jake. I'll go get your lunch."

As she turned to leave, Jake grabbed her shoulder. "I said, what did you say?"

"Nothing, Jake, honest." Alice had seen this look in his eyes before, and she was scared. When Jake got this mad, he could really hurt her. He broke some ribs one time. She'd lied to the doctor and said she fell. Then there were the times when her eyes were black. She always said she bumped into a door. *I shouldn't push him. He's my husband, and this is what husbands do when they get angry.*

Jake's hand rose high into the air and came down across her face, throwing Alice against the wall with the impact. She tried to run from the room. Jake pursued her and grabbed the collar of her shirt. "You fat bitch! Don't you ever talk to me like that again! You should be glad I stay here with you. Who else would stay married to an ugly pig like you? If it wasn't for the kids, especially Sarah, I wouldn't hang around here at all!"

At the mention of Sarah's name, a leering smile lingered on Jake's face. A sick lump formed in Alice's throat.

Clinging to the wall, Alice braced herself for more anger, but for some reason Jake's anger died. He muttered something, turned, headed into the bathroom, and left her alone leaning against the wall with rage buried deep within her belly.

Alice tottered to her bedroom, locked the door, grabbed a stash of chocolate, and began shoving it into her mouth, but her sobbing made eating impossible. Finally, she just curled up into a fetal position on the bed and let the sobs come, jamming her fist into her mouth so the sounds wouldn't escape. So Jake wouldn't hear.

A few hours later, the house was quiet and Alice was curled up on the sofa with a pile of magazines. Jake often yelled at her because she bought so many from the counter at the grocery store, but she liked reading them and looking at the pictures. *How else would I know how other people live? Do they really live like that? I wonder what Helene's house is like. I wonder what it would be like to be rich.* Alice had never had thoughts like these. But they were beginning to form in her mind and with them came a restlessness, a desire for change that had not yet fully made itself known.

As she flipped through the pages, Alice's expression changed as she came to an article, "I Was Raped by My Father." Fear overwhelmed her. She had read a lot of similar articles lately. She didn't understand why they drew her interest, but something deep within her pulled her toward the information contained in those pages.

As she read the article, something inside of Alice pulled her back toward her childhood. There was a familiarity in some of the behaviors the writer talked about, but Alice didn't understand where those feelings were coming from. While her father had often beat her, she had no memories of any type of sexual abuse. Yet the words penetrated into a place of knowingness for her. There was something about the article that felt real, both from her past and in her present, and left a sick feeling in the pit of her stomach.

After finishing the article, Alice turned down the corner of the page to mark it. She then carried the magazine to her bedroom to put in a stack that she would read again.

When she returned to the living room, Sarah was standing by the door. "Where you going?" Alice asked her.

Tossing her a disinterested look, Sarah curtly replied, "On a date."

"Sarah, you can't wear that short skirt. I can just about see your panties." Alice's voice was sharper than she intended it to be. "Are you asking for trouble? What kind of a date are you going on anyway?"

"It's none of your business!" Sarah snapped as she applied bright red lipstick.

"What do you mean it's none of my business? I'm your mom. It's my business. No daughter of mine is going out looking like that," Alice replied as she flopped down onto the overstuffed sofa that was so worn that bits of stuffing peeked out from under the fabric.

Sarah's fair complexion turned crimson as her voice rose into a scream. "You're telling me how I should look? Have you taken a good look in the mirror lately? If you weren't such a fat pig, maybe your husband would stay home more and maybe he'd leave me alone!"

Alice was used to Sarah's meanness. She'd been accepting it for years. Jake treated her that way, so how could she expect anything different from her kids? But tonight, Sarah's words caused that sickness in the pit of Alice's stomach to return. Panic charged up her body. "What do you mean?" Unable to look at Sarah, Alice's eyes stared at the peeling paint on the windowsill behind her.

"Never mind. Just leave me alone." Sarah turned and ran out of the house, the torn screen door slamming behind her.

Alice stared at the door. Horrible visions flashed before her eyes as the words from those magazine articles about sexual abuse started to play through her head like a bad movie. She sat on the couch, frozen with overwhelming foreboding, not knowing what to do, think, or feel. Denial and reality fought a ferocious battle in her mind. Finally, exhausted from the confusion and fear, she walked back to her bedroom and picked up one of the magazines in the stack by her bed.

"Mom? Why are you crying again? Has Dad been mean to you?" Sam, all clean from his bath, padded into her bedroom.

Feeling afraid and vulnerable, Alice reached out to him. Sam's surprise showed on his face. Then he smiled and curled up next to her.

"Why are you crying?" he repeated as he snuggled closer to her. With a timid smile on his face, he asked, "I ain't been that bad, have I?"

Alice remained quiet, so Sam peered into her eyes and repeated, "I ain't been that bad, have I?"

Alice was startled back into the moment by Sam's question. She glanced at her son's freckled face and remembered the mess of candy and ice cream wrappers and chip bags she had found under his bed during one of her rare attempts to clean his room. "No, Sam, you ain't been that bad. But you can't steal no more, ya hear?"

"Who says I did?" Sam pulled away defensively.

Alice felt overwhelmed. The article loomed in her mind while her fear for Sam surfaced. "I found all those candy and ice cream wrappers under your bed, and I know you don't have money for that kind of stuff." She pulled her son close to her as her world plummeted around her. She knew she was failing her kids, but she didn't know what to do about it. Behind the feelings of defeat that permeated her life, Alice began to feel a small bit of determination to make things better. She had no idea how to do it or what that even meant, but fear for her children ignited a fierceness in Alice that she hadn't known was even there.

Alice put her hands on either side of his face. "It ain't right to steal, Sam. You can go to prison for that. You gotta do better. You just gotta do better." Passion filled her voice as she continued. "You gotta make something of yourself, Sam! You and me, we gotta work on that." Her mind frantically searched for something she could do right now to help Sam. Something that would help her feel that she had some control over what happened to her kids. "I'm gonna start helping you with your homework. That's what I'll do!" She smiled at her son, then the look on her face became very serious. "You and me, Sam, we gotta make it better for you. It ain't too late for you." Alice pulled him in for a tight hug.

Over the next weeks, Alice once again pushed her fears, along with the articles, to the back of her mind as she concentrated on trying to do better with the house, herself, and especially her kids. Then, one day when she was changing the sheets on her bed, she found one of her many magazines wedged between the headboard and the mattress.

She was alone in the house and sat down on the bed to read. The magazine had an article on incest. This article was even stronger than the others, and it gave signs to watch for in your children. Alice hurried through, hoping not to see anything that she recognized in Sarah, yet the words glared at her from the page. Alice's mind fought the horror of the possibility. She knew Jake was disgusting in many ways, but even he wouldn't do something like this. He just couldn't.

Sarah was really late again tonight, but Alice waited up for her. Her stomach was in knots, and she had not been able to eat anything at dinner or even from her private stash. Jake was bowling, and Alice had tucked Sam in bed, a ritual she had just recently started with him. She had seen a program on television that talked about how tucking your children in at night gave both the child and parent a sense of security, so she had tried it and found it felt nice. She had been tucking Sam in every night for over a week now, but they always waited until Jake was gone.

When Sarah finally got home, her hair was a mess, her face was flushed, her blouse was buttoned incorrectly, and her skirt was askew. Sarah was barely in the door when Alice blurted out, "Sarah, I wanna talk to you about your father."

Sarah's expression turned quickly from irritated to scared. "What about?"

"What did you mean when you said the other day that your dad doesn't leave you alone?" The article she'd read told Alice not to talk to Sarah alone, but she didn't want someone else there when she asked her daughter these questions. A powerful motherly instinct was surfacing in Alice that pushed her to protect Sarah. A few months ago—even a few weeks ago—Alice would not have believed that Jake could do something like this, but now she was beginning to realize that Jake was capable of a lot of mean, sick things. She just hoped he hadn't done them with Sarah.

"I didn't mean nothing. I was just mad. Leave me alone." Sarah tried to walk past Alice toward her bedroom, but Alice blocked her path.

"Sarah, I don't believe you." Alice tried to make her voice soft. "You never said stuff like that before when you was mad. Why now?"

Sarah suddenly resembled a little girl. Her huge, sad eyes stared at Alice as if she was trying to decide what to do. A tiny gasp escaped through her lips. "You know what I meant."

"No, I don't know what you meant," Alice murmured, horrified. "At least, I ain't sure."

"I don't want to say it." Sarah clasped and unclasped her hands in front of her as she lowered her eyes to the floor and her voice became painfully soft. "You know what he's been doin'. He's been doing it for years."

"No, Sarah, nooooooo!" Alice cried as shock took over her senses. She had asked the question and part of her expected the answer she got, but she wasn't ready for the impact of what it meant. "I didn't know."

"I don't believe you." Sarah's voice rose in pitch. "How could you not know? My bedroom's next to yours. How could you not know?" Sarah's face contorted in pain.

"Baby, honest," Alice pleaded with her child, needing to hear the truth, yet dreading it.

Sarah started to sob as she sunk down onto the sofa. Awkwardly, Alice tried to put her arms around her daughter, but Sarah pulled away. Usually Alice wouldn't try again, but tonight she reached out and placed her arm around Sarah's shoulder. This time Sarah didn't fight her. Alice didn't touch her kids a lot. She didn't know how, but lately she had been trying. She wasn't touched a lot when she was a kid, and the only time Jake touched her was to hit her or to have sex. But now she curled her daughter up next to her. Jake could hurt her—he had for years—but he damn well better not be hurting her kids.

Yet, he was. Sarah just said he was. Earlier today, when Alice had called the 800 number listed in the magazine article, the woman who'd spoken to her told Alice that she and the kids didn't have to put up with Jake. She had given Alice a local number to call, and Alice had been thinking about it. But now that she knew Jake had been hurting Sarah like that, she had to call.

He's really hurting her, isn't he?

Alice wanted to run into the bathroom, lock the door, and puke her guts out, but Sarah needed her. As Alice held her daughter, Sarah's sobs died down and she began to talk. "He started touching me when I was just a kid."

Pain flooded through Alice, but she remained silent as she pulled Sarah closer, trying to show her that she was safe, but not wanting to interrupt the flow of words that were now coming fast from Sarah's trembling lips. "He would come into my bedroom and touch me down there. It wouldn't last long." Alice felt her daughter tremble. "He would get this funny look in his eyes, then he would go into your bedroom, and I would hear him grunting and groaning and sometimes I'd hear you cry."

Bile rose in Alice's throat, but she took a deep breath as she gently cradled Sarah's head against her chest. "I felt so bad," Sarah said. "I thought you were crying because he had been touching me."

Sarah suddenly pulled away. Her lips quivered as she spoke. "Now that I'm fifteen, he has sex with me." She broke into a sob, and Alice curled her arms around her daughter and held her tightly.

As Alice gently stroked Sarah's hair, the sobs died down, and her voice was once again just above a whisper, causing Alice to bend in close in order to hear the words. "He's been doing that since I was about twelve. And he said if I ever told you, he'd kill us both."

Small tremors of shock ran through Alice's body. *Three years! Why didn't I know? What kind of mother am I?*

Sarah turned toward Alice with anger blazing in her eyes. "But I'm sick of it, Mom. I'm sick of him. I'm sick of you. I'm sick of being afraid to be with boys unless I'm having sex. I know how to have sex with them. I just don't know how to be with them any other way." Once the words started flowing from Sarah's mouth, they were like a gushing river that couldn't be stopped.

As Sarah talked, shock and fear subtly shifted, and Alice felt strength grow from deep inside of her. Jake could hurt her, but he wasn't going to hurt her children, not any more. Alice was experiencing a devastation so deep she wasn't sure she could crawl out of the chasm of darkness, but at the same time, she knew she had to find the strength because of her children.

Alice walked with Sarah to her bedroom, told her to lock the door, and that she would figure out what to do.

Alice was in bed but wide awake when Jake came home. Tonight, he left her alone.

Chapter 10

Northern Minnesota

The next morning after Jake left, Alice called the local abuse hotline to try to figure out what to do to protect herself and her children. She knew she had to leave, but she didn't know where they would go and what she would do to support them. She had married Jake right out of high school and had only had a job one summer in her teens. The woman on the phone told her about a shelter they could go to where they would be safe until Alice could figure out the rest. So, Alice made up her mind that she would tell Jake they were leaving, and when the kids came home from school, they would pack up, leave, and go to the shelter. From there, she would figure out the rest.

The woman on the phone told her not to talk to Jake by herself. Alice was told she was in danger and that a welfare worker and the police would be dispatched for her protection when they were ready to leave, but Alice didn't pay attention to the warning. Besides, Jake wasn't home, and she hoped he was drunk somewhere and wouldn't be around when they left.

But that afternoon, Jake came home and plopped on the sofa to watch television. She mustered up some courage and told Jake that they were leaving. Jake just laughed and told her she was dreaming, that she wasn't going anywhere. She insisted she was, and Jake raged that if she ever tried it, he would kill her. Then he beat her worse than he ever had and left her lying on the floor, bruised and beaten while he stormed out of the house, warning her that she had better be there when he returned.

The kids were in school and Alice was all alone, so she just lay where she had fallen, clutching her ribs as she curled into a pitiful, hopeless heap. Reality sunk in that he would kill her if she left, yet she also finally accepted the fact that he would probably kill her if she stayed. Alice felt trapped.

Thoughts raged through her mind as the numbness left her body, and Alice took a very clear look at her life, for perhaps the first time. She knew that Jake was mean and abusive, yet she needed him. She was scared to death to be with him, and scared to death to be without him. For years it had somehow been okay for him to beat her because her small world had convinced her that it was just a part of being a wife. But now she knew he was hurting her kids too, and Alice's spirit started to rebel, yet she didn't know how she'd find the strength to change things.

Jake returned around suppertime, angrier than ever and very drunk. Alice quietly made a meal and put it on the table, feeling Sarah and Sam's eyes watching her every move, taking in the many bruises that were turning dark blue and the way she carefully moved and often put her hands on her ribs. As they ate in silence, Sam's nervous hand accidentally knocked over his glass, spilling the contents across the table.

Slamming his hand on the table, Jake yelled, "What's wrong with you, boy?"

He took his belt to Sam, followed by putting his fist through the wall before finally slamming the door behind him as he got in his car and sped away.

Alice hurriedly gathered Sam's bruised body to her, and Sarah, looking pale and scared, huddled next to them on the floor of the living room. During her hours curled up on the floor after Jake's beating, Alice had resigned herself to the fact that she would just watch Sarah very closely and not let Jake near her. She felt terrified, trapped, and unable to leave with no place to go, but as she held her shaking children against her, the fierceness of a mother lion surged forth as Alice became determined that Jake wasn't going to hurt Sarah or Sam ever again. She would see to that!

With trembling hands, Alice called the local emergency number she had been given by the abuse hotline. She was told to pack some clothes for each of them, lock the door so Jake couldn't get in, and wait for the police car that would be there within minutes. They each scurried to their rooms, stuffed clothing into plastic grocery bags, and gathered together near the window by the front door, waiting for their rescue.

Not long after he left, Jake's car came screeching back into the driveway, and he ran to the front door like a man on fire. When his shoulder hit the locked door, he bellowed like a bull, "Let me in right now! Damn you, Alice! You don't lock me out of my own house! You'll pay for this!"

He kicked in the door and was advancing, with his fists clenched, on the terrified trio just as the police car arrived. The officers ran through the open door and tackled Jake.

Jake screamed, "Get your hands off me! This is my house! You can't stop me from getting into my house!"

Two of the officers handcuffed him, took him outside, pushed him into the backseat of the patrol car, and drove away.

Alice, Sam, and Sarah stood huddled together, sobbing as a social worker arrived and a police officer helped them out of the house and to the waiting car. They remained silent as they drove away.

It was late at night and the shelter was quiet. While the beds were not comfortable, they were clean and she and the kids were safe from Jake. Alice glanced at Sarah lying next to her in the double bed sleeping peacefully. Just then, Sam moaned in his sleep, and Alice pulled herself out of bed and walked quietly over to him. She gingerly sat on the edge of his bed and watched him while love and sadness washed over her.

Up to this point in her life, she hadn't thought a lot about love. The only love she had ever received had been from her parents and Jake, and from those two experiences she hadn't found love to be something that anybody would really want. In her childhood, her father had very little to do with Alice or her sisters, unless he was yelling at them. And her mother had made sure they had meals to eat and clean clothes to wear, but if she wasn't doing housework, she was sitting in front of the television, telling them to be quiet. Any love she had received as a child had come from her sisters, and even that had disappeared as they got older and went their separate ways. Then she had married Jake, and in the beginning, he worked and she kept house, and occasionally they would get together with friends and go out dancing. She remembered some laughter and feelings of being cared about in the very beginning of their marriage, but that was over twenty years ago.

Still sitting on Sam's bed, Alice became conscious of the fact that over this last week, she was starting to feel different about love. Since realizing Jake was hurting her children, a real protective kind of love had emerged. It surprised her when it surfaced, because her kids had always been just a part of her life with Jake, something that had happened to her, like the rest of her life. She and Jake had had sex, she had gotten pregnant, miscarried a couple of times, and then when the kids were born, they just were. Not a lot of thought or energy had gone into them.

She gently touched Sam's face. While she had always made sure the kids, had clean clothes to wear and food to eat, she had never been aware that children took a lot of thought or energy, and she certainly didn't understand they deserved it.

Alice felt broken, not only in body, but in spirit. Her whole life was a shamble; her children were scared and she didn't know where to go from here. An inexplicable force kept drawing her back to Jake, and she was fighting it with all the strength she had, but she had no idea where she and the kids would go next. Maybe she should go back to Jake. Maybe he could change. Maybe everything could be okay.

The thought of facing the world and raising the kids by herself was scary and she didn't believe she could do it. Her mind was muddled and obsessed with the need to be with somebody, to be connected somehow, and the thought of being totally alone in the world brought extreme panic. For Alice, being connected, even to someone abusive, was better than being all alone.

As she left Sam's bedside and climbed back under the covers of her bed, Alice was convinced that going back to Jake was the only solution. She had convinced herself that things would be okay now. Then Sarah turned in the bed, and Alice's eyes focused on her daughter. Sarah's long, dark hair fanned out against the pillow, emanating childlike innocence as she slept. Yet Alice knew that in the daylight hours Sarah was not innocent, that she would never be innocent again because of Jake. Sarah had lost her childhood in a sick, sexually perverted experience. Alice's muddled mind clung to her daughter and her daughter's chance of a better life. There had to be something better out there for them.

Chapter 11

Dallas, Texas

It had been a long week at work for Suzanne, and the dream about Stephen had returned to haunt her every night, leaving her feeling lonelier than before. She had been divorced for eleven years, yet dreams about her ex-husband still went straight to her heart, filling her with anguish and a renewed sense of failure.

To top it off, Melanie had been on vacation all week and Suzanne had a temporary fill-in. She not only missed Melanie's knowledge about everything that went on in their area of the company, but she also missed her camaraderie and friendship.

Her ten sales reps were scattered throughout the state, and Suzanne regularly traveled during the week to work with each of them. That usually helped her cope with the pain of her personal life because it got her away from her lonely apartment, keeping her busy so that her mind couldn't dwell on either her past life or the sad reality of her present life. But this week, even that hadn't helped. The desolation had followed her as she traveled to see several of her reps. It had been hard to keep her mind on business, and fear had started creeping in on her—fear that the wall she had hidden behind for years was beginning to crack.

Friday was finally here. Her body welcomed the chance to relax, but her mind, as always, was fighting the thought of leisure with nothing to keep her thoughts busy or occupied. The walls in her condo began closing in shortly after she shut the door. She poured herself a large scotch, hoping it would relax her and help her fight the urge to go out and find the nearest bar, the quickest route to drunken oblivion.

Tonight, a part of her didn't want to go out. An almost-silent voice deep inside of her seemed to be trying to warn her—to keep her home—but the thick curtain of loneliness was heavier than usual, smothering out any warnings or rational thinking. She desperately needed the peace that a drunken stupor provided.

Racing like a haunted spirit, she slipped into jeans and a silk blouse. She was too frenzied to notice that the blouse clung seductively to her breasts. The suffocating blackness of her life was advancing so quickly that as Suzanne grabbed her purse and hurried for her car, the pins came loose in her coiled hair. She frantically pulled at them and her hair tumbled down onto her shoulders.

As she drove to her destination, that voice deep inside of her begged her to turn around and go back home. A feeling of dread burned in her stomach, but Suzanne raced away from the consuming loneliness and whirling memories. She couldn't turn around. She just couldn't. Suzanne started to regret her decision, but the ghosts of her past pushed her onward.

Billy Bob's Nightclub and Bar was noisy and crowded with country music blaring from the live band on the large stage. Suzanne was feeling relaxed from the alcohol in her system, the skillful arms gliding her around the dance floor, and the soothing hands that were moving around her back and shoulders, carefully nudging their way to the sides of her breasts.

Her head was leaning against his shoulder as she moved with him to the music. Her eyes were lazily gazing around the room as the alcohol kept her mind blurred. For a moment she thought she recognized someone on the crowded dance floor, but then they glided in another direction and her view and recognition blurred.

"May I cut in?" a familiar voice whispered in her ear.

Her partner pulled her closer to him as he said, "Buzz off," and danced her away from the man who had spoken.

Through an alcoholic haze, Suzanne thought she recognized the man who had tried to cut in, but as her partner's hold gently tightened, she relaxed against his shoulder and once again became lost in the music.

"Suzanne?" a voice behind her said with a tap on her shoulder. She turned toward it, resisting the nudge by her dancing partner to ignore it. Blinking to try to clear her vision, she gazed at the intruder who'd said her name. Recognition of the voice slowly broke through the blurriness. "Jeff?"

"That's right."

"Hey, do you mind?" her dance partner balked at the intrusion.

"Sorry, fella. We're old friends. I just want one dance. How about it, Suzanne?" Jeff was holding out his arms for her.

She smiled a faraway smile, turned toward Jeff, and stepped into his arms.

The fringes of sleep unwillingly left Suzanne in the morning as she awoke to a headache that was throbbing more than usual. Quietly getting out of bed, she didn't look at the man lying next to her. It didn't matter. He didn't matter. In fact, she would rather not know what he looked like. She would rather keep him to the foggy liquor-blurred memory of the night before.

Gathering her clothes tightly against her, Suzanne tiptoed into the en suite bathroom. She quietly closed the door and avoided looking at herself in the mirror as she pulled on her jeans and blouse. Carrying her shoes in her hands, she re-entered the crowded bedroom that was crammed with a large bed, two dressers, and a full-length mirror in a wooden standalone frame, and stepped carefully past the bed. Usually extreme silence wasn't necessary because the man typically didn't want to face Suzanne any more than she wanted to face him, but this morning was different.

Suzanne had reached the bedroom door, her hand on the knob, when a voice stopped her. "Why in such a hurry this morning, Ms. Simpson?"

Suzanne reeled at the use of her last name as panic stuck in her throat and slight remembrances of the night before started playing in her head. Memories of a familiar face danced before her.

Sitting up in the middle of the sheet-strewn king-sized bed was a naked, handsome Jeff Davidson. Everything about him was seductive and suggestive, everything except his face. His expression was cruel, and his leering smile betrayed his anger as he ogled Suzanne and threw his head back, laughing derisively. His words were sarcastic as he flung them in her direction. "You know, I never would have believed it, but you're a pretty good lay. There is some hot stuff underneath all that frigid ice."

Suzanne felt sick to her stomach. She vaguely remembered a familiar face, a soft voice, strong arms. She turned to flee the room, afraid she would throw up, but the door was locked. She desperately fumbled with the handle. In those few moments, Jeff leaped from the bed, pressed his hand against the door, positioned his naked body between her and her escape, and arrogantly glared down at her.

"Not so fast, Ms. Simpson. I'm not about to let you leave yet. We have a lot to talk about."

Drawing deeply from a sense of control and strength she possessed when she was not drinking, Suzanne replied in the voice she used as his superior. "We don't have a thing to talk about." As she spoke, she tried to keep her eyes from wandering the length of his naked form.

Jeff laughed a nasty laugh. "Why, Ms. Simpson, don't tell me you're interested in seconds. Or let me see, is it about fifths or sixths?"

Nausea took hold of her. Out of control and frightened, Suzanne's stomach began to roll as realization of what had happened began to sink in. Now she had done it. She had gone too far. *I'll get through this . . . I can do it. I just have to keep my head.*

Turning to face him, she gathered her strength. "We both had too much to drink last night, Jeff. We made a mistake, but we're both adults. We can pretend this never happened." A knot lodged in her throat as she turned to the door.

"It's not going to be that easy," Jeff said angrily. "I thought you might be interested in seeing what great pictures you take."

"Pictures? What pictures?" Suzanne placed her hand over her mouth. She was going to throw up, she knew it—right here on his rug and all over his naked form. Her stomach was going to turn inside out and leave all of its contents splattered all over his body. As she subtly gulped in air to keep her stomach from unloading its liquid contents, she tried to pretend she didn't know what he was talking about, yet somewhere in the cavern of her mind, she knew. Oh yes, she knew.

Walking to his dresser, Jeff held up a stack of pictures. "I think we have a lot to talk about." One by one he showed her Polaroid photos of herself in naked, sickening poses. She was really drunk last night. She didn't remember much, but tiny pieces of her memory flickered in and out of her consciousness—their naked bodies, the sex, the release. But she didn't remember anything explicit that would separate last night from all the other times.

Ashamed and scared, she fought for composure as Jeff gloated. Jeff Davidson was the type of man who worked to get his opponents into vulnerable positions, then basked in their defeat. During sales calls, she had watched him in action, so she knew the viciousness underneath that smile. Even though her mind was still blurred from the alcohol and her blazing headache, she was beginning to understand the situation into which she had so blindly stepped.

In business, Jeff kept his maliciousness covered with a veneer of charm and manners, but Suzanne knew it was a very thin covering. As her alcoholic blur was quickly burning away from the panic that was surfacing within her, Suzanne's sharp mind came quickly to the surface. And with that thought, the numbers in her bank account flashed across her mind as she accepted the fact that she could afford blackmail—at least for a while. But, she wouldn't make it easy for him.

Looking him straight in the eye and gathering strength into her voice, she responded, "So, you took some good pictures. What do you want me to do about it? I'm not in the photo-judging business."

"Well, now." He grinned wickedly. "I thought you just might be in the photo-buying business."

Anger welled up inside of her. "All right, Mr. Davidson, I'll bite. What the hell do you want?"

A wicked smile encompassed his entire face. "Several things, Ms. Simpson. And each one of these pictures will be traded in turn."

Suzanne's throat went dry as she scanned the stack of pictures. Her mind immediately went back to the numbers in her bank account as well as her savings and investments. She had built a nice nest egg, but if the price per picture was too high, she could be broke halfway through the stack.

Turning away from Jeff, Suzanne noticed the bedroom and adjoining bathroom for the first time. It was nice, but nothing like the large, luxurious condo she had. Suzanne knew what Jeff made because she gave him his raises and bonuses. She knew he could afford more than this and quickly calculated that he must be spending his money on something other than a place to live. Her mind circled with possibilities—maybe he gambled or had some addiction that needed cash.

As she stood inches away from his naked body and leering face, Suzanne took as much control over the situation as she could, deciding that she would play this cool, not get flustered, and stay in control. She knew she could think her way out of this the way she had everything else in her life. Having a quick mind was what had gotten her to where she was. It was her mind she relied on, never allowing herself to get caught up in having feelings about things, but just thinking about them and working them out. And once more she returned to the strategy that had always helped her step above situations that had tried to destroy her over the years. She had learned many years ago to stuff her feelings about her life or experiences deep inside of her so they didn't come out, at least not until she was drunk, when they didn't hurt so much.

"Okay, how much money do you want?"

"Oh, it's not just money." The leer on his face was menacing.

"What do you mean?" Large, invisible hands of panic tightened around Suzanne's throat.

Jeff stepped toward her and ran a finger down her cheek. "Last night was pretty good. I could go for a lot more of that."

Suzanne stepped back as though she had been hit, and her stomach lurched toward her throat. Her voice sounded like a vulnerable, little girl. "I'll give you money, but leave me alone."

Jeff ran his finger down her chest and inside her blouse, tickling the crevice between her breasts as he quietly spit out the words, "Sorry, boss, I'm in charge here. I make the rules of this game. First of all, I want you to get off my case at work. No more threats or playing big mama boss. Then, you'll give me a considerable raise. Some you can take care of with a raise at work, the rest will come out of your bank account."

"I won't do it. Forget it." Her strength was trying to surface.

"Then I guess I'll just have to send a few of these pictures to your boss, a few to the CEO, etcetera, and down, down, down goes your career. Who do you think will hire you after that? And the rumors will fly. You'll be known as a slut and a drunk. You'll be dead in the water, Ms. Corporate Ladder Climber."

Suzanne tried to fight her fear, stay cool, and think her way out of this, but she was drowning. Her stomach seemed to be permanently stuck in her throat, and her mind was clawing at a myriad of ideas and thoughts, desperately trying to come up with a solution, a way out of this problem. At the same time, memories from the past were swirling around her as she sunk into the cruel, raging waters of another man's control. She was lost in such a maze of panic that her father's face flickered in and out of her memory, merging with Jeff's. For a moment, they were both there, looming over her, with nasty smiles on their faces, and for several moments they felt like one and the same.

Deep inside, she trembled with fear. She had nowhere to turn and the vulnerable, little girl inside of her replaced the woman who was so desperately trying to stay in charge. Once again, she had been a bad girl, and she couldn't tell. Nobody could help her.

Chapter 12

Atlanta, Georgia

The shrill ringing of the telephone startled Helene awake. Turning in the bed, she glanced at Bill buried in the covers. It was nice to see him there; she hadn't appreciated that sight for quite some time, but in the predawn hours, it was nice that he was home.

Grabbing the insistent phone before it could ring another time, Helene whispered into the receiver, "Hello?"

"Hello?" The male voice on the other end seemed unsure. "May I speak with Helene Miller please?"

Helene sat up in bed. "With whom?"

The voice hesitated. "I'm trying to reach the daughter of Anna Theresa Miller. Do I have the right number?"

Helene's tongue ran across her dry lips. "Yes . . . yes, you have the right number. This is Helene Miller Foster."

"Oh, I'm sorry. Your mother's note said Helene Miller."

"I've been married for many years. My mother knows that." She paused in frustration. "But why are you calling about my mother? And how did you know how to reach me?"

Ignoring the first question, he went right to the second. "Your mother left a note with your phone number."

She has my phone number? was the first thought that popped into Helene's mind. Then her hand started to shake and her voice quivered as she answered. "Left a note, what do you mean, left a note? Where is she? Is she okay?"

Helene hadn't been in contact with her mother for over fifteen years. When Thomas was a baby, Helene had called her mother a couple of times, thinking she would be excited about being a grandmother, but her mother hadn't shown much interest at all. The conversations had been stilted and uncomfortable, so Helene quit calling and she hadn't heard from her mother since.

She hadn't really thought about her for years, until recently—until these problems with Thomas and her own visits to the therapist. She used to think that her mother, or her mother's life, would never affect her again. She believed that if her mother died, she would feel no remorse or regret, but now fear was settling around her heart. Her mother must be dead. Why else would a stranger call so early in the morning?

The voice on the other end was calm and deliberately spoke slowly. "Mrs. Foster, your mother is in the hospital. She's in a coma. I haven't been able to reach your sisters yet."

"What hospital is she in?" Her hand flew to her chest as if to stop its rapid pounding.

"The Virginia Regional Medical Center," the voice replied.

At first her mind couldn't grasp the name of the hospital until she remembered that her mother still lived in Minnesota, and Virginia was the small town not far from the farm where Helene had grown up. Still trying to get her bearings and take in the information she had just received, she quietly answered, "I'll be there as soon as I can," and hung up the phone without giving the man on the other end of the line a chance to say anything more. After hanging up she realized that she didn't even know who he was. *Where was Alice? Why wasn't she with Mom?*

Helene hadn't been back home since she left right after she graduated from high school, and a few weeks ago, Helene wouldn't have given a second thought to going back home because it was a part of her life that she had cast aside and ignored. But from the sessions she had had with Raymond Welsh, she now knew how badly she was affected by her childhood—by her father's drinking and her mother's helplessness and martyrdom.

Her mother, her mom, her mommy . . . she hadn't thought about her for a very long time. As she thought about her now, anger welled up inside of her—anger for the mother she never had, anger for what her childhood had not been. Her mother had deprived her of the loving feelings a little girl should get. Her mother had deprived her of the caretaking every child deserved. She couldn't remember being told she was loved or being tucked in at night and read bedtime stories the way Helene had done with Thomas. When Thomas was born, Helene had read every book she could get her hands on so she could understand what being a mother was all about because her memories of her mother were that she cooked and cleaned, told them to do their chores, and spent any spare time she had in front of the television set.

With her therapist's help, Helene was beginning to deal with her past and the fact that she might need to talk with her mother about all her pain. She was probably a couple of years away from the real confrontation, and now her mother was going to deprive her of that too because her mother was going to die.

Anger surged into the pit of Helene's stomach where it lodged and churned. Her body tensed and fury scorched through her as her mind traveled through conversations she would like to have had with her mother. Scenes where Helene was telling her mother about the pain, telling her how disgusted she was by her weakness, her inability to stand up to Helene's father and take care of her children the way they deserved. As Helene's mind delved farther into the possibilities of a confrontation, she relished the thought of finally forcing her mother to tell her she was special, she was pretty, and she deserved all the best. It was as though forcing her mother to say it would enable Helene to finally experience those feelings.

Now she knew that her mother was going to deprive her of even that. *My mother is going to die. How dare she die?*

"I've got to go. I've just got to go," she mumbled as she kicked the covers back on the bed, reaching for the phone and the phone book at the same time. It was too early in the morning to get in touch with their travel agent, so she called the airline directly and found out that she could catch a plane in four hours. She would first fly to Minneapolis, have an hour layover, then fly to

Duluth where she would rent a car and drive to Virginia. She called a car rental agency and reserved a car as her mind mechanically took care of the details.

As she was making her arrangements, Bill stirred. He rolled toward her and watched and listened. As she hung up the phone, he put his hand on her arm. "Helene? What's up? Where are you going?"

"Home." The word came so easy, but she hadn't thought of Minnesota as home for over twenty years.

"Home? Where? Why?" He sat up straighter in the bed, shaking his head to dislodge the sleep that still encompassed him and trying to understand what she was saying.

"Bill, I'm in a hurry. My mother's dying. I'm going home to Minnesota. I don't know the details. I don't know when I'll be back. I just know I have to go." She was walking back and forth tossing clothes from her closet and her dresser drawers onto the bed, stopping occasionally with her finger on her chin as she tried to figure out what she needed to take.

"What about us?" Bill was now sitting on the side of the bed watching her intently. "What about Thomas and the counseling?" His hands splayed out in front of him. "Who will make sure he goes and that he stays on track with his recovery?"

Helene stopped what she was doing, put her hand on her hip, and slowly emphasized the words, "You'll just have to handle whatever comes up here. And Thomas will just have to be a little more responsible because I can't take care of you two right now. I have to go home. I can't explain it. I just have to go."

Within a short amount of time, Helene was showered and dressed with her bags waiting in the hallway downstairs. She had called a limo to take her to the airport and she waited by the window, waiting for her transportation to arrive. Bill had gone into Thomas's room to awaken him. Now the two men stood at the bottom of the stairs, their shoulders slumped and bewilderment covering their faces.

A sad smile pulled at Helene's mouth. They looked like small boys who were being abandoned, and in an instant of clarity, Helene realized that in the past she would have felt guilty. She would have felt she had to stay home. But not this time. The tug of her past was so strong that nothing could keep her from going back to Minnesota. She had to go. Somehow she knew that she hadn't dealt with her feelings over her father's death more than ten years ago. Alice had called her with the news, but she had refused to go to his funeral, hadn't sent flowers, and had tried to ignore the fact that he even existed, let alone that he had died. Now that she was in counseling, she was aware that pain from the past couldn't be ignored. Somewhere, somehow, it always reared its head.

Now, she was going to have her mother's death and all of her unresolved feelings about her mother piled on top of everything else she was currently dealing with. She had stuffed her feelings for so many years that she felt like a burlap sack straining and ripping at the seams. The reality was that she had to go back and deal with whatever was waiting for her. She just had to.

"You two be good." She feebly grinned at them.

"Where will you be staying?" Bill asked. "Will we be able to reach you if we need you?"

"I just don't know details right now." Helene felt irritation at the little-boy tone in his voice. "I'll call you as soon as I get settled in a hotel. It's been so long since I've been back there, I have no idea what's available."

"What if an emergency comes up? How can I get ahold of you?"

"I said I'd call you, and I will." Her voice was firm.

Helene wanted to laugh as she recognized how suddenly the tables had been turned. For many years, it had been Bill rushing out on a last-minute business trip and she was left standing by the door not really knowing where he was going or why. In the back of her mind, she always wondered if he was meeting another woman.

Could Bill be worried that I may never come back? She'd never given him any reason to think that. For a moment, a small smile crossed her lips. *Now he'll know what it feels like.* The thought amused her.

A horn sounded in the driveway, and Helene turned to her bags. "We'll get them, Mom." Thomas was quick to grab her suitcases.

Helene felt genuine surprise at the way they were hovering over her. They didn't do that. They always took her for granted, knowing she would always be there for them—knowing she would always be home when they got there, if they decided to get there.

Thomas placed a hand on her shoulder. "Mom, I hope your mother will be okay." He didn't say "grandmother" because Thomas didn't know her as "grandmother." In fact, he didn't know Anna Miller at all. Helene had never allowed him the chance.

"Thank you, Thomas." She stroked his cheek. Typically, Thomas would have pulled away if Helene tried to do any mothering, but in these early morning hours, he just stood there with his hands down along his sides, looking helpless. Helene wrapped her arms around his neck. "I love you, Thomas. Be good, okay?"

"I will, Mom."

Helene turned to Bill and was startled as he encircled her with his arms. Pulling her close to him, he whispered into her ear, "I love you, Helene. I really love you."

Anguish choked Helene as she laid her head against his shoulder, fighting the feeling of wanting to just stay there and not get into the waiting car. Bill hadn't held her this close in a long time, and she wanted to stay snuggled in his arms and savor the deliciousness of it. It felt good; she had craved this for so long that she wanted to settle into his strength. But she couldn't today because she had to go home. She just had to go home.

Helene climbed into the limo and settled herself in the backseat. "Be good, both of you," she smiled weakly. "I'll call you as soon as I'm settled."

As the limo drove away, Helene waved from the backseat as she watched her entire world fade behind her. She knew they probably couldn't see her through the heavily darkened window, but as she watched them fade, Helene wondered what her life would be like when she came back. A swirl of fear engulfed her as she fought an impulse to tell the driver to stop so she could just return to her life as she knew it, because she somehow knew it would never be the same again—that she would never be the same again. She felt herself being pulled into the mouth of a deep, dark cavern as forces tugged her deeper and deeper into her past, and she knew with an innate certainty that she would not emerge the same person. She didn't know how she would change. She just knew that after this trip she would be forever altered. About that, she was positive.

Chapter 13

Northern Minnesota

The policeman escorted Alice, Sarah, and Sam up to the door of their house. Alice kept looking behind her. Sarah's hands were shaking, and Sam's eyes were round with fear.

"I can stay here with you for an hour," the policeman said. "That should be long enough for you to pack enough belongings to last you for a while. Then I've got to bring you back to the shelter. We've got so much territory to cover." He smiled in apology. "I'm really sorry, ma'am. I know you should be able to stay in your home and feel safe, but we just don't have the manpower to protect people from their own families. And sometimes those are the most dangerous of all."

They slowly walked through the house with plastic bags in hand; they had instructions to bring only what was necessary for the next couple of weeks. When they got to Sam's room, he shrugged his shoulders and opened the door. Sarah walked quietly to her room, and Alice trudged down the hall. As she rummaged through her closet for clothes to take, she came upon the stash of chocolate and sat still for several moments, deciding what to do. She shook her head, then gathered up her clothes, stuffed them into the plastic bags, and started for the door where she paused, quickly turned around, grabbed a handful of the chocolate bars, and shoved them to the bottom of one of the bags.

As they gathered back in the living room, the phone rang. Sarah grabbed it then turned to Alice. "Mom, it's for you. They say it's about Grandma."

Reaching for the phone, Alice brushed sweat from her brow.

"Hullo," Alice muttered into the phone. Alice hadn't called her mom in a while, but her life was in turmoil, and her mother would just tell Alice that she had made her bed, so she had to lie in it. Her mother would never believe about Sarah and Jake, and she sure wouldn't understand Alice and the kids going to an abuse shelter. She would just tell Alice that she was overreacting. Alice honestly couldn't deal with her mother now.

"Mrs. Hudson? This is the Virginia Regional Medical Center. We've been trying to contact you for hours. Your mother is in intensive care. How soon can you come to the hospital?"

Alice's mind fought through a fog of confusion. Her mother was in the hospital?

"I'm not sure," she stammered as she struggled to deal with what she was hearing. "What do you mean intensive care? How long has she been there?"

"She was brought in during the night by ambulance," the voice answered.

Anger flooded through her as Alice tightly gripped the phone. She had been dealing with her mother's life, her mother's pains, her mother's loneliness, and her mother's unhappiness ever since she was a young child. She was the one her mother talked to and complained to, even when Alice was a child. At times it felt as though she were more responsible for her mother than her mother had ever been for her. Well, she couldn't do that right now. Her own life was turned upside down and her kids needed her. She wasn't going to get pulled into her mother's "poor me" attempts like she always did. She didn't know where her own life was headed, and she couldn't deal with her mother. Not now!

Yet once again, Alice was being asked to set her own feelings and life aside to deal with her mother. Of course, she did what she was expected to do as she asked the police officer to drive her and the kids to the hospital.

Chapter 14

Dallas, Texas

It had been three weeks since Suzanne's terrible mistake, and Jeff had been pursuing her the way a hound chased a fox—never letting up. She never knew when he would appear or what he would want. She had met his demands. She even wrote letters commending his performance and gotten him a raise and a bigger bonus. In the process, she had been trying to avoid Melanie's questions and protests, but today Melanie caught her off guard.

"What's going on? Jeff hasn't changed a bit. What's going on here?"

Feeling backed into a corner, Suzanne snapped at Melanie, "Don't overstep your authority."

"What's he got on you?" Melanie asked as she stepped into Suzanne's office and sat down in her usual spot. "Come on," she coaxed as she leaned over the desk. "What is he threatening you with? You'd never do this without a reason. And why all those closed-door meetings? What is it?" Melanie sat back in the chair. "Don't let him do this!"

Suzanne spun her chair around to face the windows and stare at the view below, turning her back to Melanie. She wanted to yell, scream, punch something, but that would mean she'd have to tell Melanie what was going on, and she couldn't. *My God, I just can't.* She couldn't tell anyone.

She buried her face in her hands and just shook her head. "Please, Melanie, just let this be." She had gotten herself into this mess, so she would have to handle this by herself.

Suzanne heard Melanie get up and walk out.

Suddenly, she heard Jeff's voice. She turned in time to see him sauntering into her office. "Hi," he smiled as he closed and locked the door.

Suzanne was boiling inside. She wanted to call him an arrogant pig, to tell him to get out of her office. She'd like to fire him and get him out of her life for good, but she couldn't take the chance that he would follow through on his threat to distribute the pictures. She was too afraid to face those consequences, so she was a pawn in his malicious, spiteful game.

"Why aren't you working?" she demanded.

"Have you forgotten, boss? You don't make the demands. I do." He advanced toward her, cleared her desk with one sweep of his hand, and grabbed her.

Suzanne's stomach churned. "No, Jeff. Not here, please." Her fists clenched and her body turned rigid.

Jeff's smile turned nasty. "I think you've forgotten, sweetheart. I'm in control here." His emphasis on the word *sweetheart* turned it into something nasty and foul. "I'll say where, when, and how much. You, Ms. Simpson, are at my bidding and don't you forget it."

Suzanne wanted to resist, to tell him she would not be blackmailed, not anymore. Yet she didn't. The little girl was back in Daddy's control. Back in the darkness of secrets where nobody could know what happened, nobody could know what a really bad girl she was because of what men wanted to do to her. The darkness and pain of her childhood sucked her downward like a whirlpool into a vortex of helplessness as she bit her lip to keep the sobs inside.

As Jeff moved her up onto her desk, raised her skirt, and lowered her pantyhose, Suzanne once again pushed away the feelings and pain as she closed her eyes, gripped the desk with her hands, and silently submitted.

Suzanne fumbled with the key in the door. When she stepped inside, she dropped her briefcase and slammed the door shut, then dead-bolted it. Ripping off her coat, she ran into the bathroom, hurriedly removed her clothing, and jumped in the shower, scrubbing her skin as hard as she could. Finally, the tears came as she stood under the water, sobbing until the water ran cold against her skin.

Slowly turning off the shower, she wrapped herself in a towel and leaned back against the wall of her bedroom, slumping to the floor in utter exhaustion. She had to get away from Jeff's clutches because she couldn't handle the feelings that were pounding hard against her chest. Anger that had been buried deep inside of her for years roiled under the surface like a dormant volcano. Over the years, a hard crust had formed over her anger, keeping it contained, but that control was slipping. The horrific rage inside of her was now threatening to erupt.

Today, during Jeff's invasion of her body, she had glanced at the letter opener lying neatly on her desk and had wanted to grab the instrument and quickly and violently thrust it into his back. She had felt too helpless to even reach out her hand. When Jeff was satisfying himself with her body, Suzanne saw a flash of her father and fury had blazed so ferociously within her that she had violently thrown Jeff off her.

Pulling his pants up and regaining his balance, Jeff had grabbed her arm as anger contorted his face. But rage had burst to the surface and Suzanne had tugged up her panty hose, punched his jaw, grabbed his collar, and hauled him toward the door. Unlocking and opening the door with one hand, she had pushed him into the reception area where Melanie's desk was and quickly slammed her door closed behind him. Gathering all the strength she possessed, Suzanne straightened her clothing and resumed her day, shoving her anger into the black cavern of feelings deep inside of her.

With wet hair and the towel still wrapped around her, Suzanne headed into the kitchen to pour herself a scotch. Then, without any warning, energy oozed out of her like a punctured balloon, and she fell against the countertop, holding her head in her hands as she waited for the sobs to come once more. They didn't.

After several moments, she pulled herself into a standing position and noticed the red light blinking on her answering machine. She numbly hit the play button.

The first two messages barely touched her consciousness. They were reminders of appointments—one from her dentist, the other from a business associate. It was the third message that caught her attention as she leaned close to the machine to get every word. She hastily grabbed a pen and paper from a nearby drawer and scribbled down the number. The call was from a hospital in Minnesota. The person who'd left the message said it was an emergency.

Normally Suzanne wouldn't be concerned, but the many weeks of dealing with Jeff had uncovered feelings about her family and her childhood. Suddenly, a childhood that had been buried away had come to the forefront. In a half daze, Suzanne picked up the phone and made a call.

After hearing the news, she hung up and slipped into one of the four chairs that neatly circled the kitchen table and sat there in stunned silence. A cynical laugh slowly bubbled to the surface as she realized she now had exactly what she needed to get away from Jeff for a while: a dying mother. Who could not have sympathy with that?

Her lip curled in distaste as she remembered how her mother had never come to her rescue when she needed her all those years ago. And neither had her sisters. Suzanne had felt alone and abandoned. She had never told anyone because her father had threatened to hurt them all if she did, and Suzanne had believed him. But why hadn't her mother and sisters known? The small, wounded child that still existed deep inside of Suzanne couldn't forgive them for that.

Hysterical laughter erupted from Suzanne. All those nights that she had lay at the mercy of her father, her mother had never come to help her. The mother who had been just a few doors away had never come to her child's aid. Yet now, from over a thousand miles away, her mother was coming to her rescue from her deathbed. Was it poetic justice? To get away from the pain and torture of her present, she was rushing headlong into the pain and torture of her past.

Suzanne turned her head toward the ceiling. "God, if you really are up there, you've got one cruel sense of humor." Slipping off the chair to lay face-down onto the floor, Suzanne submitted to the sobs that racked her body.

Chapter 15

Northern Minnesota

The hospital room was dark, the blinds were closed, and the door to the hallway was shut. The only sounds were tiny beeps from the monitoring equipment. Helene stood at the end of the bed staring down at the still figure of the woman she hadn't seen in over twenty years. She knew her mother was getting older, but she was startled by the effects of aging. Her mother's skin was dry and wrinkled from lack of care throughout the years, the thin hair clinging to her head was a dull steel gray. An IV tube protruded from one of her hands. Sadness pulled at Helene as she stared at the still form.

When Helene arrived at the hospital, she'd stopped at the nurse's station to understand what was going on with her mother. She was told that her mother was in a diabetic coma. They did not know if or when her mother would regain consciousness.

Why did I come? What did I expect to accomplish? Yet she couldn't leave. Finally settling into a chair by the window, Helene closed her eyes in exhaustion. Rest was just starting to settle over her when the door opened. Because of the darkness of the room, Helene was not immediately visible to the newcomer. In quiet seclusion, she watched the woman approach the bed, expecting it to be one of the myriad of nurses that fluttered in and out, checking the tubes and equipment.

My goodness, this woman is huge. The figure seemed to waddle toward the side of the bed where she stood staring down at the patient. Slowly the woman reached out and touched Helene's mother's hand. Helene shifted her position, and the startled visitor turned toward the noise. "Hello?"

"Hello," Helene replied. "I didn't mean to startle you. I'm Mrs. Miller's daughter." She stood and walked toward the bed.

"Helene?" the woman questioned.

As Helene inched closer, a lump formed in her throat. She barely recognized her sister. Alice had been heavy for a long time, but Helene wasn't prepared for this. As she stared at her sister, Helene felt disgust. All she saw was the lack of self-control and self-discipline. Her eyes passed from the top of Alice's tightly curled hair, over her bruised face, and down her huge body clothed in a blue polyester pantsuit, and she was embarrassed. Even on noticing the bruises, the concern wasn't enough to overcome the negative reaction welling up in Helene.

As Alice and Helene sized each other up from across the bed, silence permeated the room. The stillness was broken by an entering nurse. She checked their mother and turned to the two women. "Visitors must be kept to only one at a time. We have a small private waiting room for the intensive care families. I'll show you where it is."

Alice's large body seemed to plant itself by the bed, so Helene smiled and followed the nurse from the room.

Suzanne arrived that afternoon and the three sisters barely acknowledged each other as they rotated from the waiting room to their mother's bedside. At first, they were like adversaries who stayed far away from each other, sizing up their opponents. As the evening approached and the exhaustion of the whole experience took its toll on each of them, they slowly began exchanging a few curt words here and there. Neither Helene nor Suzanne had been back to Minnesota since they graduated high school. And none of them had talked to each other, even on the phone, for close to ten years. They were strangers who shared the same childhood.

At the end of the day, Helene returned to her hotel room exhausted, and vowed that the next day would be better. She would begin trying to build a relationship with her sisters and come to terms with her childhood. She was now back in the place she had started, and it was up to her to make the best of it. She had to make sense of her family and her past so she could try to make sense of her present. She wasn't sure how she was going to do it, but she was determined that she would. While her body was exhausted, her mind would not rest, and a cauldron of convoluted feelings stirred inside of her. She cried until she was too tired to cry anymore. To Helene, it seemed as though the alarm sounded just minutes after she had climbed into bed.

Helene stopped by the nurse's station to see if there had been any changes during the night. There hadn't been. Her mom was still in a coma. "The doctor will be by to see you later this morning," the nurse behind the desk informed her.

Upon entering her mother's hospital room, she was surprised to see Suzanne already there. Suzanne rose to leave as Helene entered, but Helene motioned her to stay when she noticed that Suzanne was crying. "Are you crying for Mom?" Helene asked the question without being aware that she'd asked it.

Suzanne shook her head and in a very soft voice replied, "No . . . for me."

Helene sat in the chair on the other side of the bed. "Me too. I cried myself to sleep last night, but it was more for what I missed and what I wish I felt than it was for Mom."

Suzanne eyed Helene. "I thought you and Mom were close—you being the oldest one and all. She always seemed to be so proud of everything you did. Alice and I couldn't come close."

Helene's mouth fell open in surprise. "Mom? Proud of me? She never said so. When I used to stay in touch with her, all she did was complain about what I wasn't doing or how good I had it and how bad she had it." Anger flushed through Helene's body. "She always made me so damn mad. Why didn't she ever do anything about her life instead of just complaining about it? Why did she put up with Dad? Why didn't she stand up to him and protect us and make life better for us? She was our mother for God's sake! If we couldn't depend on her, who could we depend on?"

Alice walked into the room as they were talking and sat down in a chair close to the door. "You both think you have all the answers, don't you? Life has always gone so smooth for you two. What do either of you know about being trapped with a man? Feeling you can't do any better and you've got children to support. What do either one of you know about that?" Her voice began to rise. "You come home with your fancy clothes and your fancy lives and you sit here and judge Mom. Sure, she whined a lot. She drove me crazy with her whining and she was always nagging on me, but I understood her."

Alice lowered her head to look at the floor. "I understood how life had given her a raw deal and she didn't know how to get out of it, and being so scared that you're gonna lose the man you have. No, he might not treat you very good, but deep down inside you don't believe you're good enough for him to treat you better. And you don't know who you are except by the way he treats you. So, if he leaves, you just become an empty box. What do you know about that?" She raised her head and her hollow eyes peered in their direction. "If you can't understand that, you can't understand Mom."

Helene felt pinned to the wall. *Is that how Mom felt?* Despair plummeted into her stomach and twisted and turned as Helene recognized that her feelings were the same as Alice was describing. She was afraid of losing Bill. Afraid of what she would be without him.

Silence permeated the room as the women withdrew into their own private worlds of despair, remorse, and confusion. A nurse came into the room. Helene knew they shouldn't all be in here at one time, but the nurse just glanced at each of them and quietly left.

Helene's eyes softened and a single tear slid down her cheek as she observed the woman lying motionless in the bed. Being secluded away in that darkened room with her mother and sisters made her feel safe. Like being sequestered in the warm, safe womb where you were protected before being released to the harsh realities of life. Maybe it was the room, maybe the presence of her mother and sisters, or maybe the timing in her life, but almost without realizing she was doing so, Helene began to talk—at first to her mother, then to her sisters, and finally to the whole room as a release.

"Maybe I've been unfair. Maybe I really didn't know you. Maybe I've judged you unfairly all these years." Turning her head to Alice, her voice took on a slight edge. "It's her fault. How could we know what she was going through if she didn't say so? She told you. Why didn't she tell me?"

"Mom didn't tell me," Alice said defensively.

"Then how do you know how she felt?" Helene asked.

Sitting back in her chair, Alice's voice lowered. "I just know."

"But how? I didn't know, yet here I am doing much of the same thing." Helene stood up from her chair and began to pace around the room. "Bill cheats on me. He's cheated on me for years. I never say anything. I'm too afraid. I don't want to lose him. Without him, I'm nothing." She quickly sat back into the chair, her eyes dropping to her hands in her lap.

Alice's mouth fell open in surprise. "But you've always been so sure of yourself. You could make something of your life, and lots of men could fall in love with you. Not like me. Jake was my only chance, but I can't let him hurt my kids no more."

"What do you mean hurt your kids?" Helene demanded.

"He was hurting both of them, especially Sarah."

"Did he beat them? Did he beat you? Is that how you got those bruises?" Helene's words shot out like bullets from a machine gun.

"Yeah, he beat me and he sometimes whipped the kids, but he was hurting them different, especially Sarah."

Suzanne shifted in her chair. "How was he hurting Sarah?" she demanded.

"I don't wanna say." Alice pulled on the edges of her jacket. "He was just hurting her." She made a weak attempt at a deep breath. "Somehow it was my fault, and I just had to stop it. I didn't know." Her eyes look pleadingly at Suzanne, begging her to understand. "I mean, it was okay when he hurt me, but not my kids. You understand?" Strength ebbed into her voice. "But not my kids!"

"Yes, I understand," Suzanne snapped. "He was having sex with Sarah, wasn't he?"

"Well . . ."

"Damn it, Alice. Was he molesting her?"

Alice began to cry. Sobs flowed from her huge body and she leaned against the bed, putting her face against the sheet as she gently touched her mother's leg. "I didn't know. I would have stopped it, but I didn't know."

"How in the hell can you live in the same house and not know?" Suzanne was now standing with her hands on her hips, glaring at Alice. "You had to know! Just the way you all knew when I was a kid. You don't want to do anything now, and you didn't want to do anything then!" Her voice was edging up and her face was flushed.

"Suzanne, keep your voice down. You're gonna get us kicked out of here. And leave Alice alone. You can't know what she's . . ." Helene trailed off as Suzanne's words penetrated her mind. "What do you mean she didn't do anything then? When you were a kid? What are you talking about?"

"Helene, quit playing dumb and cute." Suzanne swung her entire body in Helene's direction, looking as though she wanted to throw a punch at her. "You all knew, but you knew if I was the one, you wouldn't be."

"You were the one for what?" Helene leaned forward, her mind trying to figure out what Suzanne was talking about.

Alice gripped her mother's foot as she stared at Suzanne. "Tell me what you're talking about," she demanded in a low but powerful voice.

"I'm talking about Dad, damn you. Don't make me say it." Suzanne slumped back into her chair and buried her face in her hands. "You know. She knew. You all just abandoned me to him."

"I still don't know what you're talking about," Helene burst in.

Alice's voice was quiet and calm. "She's telling us that Dad had sex with her. Aren't you, Suzie?"

"Don't call me Suzie!" she sneered. "I'm not Suzie. That was Suzie way back then. I'm not Suzie! Don't ever call me Suzie."

Alice and Helene watched as Suzanne broke down before their eyes. Sobs burst loose from her as she clutched her mother's hand. "Why didn't you protect me? Why did you just abandon me to him? Why did all of you abandon me?"

A nurse came into the room with a stern look on her face, apparently intending to tell them to leave. Helene turned toward her and said, "We'll keep quiet, but please let us stay. Now's not a good time." Helene half-expected her mom to lift her head and snap at them to be quiet the way she often had when they were children.

Alice walked over to Suzanne, placing her hands on her sister's shoulders. "We didn't know. And I don't think Mom knew. It's not something you think is gonna happen with the father of your kids. It's too creepy. You don't think a father would do that, not to his own kids. You'd have to have told her." She paused for a moment as bewilderment filled her face. "Even then I don't know if she'd have believed you. It's hard—it's just so hard." Placing her head against Suzanne's back, Alice began to cry. "I'm sorry, Suzanne. I'm just so sorry."

Chapter 16

Northern Minnesota

Sleep did not come easy for Helene as nightmares haunted her throughout the night. The faces of Suzanne, Alice, Thomas, and Bill all mingled together in a collage of feelings, each of them pulling at her, needing something from her, but she didn't know what.

As the morning light filtered in through the nearly closed drapes, Helene struggled to pull herself awake. She lay in bed staring at the ceiling, not wanting to get up, yet not wanting to stay where she was. Yesterday filtered through her mind as she tried to understand all she had learned. How could they have lived in the same house and not known what each other was going through? Their father had been easy to despise because of his constant drinking and his downright meanness, but yesterday Helene began to understand that the feelings she, Suzanne, and Alice had for their mother were a tangled web of love, resentment, and anger.

Helene was still trying to absorb the fact that their father had sexually molested Suzanne and none of them had known about it. Could Mom really have been blind to that kind of abuse? Then again, who would expect that a father would do something like that to their child? Helene shivered. She would never understand a parent who would intentionally hurt a child. As far as she was concerned, anybody like that was a monster.

Her thoughts wandered to Bill and Thomas. Bill was not the attentive father that she wanted him to be and he spent far too much time away and not enough time with Thomas, but Bill would never intentionally hurt their child. When Thomas was first born, they both doted on him, then Bill's law practice took off and he was gone a lot. By the time Thomas was a toddler, he and Helene got used to doing things without Bill.

For many years, she was Thomas's world, and he would come to her for everything. They spent many Saturdays at the zoo and would drive to Stone Mountain and take the tram to the very top where Helene would worry about him getting too close to the edge, Thomas exclaiming with wonder at how high up they were.

Helene wasn't sure what had changed, but something had, and while it was easy for her to blame it all on Bill for not being a good father, she knew from her sessions in therapy she had to look at her own choices as well. Being with Suzanne and Alice yesterday had opened her eyes to how easily she had slipped into the role of victim, shuffling out blame instead of dealing with what was.

Sitting up in bed, Helene decided that she needed to talk more with her sisters, but not in the quiet, morgue-like hospital room where their mother rested in a deep sleep. But, she didn't know how to reach either Alice or Suzanne.

Helene leaned back against the bed. What did she know about her sisters? She didn't know anything about Alice and her life. She didn't know Jake, and she'd never met her niece and nephew. Her life had been so separate from them, and she had intended it to be that way. Other than the few brief attempts she had made when Thomas was young to connect with them, she had never gone out of her way to be close. She had never really wanted to be a part of their lives or them be a part of hers. If she had let them close, they would have brought all the past with them. She had felt that she was free of her past as long as she stayed free of her family.

In the quiet hotel room, sadness encased her as she understood that the only thing she had freed herself from was the possibility of closeness to her sisters. Questions circled through her mind. Did she want to be close to them? Would she like them if she got to know them? Would she like the experience of closeness with them? She had no idea. Alice's appearance appalled her, yet there was a possibility of bonding and closeness she could not escape. She felt the same about Suzanne and, she reluctantly had to admit, even about their comatose mother lying silently in that bed.

Helene leaned back against the headboard and covered her face with her hands, fighting the feeling of loneliness that rushed over her. She had two sisters, a husband, and a son, and she didn't feel close to any of them. She felt like a very small child in a big, dark space, all alone and afraid with no one to run to, or even to call out to. She couldn't call out if she wanted to—she didn't know how.

Curling into a fetal position, Helene slid down onto the bed and cried like a small girl yearning for her mother—a mother she never had but one she had longed for her whole life.

Chapter 17

Northern Minnesota

Sam curled next to Alice in the bed at the shelter. "Mom, are we gonna go home again?"

"I don't think we can, Sam." She pulled him closer.

"Why? 'Cause Dad will hurt us?" His innocent freckled face gazed up at her.

"Yeah, he might."

He pulled away from her, and his voice filled with worry. "So, where are we gonna go?"

"I don't know, Sam."

"Does that mean you'll have to take care of us now, Mom?"

As Sam's words reached her ears, reality hit Alice in the face like a baseball bat, leaving her head swirling with worry and concern. She was going to have to do more than just leave Jake and sit with her children in a women's shelter for the rest of their lives. She was going to have to do something. She detested Jake because he sat on his ass waiting for the welfare checks, not making things better for them, not trying. Yet she hadn't been doing much better than Jake. Thoughts careened around in her mind, bringing up visual memories that choked the breath from her.

Refusing to give in to hopelessness and disgust, her arms curled tightly around Sam. "Yeah, I'm gonna have to take care of us now. I'm not sure how, but I'll do it."

"I know." He curled further into her large, soft body. "Mom?"

"Yeah, Sam?"

"I never really liked Dad."

Alice peered down at her son, surprised. "Why not?

"'Cause he was always mean to you, and he made Sarah cry in the middle of the night." He gazed up at his mother. "And that's not what nice dads do."

Alice closed her eyes. He knew that Jake had been hurting Sarah. They had all known. Everybody but her. Why? Why hadn't she known? She couldn't find the words to answer Sam. There were just no words. Guilt overwhelmed her. How could she have missed it twice? First her father with Suzanne, then her husband with her daughter. What was wrong with her? What was wrong with their family?

"Mom," his sleepy voice persisted, "things are gonna be nicer now, aren't they?"

"I hope so, Sam." She gulped away a sob.

"I know they will."

"How do you know that?" Alice placed her cheek on the top of her sleepy son's head, feeling his innocence and hope.

"'Cause you love us." He yawned and finally fell asleep curled in her arms.

Huge sobs escaped from deep within her belly. Even though Alice tried hard to hold them back so her children wouldn't hear, Sarah stirred and sleepily whispered, "It'll be okay."

Snuggled between her children, Alice nestled in the love they were finding with each other and clung to a wisp of hope that had started to emerge over these last days, now that they were safe from Jake's meanness and anger.

It was early morning and Suzanne sat alone in the hospital room. She thought Helene and Alice would be here when she arrived. Suzanne didn't want to be alone with her mom, even in her comatose state. She felt as though her mother heard the conversation yesterday and was now staring at her in anger—silently screaming at her that she was lying, telling her to stop making trouble. Dad had always said that there would be trouble if she told. He always threatened that her mother and sisters would leave if she told or if she wasn't good to him. He had made it all her responsibility, and she had believed him. And she had hated them all.

And now Alice's daughter was being hurt by *her* father. It seemed like a never-ending cycle. She had blamed her mother for not keeping her father happy, then she had blamed herself for her mother's constant unhappiness. Her thoughts had always been helter-skelter—angry, distrustful, and hateful regarding men and fathers. She had built this huge shell around herself and her feelings. Nothing had ever cracked it—nothing until Alice had talked about her daughter. Suzanne cringed at the thought of another child going through what she had gone through, yet in a way she also felt less alone. It was as though Sarah's abuse reaffirmed that it hadn't been Suzanne's fault.

Her mind raced and her feelings bounced around the hospital walls as she sat at the end of her mother's bed. "You really didn't know, did you?" Her voice echoed into the silent room. "How could you know? How could you have guessed? It doesn't seem real or possible, even now, even after living through it. I've hated you all these years for nothing. I've hated you so I didn't hate myself. But yet, I hate myself. I hate him. Damn it, but I'm full of hate." Her voice started to rise. "Why me? Or Sarah. Why, Mom? Why? God, I wish I would have killed him!"

Suzanne suddenly felt her mother's foot move under her hand. At least, she thought it did. She sat still and waited for another movement, but there was nothing. Maybe she'd imagined it.

"You hear me, don't you, Mom? You hear me. I know you do! How could you have stayed with him all those years? You deserved better. You did. I did. We all did." Silence quietly washed over Suzanne; her voice dropped to a whisper. "How can I judge you, Mom? Look at me. How can I really judge you?"

Suzanne was quiet for several moments before she touched the still form on the bed and whispered, "I'm sorry, Mom. I'm so sorry for all of us."

Chapter 18

Northern Minnesota

A large pizza sat on the table in Helene's hotel room. It was late, and the three sisters were all exhausted, but the need to be together was strong. It was a need they were not familiar with. The closeness was something they all yearned for. Throughout the day, they had each spent time in their mom's room. Suzanne had spent most of the day, Helene had come in later, and Alice had joined them after her appointment with the counselor.

During her hour with her counselor, Alice had talked mostly about Suzanne being molested by their father. She had been shocked to learn that incest was more common than most people realized.

Now that she was with her sisters again, Alice wasn't sure what to say. None of them were saying much, and they were definitely staying away from the topic of Suzanne's sexual abuse. Helene tried to bring it up when they were waiting for the pizza delivery, but Suzanne had snapped that she didn't want to talk about it. Helene had changed the subject. Now they were talking about every subject but that, and Alice was glad. She was still trying to get her mind around the fact that Jake had sexually molested Sarah, and now she found out her father had done the same thing to Suzanne. It was more than she could handle. Tonight she was glad for a small reprieve.

After they left the hospital, Helene had driven Alice to pick up her kids from school and they had come back to the hotel where Suzanne was waiting. It was the first time her sisters had met her kids, and Alice had been nervous that the meeting wouldn't go smoothly. But it did. Sarah had been a bit withdrawn, but Sam had curled into hugs from both Helene and Suzanne and had chatted their ears off for at least an hour once they were all together. On the way to the hotel, Helene had asked the kids if they wanted burgers and fries or pizza for dinner. Both kids had decided on burgers and fries, and the adults had opted for pizza.

Now, the kids were curled up on the bed in the bedroom of Helene's two-room suite, sleeping soundly as Alice sat quietly with her sisters, nibbling on a slice of pizza. No one had said a word for several moments and Alice was enjoying the quiet.

"Is that all you're going to eat?" Suzanne watched her.

"I'm full," Alice murmured as she glanced down at the piece in her hand.

"How can you be full on one piece?" Suzanne asked as she grabbed her third slice.

"I guess I really don't eat a lot."

Helene stopped mid-bite. "Then how come you're so—"

"Fat?" Alice finished her sentence.

"Well . . ." Helene paused. "Yes."

"Helene, I know I'm fat." Alice threw her slice of pizza down onto the napkin in front of her. "How can I not know it? I have to carry this load around all the time." She grabbed large portions of her stomach as her face contorted.

"But how can you be fat if you don't eat much?" Helene calmly asked.

"I don't each much when other people are around," Alice admitted as she stared at the floor.

"You mean you sneak food?" Suzanne chimed in.

"Yeah. Especially chocolate." It seemed to be time for honesty between them. "I can eat twelve candy bars at one time. And then I hate myself." She blushed from embarrassment of admitting her addiction.

"So, why do you eat them?" Helene's voice was matter-of-fact.

Alice glared at Helene. "For cripes' sake, Helene, if I knew that, I'd stop. Chocolate calms me, that's all I know. When Jake would be really bad to me, or Mom would call and whine and nag, or the kids would act up, I would eat candy bars and then I would feel calm. I don't know why."

"Have you gone to a doctor?" Helene asked as she placed her piece of pizza down on the paper plate in front of her. "Maybe you should get your thyroid or something checked. There's got to be a health problem."

"Helene," Suzanne glared at her, "things are not always that simple. Why can't it be an addiction? Why can't Alice be addicted to chocolate the way I am to alcohol?"

Alice and Helene's mouths dropped open. "You can't be an alcoholic," Alice said. "You're not like Dad."

"That's what I've been telling myself for years." Suzanne's voice became quieter. "But sitting alone in that hospital room today I came to grips with my drinking problem. I've gotten myself into a mess back in Dallas because of my drinking," she slowly admitted.

"What kind of mess?" Helene asked warily.

"Just a big mess, that's all." Suzanne would not look at her sisters.

"Are you going to tell us about it?" Helene asked.

"No." Suzanne's eyes were focused on the table where her fingers were busily tracing the wood grain.

"Then why did you bring it up?" Helene's voice rose.

"Don't use that tone of voice with me, Helene," Suzanne snapped. "I hate it when you go into your 'big sister' voice. That voice won't work on me anymore."

"I don't have a big sister voice," Helene defended herself against the accusation.

"Wanna bet?" Suzanne leaned forward, her eyes warning of trouble and confrontation. "You used it so much that me and Alice used to wish you'd get laryngitis or run away from home." Her eyes returned to the table where her fingers resumed their tracing. "Until you did run away. Then I felt like it was my fault. Dad used to tell me that both of you left because of me. And I believed him."

Alice quietly watched the exchange between her sisters.

"Dad really hurt you, didn't he?" Helene asked Suzanne. "I mean more than physically."

Suzanne's head barely nodded.

"How did you deal with that?"

Suzanne's eyes stayed focused on the table as she answered, "I haven't, and I don't."

Helene's eyes widened in surprise. "How can you not have dealt with it?"

"I bury it. During the day I'm a businesswoman, and no one knows anything about me. I don't share. I don't talk. If we were taught anything as kids, we were taught not to talk, not to tell anybody anything about ourselves and about our private lives. That's what I do."

"Well, what about with men? It's got to affect you with men," Helene stammered.

"I don't spend time with men. At least not when I'm sober. When I get drunk, I do anything with men I want to."

"What about when you were married?" Helene persisted. "How did you handle that?"

"I didn't," Suzanne's voice was barely above a whisper. "It's the reason we got divorced. I couldn't have sex with my husband unless I was drunk."

"I'm so sorry," Helene murmured.

As the exchange was taking place between her sisters, Alice sat there stunned. She couldn't believe it. She'd always thought that her sisters' lives were perfect. She had always been the loser, the one who didn't go on and do anything with herself. Yet Suzanne was sitting there talking about being an alcoholic and having sex with men she didn't even know, and Helene knew her husband was cheating on her but wouldn't do anything about it. *They're both nuts. I'm not the only one.* And for some reason, Alice felt better about that.

"Suzanne, have you tried quitting?" Helene's voice was filled with concern.

"Are you kidding? I try quitting all the time. Each time I wake up in a strange man's bed, I vow I'll never drink again. But I always do."

"What about one of those clinics? Famous people go to them all the time. If you can't afford it . . ."

Suzanne scoffed. "I don't need a handout, and I don't need you to fix my life. Fix your own instead of trying to fix other people's lives! You always did that, even as a kid."

"Did what?" Helene asked.

"Tried to fix everything." Suzanne's chin jutted as she strongly pronounced each word.

"I did not." Helene straightened her shoulders in defiance, daring Suzanne to continue.

"Helene, you did too!" Suzanne responded. "You always had a solution. Well, I'll figure out my own solution. You figure out yours."

"I'm not an alcoholic," Helene spat.

Alice watched as Suzanne unfolded before her eyes and began to cry. "I just can't take any more of this. I'm in such a mess. I could lose my job, my reputation. Everything. I just don't know how to get out of it."

"Get out of what?" Helene asked.

Suzanne leaned her head back against the bed and began to talk.

As she listened, sadness settled over Alice. Her momentary feelings of being glad her sisters' lives were a mess began to quickly subside as she listened to the agony in Suzanne's voice as she talked about Jeff and how he had taken naked pictures of her. Suzanne's life was far from perfect. She was lonely and scared.

Alice reached over and touched her sister's cheek. "I always thought you had everything. Your big-city life and big-city job. I never knew. I would have tried to help somehow if I had known. I just always thought it was all so good."

"See," Suzanne smiled weakly at Alice, "Helene's the one with the perfect life, not me, that's for sure."

"Do you really think that?" Helene asked.

"Well, you have it all." Suzanne listed things off, finger by finger. "Big house, big cars, handsome husband, great son. What in your life is not perfect?"

"My marriage." Helene stared down at the floor.

"Ah, come on, Helene." Alice turned to her. "So it's not perfect. It's not hell like mine was. Does it all have to be absolutely perfect before it's okay for you?"

"Bill cheats on me." Helene raised her head slightly, her voice just above a whisper. "He's had so many affairs these last twenty years, I can't count them all." Lowering her head again, she continued, "He doesn't have sex with me very often. He finds it elsewhere."

"So you said, but if it really bothers you, you wouldn't stay with him," Suzanne responded.

Helene's lip quivered. "It kills me inside each time I discover another lipstick mark or telephone number. Every time a woman calls, I want to scream at her."

"So, tell him!" The tone in Suzanne's voice registered impatience and Alice squirmed. She didn't want to have to deal with a fight between Helene and Suzanne. "Tell him to shape up, or you'll leave!" Suzanne declared.

"I can't." Helene murmured.

"Why in the world can't you?" Suzanne's hands flew to her hips, and she leaned toward Helene angrily.

"Because I don't think I deserve what I have. How can I ask for better?" The words seemed to fly from Helene's mouth without any forethought, and as they settled into the air around her, Alice winced.

"That's crazy." Suzanne sat back and reached her hand toward Helene. "You deserve the best of everything. You are a terrific person, you always have been."

"Me?" Helene croaked.

"Of course you." Softness now etched Suzanne's face. "You were were always such a great example. You never let anything stop you. You always felt you could do whatever you wanted, and you did. Look where you're at."

"I'm not anywhere. Bill's the one with the job and earning the money." Helene slumped back in her chair. "I'm just his wife. I'm not capable of anything. I always thought I'd at least be a good mother, and now I know I wasn't even that." She paused for a moment. "You're the one who worked your way up in the business world, Suzanne. And look where you are now. You've accomplished something. All on your own, you're not clinging to a man's shirttail."

"Sure, and I don't have a man who loves me either!" Suzanne pushed the pizza box away from her. "I can't even have a relationship with a man. What good is a great career when I have to be drunk to have sex with a man? Just because of our drunken, sexually depraved father, I panic just having coffee with a man when I'm not drinking. If it's not business, then I've gotta be drunk. What kind of accomplishment is that?"

Alice had had enough. "You two make me sick." She slapped her hand against the table. "Helene," she glared at her older sister, "you with your big house, great husband, neat kid," then she pointed at her younger sister, "and you, Suzanne, you have a good job." Lifting her hands in the air, she raised her voice in frustration. "What have you two got to bitch about?"

Pushing her chair away from the table, Alice's words came quickly. "Helene, you can figure out what to do about Bill's affairs. You've always figured everything out. What's stopping you? Maybe you just want an excuse. And quit whining, Suzanne. You sound just like Mom! Sure, life has kicked you in the ass. So what? Who hasn't it kicked? I've got two kids to raise, no education, have never worked, and I'm a huge, fat slob with a husband who's threatening to kill me if I don't go back to him. Give me a break! I'd trade places with either of you right now. Your problems sound stupid compared to mine." She slammed the cover down on the pizza box and sat back, a bit out of breath from her tirade.

"Who are you to judge?" Helene snapped, and the air in the room seemed to crackle with intensity. "Just walk a mile in my moccasins, as the old saying goes. And why can't you do something about your problems the way you're preaching to us? So you're fat. Haven't you heard of diets? There are diet clinics all over the place. And why can't you learn a trade? And move if Jake is threatening you. Do something about it, Alice." Helene leaned forward. "Or are you all mouth and no guts?"

"You forget one little detail, Miss Know It All," Alice snarled. "That all takes money, and I don't have any. Right now I'm living in a women's shelter, dependent on other people to feed us and keep us safe. I know I'm going to have to figure out a way, I just don't know how 'cause it all takes money."

"Well, that's no big deal." Helene slowly shook her head as if Alice had just lost her mind. "I've got money. I can help."

"Damn you and your money!" Alice quickly stood and began pacing, agitation contorting her face. "I can't take your help!"

"Why not?" Helene asked.

Alice stopped pacing for a moment and slowly wrapped her hands around her stomach. "'Cause I can't."

"Why in the world can't you take our help?" Suzanne demanded.

"I don't wanna owe nobody nothing." Alice huddled back against the wall.

"Now who sounds like Mom?" Suzanne snarled.

Alice was quiet for a moment. "I do, don't I? Mom always told us not to owe anybody anything. And that nobody ever gave nothing for nothing. That's what I'm afraid of. If you help me, you'll want something in return. I don't have nothing to give."

"You're my family. That's all you have to give," Helene said softly.

"But you never wanted nothing to do with us before. Why now? What's the difference?"

"I don't know." Helene shrugged her shoulders. "I've been asking myself that same question. But for some reason, I really need to be close to you two. It's like if we can be close, then everything wouldn't have been for nothing, and all the bad things that happened when we were kids will just fade away and not be as important."

Silence gently settled over the three women as Helene's words permeated each of their thoughts. After several moments, Suzanne gently whispered.

"Now I remember why I always looked up to you and loved you."

"Looked up to me?" Helene's tone was suspicious. "I thought you two could never stand me. You always said I was too bossy."

Quickly lightening the mood, Suzanne tossed a napkin at Helene, stuck out her tongue, and grinned. "Well, you were!" Then she became serious. "But we always knew we could count on you even when we couldn't count on Mom and Dad. That's why it hurt so badly when you pulled away from all of us. You left home first, and then Alice left. I was all by myself in that house, and I was terrified."

Agony encompassed Alice as she listened to Suzanne. She didn't know what to say or do. So much was changing so fast between the three of them, and Alice wasn't sure she understood the changes or was even ready for them.

When Suzanne reached for Alice's hand and tightly squeezed it, Alice was taken aback by the tears that glistened in Suzanne's eyes and the words that she spoke in a voice that was barely above a whisper. "And, Alice, I didn't have you to mother me. I really missed that. I hated it when you married Jake. He wasn't good enough for you. I could tell he wasn't going to take care of you, but you wouldn't see it. Remember when I tried to talk with you? You said I was jealous because you were getting married when I couldn't even get dates. I turned down dates all the time. I just studied. I decided I was never going to risk having to depend on a man." Suzanne choked up. "Then I met Stephen, and I really thought it could work, but I couldn't have sex unless I was drunk, even with him. So I started drinking more, and that really ended the marriage. I still grieve for him, for what could have, should have been. Something I'll never have."

"And just why won't you have it, Suzanne?" Helene demanded. "Just answer me that."

"I told you I hate it when you go into your big sister voice." Suzanne grinned. "Yet I sorta like it. When you used to do that, then I'd know everything was going to be okay. Because if Helene said there was a better way to do it, we knew she'd find the better way. I never doubted you'd have a good husband and great marriage and all the trappings."

Suzanne grabbed Helene's hand. "Do you remember when we used to play paper dolls? I used to get so mad at you. You would spend hours cutting out all this special furniture and arranging it just so. You knew exactly what you wanted. I bet your home is a dream house. You always said it would be, and you always made your wishes come true."

"How can you say that?" Helene cried out. "My wishes haven't come true. My marriage is a disaster, my son is an alcoholic, and the only close friend I have is my maid. Quit painting this perfect picture of my life. It's not perfect. Dreams don't come true. There's always a black cloud somewhere. Nothing is perfect. We can't make it perfect no matter how hard we try."

"Have you stopped trying, Helene?" Alice urged. "There's always a way. That's what you always told us, that there are always options. You used to always tell me, 'You just haven't considered all your options, Alice. The best ones might not be perfect, but there are always options.' Why are you just accepting that your marriage is a wreck and your life is awful?" Alice huffed in desperation.

Helene's eyes grew large as teardrops hugged her cheeks and dropped from her chin. She didn't stop them from falling . . . just sat there and stared at her sister.

Alice moved closer and pulled Helene's head onto her shoulder. Suzanne moved to the other side and placed her head on Helene's shoulder. Silently, they sat there as tears ran scattered patterns down their faces.

"Everything will be okay, you know," Alice whispered. "We've got each other, right? Mom and Dad gave us that. They gave us each other. Maybe we just gotta check out all the options that come with that."

Helene curled her sisters closer. "I love you two. I don't think I've ever really realized that. But I really do." She gently placed a kiss on the top of their heads as the sisters lapsed into a peaceful silence.

Chapter 19

Northern Minnesota

The breakfast clatter in the restaurant was pleasant to Alice's ears. She couldn't remember the last time she had eaten out in a nice restaurant. This was just a diner as Helene said, but to Alice it was eating out. She had dressed in her best polyester pantsuit and had taken special care with her hair this morning. In fact, she had even borrowed some of Sarah's makeup, and her daughter had shown her how to apply it.

"Mom, you could be pretty if you just took some time with yourself and—"

"And wasn't so fat." Alice had slapped her hands against her stomach in disgust.

"No, Mom," Sarah had sighed. "I wasn't gonna call you fat. I was gonna say go on a diet. Why don't ya? Why don't you take care of yourself?" Sarah had gazed at her mom in the mirror in the tiny bathroom.

"I don't know."

"Yeah, I know." Sarah had grabbed Alice's shoulders as they continued to gaze at each other in the mirror. "Me either. I don't know why I let myself be used by boys just 'cause of Dad. I don't know why I think I'm not worth anything."

"You been really talking to the counselor, huh?" Alice had asked.

"Yeah, we've been talking a lot." Sarah had paused for a few moments as if she was deep in thought, then she had continued, slowly and deliberately. "She's helping me see it wasn't my fault or yours. It was him. He's an adult, and what he did was wrong. I hear it with my ears. I just don't feel it with my heart yet."

Alice had wrapped her arms around Sarah as her mind raced. Maybe she could make it all better. Helene had done it. She'd done it for years. Maybe dreams could come true. Helene had just stopped believing in dreams and herself for a while. But she'd come around. Alice knew she would. And if Helene could do it, maybe Alice could too. Maybe she just needed to look at all her options.

Maybe she did have a lot more options when she married Jake. She wasn't as pretty as Helene or as smart as Suzanne, but there had to be something she was good at. The counselor had told her that everybody was good at something. The secret was finding what you were really good at and what you really liked. Alice could do that. Maybe, just maybe, she could do that.

Her thoughts came back to the table as she glanced over at Helene and Suzanne. "I feel really bad and dumb," Suzanne was saying.

"Dumb about what?" Alice asked.

"Haven't you been listening? Dumb about being so caught up about ourselves and the past that we really haven't put a lot of thought into Mom. I mean, for heaven's sake, she's in a coma, and we've all been dealing with the past. That seems pretty stupid to me. She raised a bunch of selfish brats. Maybe it's about time we just closed the door on the past."

"Quit being so hard on us. I don't think we can close that door until we shovel all the crap out of the way," Helene insisted.

"Yeah, Suzanne," Alice interjected. "The doctor told us they were doing all they could for Mom. What can we do? Besides, we're working on getting close to each other, and I think Mom would like that."

Helene smiled. "I think she would too."

"What did the doctor say this morning when you called him, Helene?" Suzanne asked.

"He just said not much has changed." Helene glanced at her sister. "He mentioned that we should think of putting Mom in a nursing home where she'll have constant care without the high cost of the hospital. He said if it doesn't change after another week, he'd highly advise it. He said it was time for us to go on with our own lives."

Silence settled over the table.

Chapter 20

Northern Minnesota

It was the end of their third week together. The beginning of the week had been windy with thick rolling clouds tumbling across the sky, bellowing their warning of oncoming storms, but today was eerily quiet with a gentle breeze. Gray silent clouds hovered in the heavens as the three women rode in Helene's rental car. They were heading out to the farm, the home of their childhood. Alice had recently been there, but Helene and Suzanne had not stepped foot there since they left many years ago.

It was time. They needed to go back. They felt a force pulling them back to the house, back to the setting of their childhood, back to the bad memories and perhaps buried somewhere, the good ones as well.

The camaraderie in the car was strong. In the short time they had been together, the bond of being siblings had been ripped from its hiding place and slammed solidly into their hearts. They needed each other. They couldn't put their fingers on what they needed or why, but the need was apparent. They weren't sure they liked each other, or that they agreed with the lives each had chosen; they just knew at this moment that they needed the bond of common genes.

It had been Helene's idea to go out to the farm. She had been shocked to hear that her mother hadn't changed the farm over all these years. "I can't understand it. Was she that bad off financially?" Helene asked Alice.

"She didn't have a lot, but that wasn't the reason. It was dumb, but she seemed to take comfort in keeping things the way they were. She and Dad didn't get along, not even in the end. He was still mean to her, but somehow it was like she was used to that. She still has his things all over the house, and he's been gone for years. It's kinda freaky. I'd try to talk to her about it. She'd just say that maybe her life with Dad hadn't been perfect, but it had been her life and that's all she had."

"I can't understand it," vehemence seared into Helene's voice. "I can't understand not fighting for better."

"Can't you?" Suzanne whispered. "Are you really fighting for better with Bill, or are you just settling?"

"That's different," Helene bristled.

"Why? Because you're at a different socioeconomic level than Mom? You're still settling. Why are you so pissed at Mom when you're doing the same damn thing?"

Helene stared at the road ahead of her. "Now if I could figure that out, maybe I could figure out the rest of the puzzles in my life. I guess it's just so much easier to look at somebody else's life and tell them what's wrong. We can't see the forest for the trees and all that stuff."

"Maybe that's why we're all clinging to each other right now," Alice quietly observed.

"Are we clinging?" Suzanne mused.

"I am. That's for damn sure," Alice spurted out. "I'm scared. I ain't got nobody except the kids and you two. I ain't never faced life before, not where I've had to take it by the straps and figure out what to do with it, and I'm scared as hell."

"Alice, do you have to swear so much? And don't use 'ain't.' It makes you sound so dumb." Helene's eyes were dark and intense as she briefly gazed at her sister through the rearview mirror.

"I am dumb!" Alice's eyes met Helene's without flinching. "So how else do you want me to sound? I ain't got no education beyond high school. What do you want me to do, Helene? Try to copy you? I couldn't do that. I'd be a fake. You're sophisticated and live in a different world. You've always had that air about you, and it's gotten you far. I ain't got it."

"Alice! You're not dumb," Helene fumed as she turned her head toward Alice in the backseat and then back to the road. "That really makes me mad when you say that. Quit pulling yourself down. You've got talents, abilities, skills. Maybe you haven't researched them yet or brought them to light, but you've got them. I won't accept that attitude. It's a loser's attitude, and you're no loser."

"It ain't your attitude to accept or change. It's mine." Alice leaned forward toward the front seat. "I'm doing the best I can. I'm dealing with me, Helene— with what's inside of me, not what's inside of you. I gotta be honest. I think that's been the problem for too long. I ain't been honest about how Jake treated me, about how I hated my life, about how I felt, or maybe didn't feel. So, I've gotta be honest, the counselor told me that. She said that my opinions and feelings don't have to agree with nobody else's, 'cause they're mine. Maybe you don't like them or like the way I talk, but you don't have a say. This is me. I may change it and become better, but it's gotta be on my time and my choices. So, get off my back, okay?"

"Do I do that? Do I get on your back?" Helene asked.

"Yeah." Alice flopped against the backseat.

"I don't mean to," Helene apologized as she continued to navigate roads that were now gravel as they got nearer to their homestead. "We just deserve so much better than we were taught."

"Then why don't you have better than what you have with Bill?" Suzanne chimed in.

"Suzanne!" Helene pulled the car over to the side of the road and turned toward her sister, her hands gripping the steering wheel. "Why, oh, why do you keep going back to the Bill thing? I told you that in confidence, not to be harped at about it. Not to be belittled by it! Not to have you use it as a knife to cut into me! You find my weak spot, my turtle's tummy, and you chop it into pieces or pick it full of holes. Just stop it. It hurts too much. I can't handle it. I'm too vulnerable right now. I don't know if I can deal with Mom, Dad, going back to the farm, you, Alice, everything about our childhood, let alone trying to deal with Bill and Thomas. I'll have to do that later. So, let it lie, will you?"

"I didn't mean it like that, Helene." Suzanne reached out to touch her arm, but Helene quickly pulled it away. "It just makes me mad because you deserve better. You're beautiful, your figure is great, you're classy, and you've always accomplished everything you set out to do. Bill doesn't know what he has, and it really grinds me to the core that you're letting him get away with it because you're scared of losing him. What would you be losing that you couldn't get again?"

"It's just so different with a man," Alice said softly. "You just seem to put up with stuff you'd never put up with from your friends. Dad used to tell me how worthless I was and that I'd be lucky to get any man. I believed him. I think I still do. Now that I'm fat and yucky, I believe him even more. If you've never been like that with a man, Suzanne, it's hard to explain. I understand Helene. Don't push her. Just sorta help her see that she is special and that she deserves better. Help her see that the chances she has to take will be worth it in the long run."

Helene quietly put the car in gear and steered the car toward their destination. The sisters seemed to have run out of things to say and the nearness of their destination drained all words and emotions out of them; they weren't sure which it was, but silence permeated the car as their trip was coming to an end.

Helene pulled into the long driveway, then stopped the car and broke the stillness as she turned to Alice. "Is that what you need, Alice? For us to help you see that you're special?"

"Yeah." Alice sighed.

"I've been trying to do that. I guess my words were just pushier than they needed to be." Helene examined the long curving driveway. "I'm scared," she whispered. "There are a lot of ghosts here for me."

As Suzanne gazed toward the house, her face was pale. "I wish mine were just ghosts. Mine are big, treacherous demons."

Alice placed an arm on each of her sister's shoulders. Helene and Suzanne leaned in together and the three women sat with their heads touching as they experienced their pasts merging with their presents and futures.

After several moments of silence, Helene maneuvered the rest of the driveway, turned off the car, leaned back in her seat, and stared at the house she had grown up in. "It doesn't look as though the house has been painted since I left over twenty years ago."

The paint on the huge, old farmhouse was almost completely peeled away. The front porch was sagging and screens were ripped at the corners. Grass was out of control and working its way into the cracks on the porch steps. The outer buildings—the pump house, the chicken coop, and the barn—were all in disrepair. The farm had the look of abject poverty, and Helene cringed as she remembered it much the same when she was growing up. Now she was seeing it as she imagined others saw it then, and an embarrassment even worse than what she suffered as a child crept over her. "I can't stand this place. Why did we come here anyway? What are we trying to prove? What are we trying to accomplish?"

"Maybe we're searching for the missing link, like scientists." A small, almost hysterical chuckle escaped from Suzanne's lips. "The link that will tie what was in the past to what we are now and show us the connection," her voice wavered. "Maybe if we can understand that connection, the forces that went into creating that beginning, maybe—just maybe—we can understand where we are now and do something different to change the future. Maybe that's why we're here." She paused, seemingly lost in her thoughts, then her voice was quieter as she continued, "I know it's why I'm here. I'm searching for a clue as to what created me as I am. Because maybe then I can make some changes."

Suzanne turned toward the barn. "He used to take me out there sometimes. When Mom was in the house. He used to say I had to help him. I never understood why Mom didn't know that Dad never did any work out in the barn. We didn't have cattle anymore. I never understood why she didn't realize. I still don't."

The three women were quiet. This was the first time that Suzanne had been willing to talk about their father and her abuse since she had first told them about it.

Helene was the first to break the silence. "I just feel so sick, Suzanne. So sick that our father was like that. It makes me feel dirty. It makes me want to hide my family and my background even more." A weight of sadness drifted over Helene. "I want to race back to the hotel and take a hot bath. How could he have been so awful? How could he have done that to you? How could we not have known?"

"If you think you feel dirty now, maybe you can understand how dirty and ashamed I've felt for years." Suzanne bit her lip as she clenched and unclenched her hands. "I went through a time when I couldn't bathe enough. I was fanatical about it." She sighed a deep, sad sigh. "I guess I dropped that compulsion for drinking."

"Maybe we just need to go inside and find some of those answers. Maybe they're hiding in there. Mom kept it pretty much like it was when we were growing up." Alice gulped. "You know, I've been in this house lotsa times, but today I'm scared. I didn't know all that happened, even to me, but now I'm having to look at it."

Alice gripped the back of the front seat, her eyes large and round. "I'm scared. I feel as though Dad is in one of those rooms. Like he's gonna be mad at us and get into one of his rages. You remember how mad he used to get when we stood up to him?" She gently touched Helene's shoulder. "Especially with you, Helene. Remember when he used to whip you when we were little? Until that day when you told him you'd kill him." A small smile touched her lips as her eyes focused on the past. "I used to think you were so brave. I used to want your courage. I used to envy you. I still do. You ain't afraid of nothing."

Helene uttered a frantic chuckle. "Well, I'm scared to death right now. I don't know what you'd call that if it's not being afraid." She took a deep breath. "I don't think it will ever get easier though, so I guess we might as well tackle this together. We just have to remember that we are here for each other, and I'm just beginning to realize how good that can be. We can handle it." She smiled weakly at her sisters. "We can get our answers, Suzanne. We can find that missing link. I know we can." But she wasn't feeling as strong as she tried to sound.

They got out of the car and stood together staring at the house, willing themselves to make that first step. A small whirlwind gathered in front of them in a mighty puff, spitting sand against their skin.

"Do you think that's Dad?" Alice whispered.

"That's ridiculous," Helene answered, but the three women sidestepped the spot where the whirlwind appeared as they carefully made their way toward the house.

Chapter 21

Northern Minnesota

The squeaking of the back screen door made them all jump. As children, they always entered the house through the back porch, so today they did the same. They entered where coats were still hung and boots still sat on the shelves. "For God's sake, those look like Dad's boots," Helene exclaimed.

"They are," Alice countered. "I told you Mom didn't change much after Dad died." Alice picked up one of the shoes, held it for a moment, then roughly threw it back onto the shelf. "She used to bitch like hell about how he treated her, and then she'd tell me she missed him. I never could understand that before. Now maybe I think I do."

Suzanne spun toward her. "Don't tell me you miss Jake."

"I don't, and I do." Alice shrugged her shoulders, and Suzanne shook her head, then they turned back into the room.

Helene walked ahead into the kitchen and ran her hand over the old gas stove. "Do you remember the cookies and breads Mom used to make? I can almost smell them cooking." She surveyed the kitchen, with its old appliances and linoleum-covered floor. "This room has good memories for me. And that surprises me. I couldn't remember having any good memories about this place or about my childhood, but the minute I walked in, I could almost smell that fresh bread coming out of the oven. And do you remember the fry cakes?

When Mom would take a ball of the bread dough and stretch it into an oval, then deep fry it? I used to sprinkle sugar on the warm cake before eating it. I still remember how delicious they were."

She glanced at Suzanne and Alice. "Why didn't I remember that before? Why did it take coming into this room to remember that? In fact, it rattles the heck out of me to realize what a good memory that is. I didn't think I had good memories about this place, about my childhood, about them. But this kitchen has good memories."

Her eyes wandered around the room as a small smile touched her lips. "I remember sitting at that big oak table when Dad was gone and you two were sleeping. I'd be working on my homework and Mom would be puttering by the stove. It was a quiet time." Helene sighed. "Mom never talked much. I don't think she knew what to say to me. But I remember one time when I read her a poem I wrote for English. She pulled out a chair and sat down by me. Then she took my hand and said, 'You're gonna be something, Helene. I just feel it in my heart.'" Helene's eyes began to mist over, and she turned away from her sisters as embarrassment overtook her.

Alice gently stroked Helene's back. Helene turned toward her. "I've hated her all these years. She disgusted me because she didn't do better for us. Then I come in here and remember a soft moment like that and guilt takes over. She wasn't all bad. Why haven't I been able to see that before? Why did I only remember the bad?"

"Maybe 'cause there was so much of it," Alice gently soothed Helene.

"Maybe. But it doesn't seem okay. I wouldn't want Thomas to just remember the bad about me. In fact, it often scares me that he might feel about me the way I feel . . . felt . . . about Mom." Helene's arms circled around herself as she shuddered at the thought.

"Helene, can you honestly say that?" Suzanne pulled out a chair from the big wooden table that sat in the middle of the kitchen. "Can't you see how much better you've done than Mom did? Can't you give yourself credit for that? Thomas might not like everything you do, but that's part of being a parent, isn't it?"

"I don't really know." Helene's fingers ran patterns on the tabletop. "Maybe that's why I'm so soft with him. Maybe that's why I've let him get away with so much. Why did I have to come here to really look at myself as a parent? Why did I have to see both sides of Mom before I could look at me? It doesn't make any sense. We are all mature, grown women. Why does the way our mother responded to us, or didn't respond for that matter, affect us? Why does it take dealing with this for me to be able to really look at my own parenting?"

"You don't really expect answers from us, I hope." Suzanne smiled. "Of the three of us, you've probably got your life most together. We certainly aren't going to be able to give you answers."

"But you have. Don't you see?" Helene sat down in a chair next to Suzanne, the wooden slats of the chair gently pushing against her back. "In these last weeks, you've given me a lot of answers. You've given me a glance at myself that I haven't had before. You've opened up new worlds of thought. And it had to take you two to do it, because you've lived where I've lived, you felt much of what I've felt. It's like you touch a part of me that nobody else can ever touch. It's crazy." She stretched out her arms on the table and was silent for just a moment. "I've shut out my family—both of you, Mom, Dad . . . I haven't wanted to need you. But yet it seems that's exactly what I do need in order to get my head together."

Helene sat up. "Don't you see? These weeks have just culminated in our visit here. It all came together when I walked into this house, into this room." Her eyes circled the room, noticing the small rooster salt and pepper shakers on the stove, the dish towel draped over the oven handle, and the metal canisters that held flour and sugar on the countertop. "I've remembered that there were good times. They might have been few in comparison to the bad times, but they existed. They were there all the time. If I hadn't ostracized myself from all of you, maybe I would have remembered the good sooner. I don't know. But I do know that I was kidding myself. You can't ignore your past. You can't shut it away from you, because all you do is trap it deep within yourself, not giving it room to grow or expand or touch your life."

Helene's words were coming fast, as if she had so much to say and no time to say it. "I've been living like I was caught on the middle step, never able to go forward because I wasn't taking with me what I had learned from the first steps, so I didn't know how to do it. But it makes sense now. I can't explain it. It feels eerie or even weird, but I feel more complete now. I understand me better and maybe even Bill and Thomas. It's weird, but I really do." Helene sighed with relief. She had not expected that so many unresolved issues and feelings would seemingly melt away just by stepping back into the house.

"I sure wish I felt like you do, Helene." Suzanne's voice was sad. "I'm scared as hell to leave this room. It certainly hasn't evoked any of those memories for me. I remember the cookies and the bread, but they still don't take away the taste from all the rest of it."

Suzanne pushed her chair back from the table. "I don't know. Maybe I need to go beyond this room. Maybe what I really need to do is to go back to my bedroom. I was going to stay out of that room, but now I'm beginning to think that's the first place I need to go."

"Do you want us to come?" Helene asked.

"No." Suzanne stared at the floor.

Helene lightly touched Suzanne's arm. "We'll wait for you here."

"No, don't." Suzanne pulled her arm away from Helene's touch. "Wait in the car."

"I'm not leaving you in this house," Helene declared.

Suzanne's face displayed a combination of sadness and fear. "I've made it this far without you, Helene. I'll make it through this."

Suzanne stood up, grabbed her purse from the floor, and walked slowly to the stairs at the back of the house without glancing back at her sisters.

Chapter 22

Northern Minnesota

As Suzanne climbed the stairs, she kept scanning the space all around her. She had an eerie feeling that her father was watching and that he was either following her up the stairs or waiting for her at the top.

The door to her bedroom was closed, and Suzanne's hand trembled as she reached for the doorknob. Then she quickly pulled her hand away as if the doorknob was hot and just by touching it she would be harmed. After a moment, she tapped on the door. "Hello?" Her voice was small and childlike. "Is anybody in there?"

Silence.

Cautiously, Suzanne turned the doorknob. As the door opened, her heart pounded. Her eyes scanned the small room. The walls were white, the small twin bed was covered with a quilt, and a wooden chair sat next to the lone window that was opposite the bed. It looked so much the same that she was mentally transported back to the age of eight. She heard the voices of that long-ago time—Mama, Helene, Daddy, and Alice. Daddy was yelling, and Mama was crying. Suzanne was hiding in her room. She was so afraid when Daddy yelled at Mama. Not because he yelled at her, but because he always came to Suzanne's room later in the night. He touched her and made her do things she didn't want to do.

The adult Suzanne fought the memory. "No, no, no," she screamed into the room. Then she grabbed her purse and pulled out the bottle of Jack Daniel's. Raising it to her mouth, she took a large gulp. Immediately, she felt calmer. She put the cap back on the bottle and looked out the window. She had vowed she wasn't going to drink on this trip, and she hadn't gotten drunk the way she often did back home, but she did have a drink or two each night, just to help her cope. And now . . . she turned back toward the bed and sunk down into it. She tightened her grasp on the bottle. That was all she needed—just a drink or two.

As Suzanne scanned the room, she took one long swallow after another. Moments passed. As the liquor made its way into her system, her vision started to blur. Her father's face appeared on the wall. Anger gushed from Suzanne. "Bastard! Don't you touch me anymore. Do you hear me?"

Between each sentence, she raised the whiskey bottle to her lips. "Don't you ever touch me again. I'll kill you!! So help me, I'll kill you!" Her voice rose to an hysterical pitch.

"You cheated me, you son of a bitch! You took my childhood away from me. I can never be a little girl again. I wanted to be Daddy's girl, but not that way, never that way." The sound of her sobs echoed in the room. "How could you do that to your own daughter?" Her voice grew childlike. "You were supposed to protect me from harm. Daddies are supposed to take care of their little girls—not rape them." She lifted the bottle to her lips , taking another large gulp.

"You had sex with me!" she screamed. "You dirty rotten bastard! I hate you. Do you hear me? I hate you, I hate you, I hate you!"

She stood up and hurled the bottle at the wall, breaking it into pieces as the liquor oozed down the wall and onto the floor. During the throw, she'd lost her balance and stumbled to the floor, cutting her hand on a piece of shattered glass. She started to cry as she sat among the shattered glass and the memories of her shattered childhood while she clutched her bleeding hand against her.

"It's your fault. It's all your fault. My messed up life, Stephen, my drinking, and even Jeff. You did this to me. If you hadn't raped me, I could be normal. I could love a man, get married, and have kids. It's your fault, and I hate you."

Blood streamed from her hand onto her blouse. In her drunken haze, Suzanne stared at the blood. *Red is a pretty color, but that's a lot of blood.*

Should a little cut bleed so much? I should go find Helene. While trying to stand, Suzanne stumbled again and reached out to steady herself. She grabbed the closet door handle and pulled it open. She slipped and landed on her knees, gazing into the full-length mirror on the inside of the door. For a moment, she was sober as she peered at her image. Her hair was wildly flying around her face. Mascara had streaked under her eyes, and the front of her blouse was soaked with blood. "Oh my God. Oh my God. Oh my God."

"Daddy please help me. I'm sick. Oh my God. I'm sick." Nausea gripped her. "I did this. How could I do this?" She shook her head. "You're dead. You can't hurt me anymore. I'm hurting me. Me. Why am I hurting me, Daddy? Why?"

"God," she screamed, "help me. Somebody help me. I love you, Daddy. Oh, God help me. I still love you." Clutching her bleeding hand, Suzanne raced from the room, started down the stairs, tripped, and tumbled down. Intense pain pierced her chest as she hit the floor. Gasping, she pulled herself up on her knees and half crawled, half walked to the front door. She pushed against the screen door and fell onto the porch.

Through blurry eyes she could see Helene and Alice waiting by the car.

"Oh my God, Suzanne!" Helene screamed.

Helene and Alice ran to her. "She's bleeding, Helene. God, she's bleeding."

"Look at her hand. She's cut bad." Helene grabbed the scarf that was draped around her neck, covered the wound, and put pressure on it to try to stop the bleeding. Helene commanded, "Let's get her to the hospital. Quick!"

And the world spun in circles.

Suzanne groaned as she tried to move in the hospital bed. "Shh, don't move. You're okay." Helene's voice was soothing.

"Where am I?" Suzanne groaned again.

"In the hospital." Helene gently rested her hand on Suzanne's arm. She told her that Alice had gone to pick up her kids from school, so Helene and Suzanne were alone.

"Hospital? Why?" Suzanne tried to sit up but it was too painful, so she gently lay back against the bed.

"Two broken ribs, a nasty gash in your hand, and a big bump on your head."

Helene leaned in closer and tenderly touched her cheek. "Geez, Suzanne, what did you do up there anyway?"

Suzanne was silent.

"The doctor said if you hadn't been so drunk, you might have been hurt a lot worse. How did you get drunk so fast?"

Suzanne smiled a weak, crooked smile. "Drank a whole bottle of whiskey."

"A whole bottle? Why?"

"That's the only way I know how to cope with demons."

"Suzanne!" Helene was angry. "You could have bled to death!"

"I know." Suzanne turned toward the window that had a view of another section of the hospital.

"Damn! I'm mad at you!" Helene gripped the side railing on the bed. "How could you do that? Don't you ever do that again!"

Just then, the door to the room opened. "Leave her be, Auntie Helene," Sarah said as she, Alice, and Sam stood in the doorway. "She's hurting bad, especially on the inside." Sarah quickly moved to Suzanne's bedside. "I'm sorry, Auntie Suzanne. I'm so sorry. Mom told me this morning that you and I had the same thing happen to us by our dads."

Suzanne brushed Sarah's hair away from her face. "Get help while you're young, Sarah. Don't let it eat away at you. Don't let it kill you."

Alice's kids didn't resemble each other at all—Sam with his red hair and freckles and Sarah with her dark brown hair and almost porcelain skin. Neither of them took after Alice, except for their smiles. Suzanne had always thought that Alice lit up when she smiled, which wasn't very often, and her kid's smiles were just as infectious.

"What happened to them, Mom?" Sam asked.

"Their dads hurt them, Sam."

"Like when Dad used to beat me?"

"Something like that," Alice said, as she and Helene steered Sam toward the door to go to the cafeteria for a treat, leaving Suzanne and Sarah alone.

After the door closed, Sarah gently folded her arms around Suzanne's neck as they cried about their shattered childhoods and broken dreams.

Chapter 23

Northern Minnesota

Several days later, Suzanne was in her hotel room resting, and Helene was spending the evening with Alice, Sarah, and Sam. They were sitting in the small restaurant that was a part of the hotel where Helene was staying. Helene and Alice sat in the booth munching on the leftovers from a dinner of hamburgers and French fries while Sarah and Sam were across the room at one of the video games, armed with a handful of quarters that Helene had dug from her wallet.

"They're neat kids, Alice." Helene smiled as she watched Sarah and Sam. "How is Sarah doing? Did it help her to talk with Suzanne?"

"I think so." Alice gazed at her children for several minutes. "She said she doesn't feel as weird and all alone anymore. But I dunno. She still doesn't talk to me about it much. And she misses Jake. I think it makes her feel weird that she misses him. She's just trying hard to deal with it all."

"They really are great kids, Alice. It's amazing with all they've been through that they aren't acting out more." Helene's mind was trying to understand how these two kids, with all of the challenges and abuse they had endured, seemed relatively normal, yet her own son, who had many more opportunities and a much easier life, had turned to alcohol.

Over the last weeks, Helene had talked to Thomas several times. He sounded good. He talked quite a bit about his counselor and about school. He seemed to be getting back to "the old Thomas," and from what Helene could tell from their conversations, he and Bill were learning to communicate better. Even Bill had mentioned that when Helene had talked with him last night.

"Yeah." Alice sadly watched her children. "They just deserve so much more."

"You'll give it to them," Helene assured her.

"I don't know how to start." She glanced at Helene. "Thanks for renting a room for us these last weeks. The kids needed to get away from the shelter and try to be a little more normal. And thanks for dinner tonight. The kids love it."

"It's been a rough month. We all needed a break." Then she asked, "Why don't you move, Alice?"

Helene's question obviously startled Alice. "Where would I move to?"

"Where would you move if you could go anywhere you wanted?" Helene's arms opened to indicate a wide selection.

"To a larger city—maybe Minneapolis." Alice mused with a smile.

"Then go to Minneapolis," Helene said.

"Sure. How?" Alice glanced back at Sarah and Sam.

"I said I was willing to help, and I am. I care about you and the kids. I'm just not very good at showing it."

"But how could you help?"

Knowing she was entering tender ground, Helene lowered her voice. "I could give you money to make the move."

Alice pushed her body back against the booth seat and gripped the edge of the table. "Damn it, Helene! Money isn't the answer to everything!" She leaned in closer and whispered, "We know you have lots of money, so quit throwing it at us, okay?"

"I know it's not the answer," Helene seethed. "If it was the answer to everything, my life wouldn't be as messed up as it is. But it certainly can make things a lot easier. Why don't you just take that stupid pride and can it for a while, okay? Can't we just help each other? Do we always have to be competing? Do you always have to make me feel like I'm shoving answers down your throat when all I'm trying to do is care about you?"

Alice's voice was gentle now. "I don't compete with you. I never have, 'cause I could never win."

"No, your competing is never to win, Alice. It's done to cripple your opponent so you won't even have to get into the race." Helene glanced toward her niece and nephew, who were still totally involved in the video game.

"How would I decide where to go and what would I do when I got there?" Alice asked meekly. "The only job I've ever had was when I worked in that restaurant that one summer in high school. Jake said he wanted his wife home to take care of him," she sneered.

"I don't know exactly what you'd do. But we can figure it out." Helene sighed, then a quick grin flashed across her face. "Are you interested in going to school? If you could do anything, how would you like to make a living? Have you thought about things like that?"

"Yeah." A long silence followed as Alice lowered her head and studied the tablecloth. Speaking softly, she answered, "I'd like to be a teacher."

Helene stared at her. "A teacher?"

"Yeah. Do you think I'm too dumb?"

"No, you're not dumb. But why in the world do you want to be a teacher?"

"So I could help others learn."

"That takes college you know." Helene watched her sister. *Maybe I do think she's too dumb.* She just couldn't imagine Alice being a teacher.

"I know it takes college. That's why I can't do it."

"I hate it when people quit before they even start," Helene said. "Why can't you do it?"

"You have to be smart, and it takes money." Alice shifted in the booth. The two sisters sat quietly for a few moments.

"You'll get smarter as you go through college." Helene took Alice's hand. "As for the money, you can get scholarships and grants. A lot of people do."

"Do you really think I could do it?" Alice asked.

"I know so."

"But I don't know how to start. I'm too old to still be asking my big sister to fix it for me." Alice said in frustration.

"Well, guess what?" Helene smiled. "I don't have the answers, but we'll figure it out."

Alice thought for a moment before looking at Helene and saying, "Helene?"

"Yes?" Helene responded.

"It's kinda nice having sisters help you figure things out." Alice smiled as she wrapped her fingers around Helene's.

"Yes, Alice, it is."

Chapter 24

Northern Minnesota

"Hello, Bill." Helene leaned her head against the headboard of the bed in her hotel room as she spoke into the phone.

"Helene! What a surprise. What's wrong?"

"Nothing." She toyed with the ends of her hair.

"But you're calling in the middle of the day. When my secretary said it was you, I got scared. Is something wrong?"

"No. I just want you to wire me some money." Her voice wavered a bit as she tugged harder on her hair.

"Did you run short?" he said anxiously. "Use your credit cards. I'll pay them off when the bills come in."

"No, I need a lot of money." She sat up on the bed and dangled her feet off the edge.

After a few moments, Bill said, "How much money?"

"Twenty thousand dollars." A gulp formed in her throat as her foot drew nervous circles in the air.

"Please, Helene, think this over," Bill said frantically. "Don't just leave without giving me a chance. I know I don't deserve it."

Helene's foot stopped dangling, and she paused for a moment, not sure she was hearing what was being said. "Leaving? Who's leaving?"

"You."

"No, I'm not."

"Oh," Bill said quietly.

Taking a deep breath, Helene softly asked, "Did that scare you?"

"What?"

"The thought of me leaving?" Helene was perfectly still without the slightest movement.

Silence.

"Bill?" Her foot started moving again.

"Yes," he said, but she barely heard him.

"Yes, what?" she asked as she tugged her hair once more.

"Yes," he whispered, "it scared me."

"Why?"

"Why do you think?"

"Tell me." Helene gazed out the window of her hotel room.

"Because I love you, and because there isn't anything I wouldn't do for you." His voice was so soft Helene strained to hear.

"You don't say that often."

"I know," Bill said. "There are many things I've left unsaid that you have deserved to hear."

"Why?"

"I don't know. But I know I've made a lot of mistakes, and you have every reason to leave me," he paused, "but I hope you don't. I'm changing, Helene."

Helene didn't know how to respond. This was a side of Bill that she had seldom experienced.

"Why do you want twenty thousand dollars?" Bill changed the subject.

"Do you have to know why?" The circles she was tracing on the bed became larger.

"No," he answered.

"You'd just wire me twenty thousand dollars without knowing why? How come?"

"Because I trust you. And because half of everything I have is yours."

Helene gently placed her lips against the phone. "Do you really feel that way?"

"Yes."

"I love you, Bill," Helene whispered.

"I love you too."

The silence that flowed between them was like a soft blanket of snow warmly covering the landscape. Neither of them wanted to tread on the virgin ground. Finally, Helene spoke, "I need the money to move my mother into a nursing home and to help my sister and her family move."

"Okay." Bill responded. "Where do I wire it?"

She gave him instructions and then asked again, "You really don't mind?"

"No, honey, I really don't."

Silence.

"You called me 'honey,'" she stated, bewildered. "I like that."

"I'm glad," he stated. "I'll take care of this right away."

"Thanks, Bill." She hugged her knees with one arm.

"You're welcome."

Suddenly, Helene needed to get off the phone because of all of the feelings that were surging through her. The two of them had not interacted like this since the beginning of their marriage. Over the years, they had grown apart and had lapsed into politeness without much intimacy, but today the intimacy felt natural. Yet, she didn't know how to handle it and needed to get some distance between the two of them, so she quickly said, "Bye, Bill," and hung up the phone.

Helene just sat there as she thought about Bill, their marriage, and her feelings toward him. From the way her heart had skipped a beat when he called her "honey," she knew that she still loved him and wanted a strong, loving marriage. She still wasn't sure if that was possible and if she could forgive him for his infidelity, but she did know that she wanted to try.

Chapter 25

Northern Minnesota

"We could move her out of Minnesota," Suzanne murmured as she lounged on the sofa in Helene's room.

"To where?" Helene sat at the table, absentmindedly twirling a tea bag in the cup of hot water in front of her.

"To Texas or Georgia. Just close to one of us." Suzanne propped her feet up on the coffee table.

"Mom wouldn't like that," Alice said from the small kitchenette. "This was her life. She wouldn't wanna die someplace strange."

"She's not dying. The doctor says she could be in a coma for a long time." Suzanne stretched her arms over her head, trying to ease some of the tension from her body.

"I know, Suzanne, but she's gonna die sometime. I think she'd want to die in Minnesota." Alice grabbed a juice drink from the mini refrigerator.

"But nobody's going to be up here," Suzanne protested.

"We can come and visit," Helene offered.

"Visit what? Her still body lying in the bed? Do you really think you'll do that?" Suzanne stared at Helene for a few moments, then stood and started pacing the room.

"I don't have to move to Minneapolis," Alice suggested.

"Are you willing to give up your life again, Alice?" Helene took a sip of her tea.

Alice squirmed. "No."

"Then what do we do?" Suzanne stopped pacing and stared out the window.

Helene firmly placed her cup on the table. "Find the best place we can for Mom for as long as she may live, even if she's in a coma. And I think Alice is right—Mom wouldn't want to leave Minnesota. Strange as it may seem, I think she'd want to be close to Daddy and buried next to him when she dies."

"I don't understand that, Helene," Suzanne said.

"Neither do I, Suzanne," Helene admitted, "but I believe it's how Mom would feel."

"Okay," Suzanne gave in. "So we look for a good nursing home or critical care home or whatever it's called. Then I guess we go on with our lives." She plopped back down on the sofa and stared at the ceiling. "Does that sound heartless?"

"No. It's reality," Helene replied.

"We're making sure Mom is comfortable," Alice agreed. "There isn't anything else we can do."

"Speaking of that, what are your plans, Suzanne?" Helene asked.

"I'm entering a treatment clinic."

"What?" Helene asked, wide-eyed.

Suzanne's head flopped back against the sofa. "A clinic for my alcoholism. I've taken a leave of absence. I talked with the doctor at the hospital, and he didn't pull any punches." She took a deep breath. "He said I'd better take a good look at my drinking. After asking a lot of questions, he asked me if I was an alcoholic. I said yes." She sighed again. "I think it's pretty evident. So, he recommended a good treatment program, and I asked him to help me make arrangements. I go there in two weeks."

"Two weeks!" Alice and Helene exclaimed in unison.

"Why so soon?" Helene asked.

"I don't want to back out." Suzanne paused a moment. "Besides, I don't have anything to go back to, so I'll spend two weeks taking a road trip through Minnesota to get my head together before I check in to treatment. We've uncovered a lot of 'stuff' for me, so I want some time to just think about it."

"What about your condo, clothes, and all those things?" Alice asked as she pulled out a chair and sat at the table.

"I called my secretary," Suzanne stated. "She's quite a woman and a very good friend. She'll be handling a lot of it for me."

"When did you get the leave from work?" Helene inquired.

"Today."

"Will they hold your job?" Helene asked.

"I don't know." Suzanne closed her eyes. "And I honestly don't care. I've got to get my life in order." She smiled sadly at her sisters. "I don't want to be a drunk floozie and a lonely businesswoman forever."

"I'm proud of you." Helene smiled. "When did you decide to do all this?"

"That day—in my bedroom on the farm. I knew I had to face my problems. I knew I couldn't run from them or blame my pain on somebody else forever. That was when I ran. I know Daddy isn't causing my pain now—I am. When I was in my old bedroom, the pain got strong enough to pierce my hard shell. I knew it was time for a change. I just didn't know how to change. I'm still not certain of everything I need to do, but I'm taking one step at a time."

Abruptly switching the subject, Suzanne turned to Alice, "Are you all set? Are you still determined to move to Minneapolis? And you're okay with us having Mom moved to a facility close to where you'll be living?"

Alice sipped her juice. "Yeah. I think that's best. I can keep you both posted on how she's doing." Her fingers traced circles on her juice glass. "And, I don't want the kids to hurt no more. This way we can get away from Jake, the kids can find new friends, and maybe we can have a new start."

Alice's voice began to fill with excitement. "I'm going to find a job. There's got to be something I can do. And then I'll start at a two-year college in September. I don't know if I can do this and support the three of us as well, but I'm certainly going to try."

Suddenly, sadness washed over Alice. "I called my friend Thelma today. She says I'm dreaming. She says I'll never pull this off and that I was stupid to piss Jake off."

"You are dreaming." Helene walked over to Alice. "But that's how we make our lives better. First, we dream how we want them to be, then we take steps to make our dreams come true."

The room grew quiet as the sisters sat together.

"I guess next week we all go back to our lives," Alice said. "They just won't be the same lives. So much has changed so fast. It's like a whirlwind has puffed me up, spun me around, and dropped me off at another spot. I'm the same me, but everything around me is different."

"You're not the same you." Suzanne smiled. "You're different. We're all different."

"But how can we be? It's only been a little over a month." Alice asked.

"I guess when life's whirlwinds pick you up and spin you around, you've got to change or give up and die, and we're not the kind to give up and die," Helene said.

"What about you, Helene? Will you keep trying?" Alice asked. "Or will you go back to what you had?"

"I can't go back to that," Helene admitted. "You two have shamed me into doing something about my marriage. My problems seem small compared to the ones you're both tackling, and neither of you will give me a moment's peace if I quit."

"You're right," Suzanne said.

"And we're gonna keep checking up on you." Alice playfully pointed her finger at Helene.

"And I'll be checking up on you too. You're no longer going to be rid of me." Helene placed her arm around Alice's shoulder.

"Good." Alice leaned her head against Helene.

"I don't think we'll ever be the same after these last weeks," Helene said.

"And who would have thought it would be for the better?" Alice's grin covered her entire face.

Suzanne laughed. "We came face-to-face with our past, held it in a death grip, and came out winners." She paused. "We did come out winners, didn't we?"

The three sisters sat in silence. Only the future could answer that question.

Chapter 26

Anoka, Minnesota

"Well, Suzanne," the doctor said, "our tests don't show any medical problems that we need to deal with. So, let's deal with the addiction."

"Okay." Suzanne was jittery. She wanted it to work this time. She had read all of the pre-treatment paperwork and knew what the treatment would be like—on paper anyway. This was the fourth treatment center that she had signed up for in the last several weeks, and all of the previous times she had backed out the day she was supposed to get started. Then she would spend a few days drinking in the hotel room, get disgusted with herself, and start the search all over again. It had been six weeks since she was supposed to have started treatment, and she kept promising Helene and Alice that she would, so she had to go through with it this time. There was a good selection of treatment facilities in Minnesota, but she would eventually run out of options, and she was determined to get treatment close to where all of her issues had begun.

"Well," the doctor continued, "step one, as you know, will be detoxification. We'll put you in a room that's much like a hospital room. It typically takes three to five days, however long it takes your body to adjust to no alcohol. As I've explained, you will be in a hospital gown for the first phase. Nurses will monitor your heart rate and pulse rate, and we'll be there to comfort you as much as we can. But, Suzanne, this is not going to be easy. Your body has gotten used to a chemical dosage—in your case—alcohol, on a regular basis.

The reaction that each person has varies. As I've explained, fever, chills, and nausea are all common side effects. And don't be surprised by bouts of rage or anxiety. Remember, we're here to help and support you in every way we can, but you're the one who has to do the work because it's your recovery."

Suzanne was silent.

"Are you scared?" The doctor's voice was gentle.

Suzanne nodded.

"That's normal and a good sign, I might add." He stood up. "Let's get you checked in, shall we?"

The room was bare except for a bed, a nightstand, and a few magazines. The bed was equipped with a switch that Suzanne could turn on to call a nurse. She scanned through some magazines and gazed out the window. The nurse checked in from time to time.

It was now evening. She'd checked in just before lunch, and so far she'd had no side effects except boredom. She could go to the group room down the hall and watch television. *Forget it! I don't want to deal with other people right now.* Maybe she was wasting her time. Maybe she wouldn't have any of those side effects they kept telling her about. Maybe she could stop drinking anytime she wanted. Maybe it was just a lack of willpower.

The nurse, Cindy, brought her dinner on a tray, and they talked for a few minutes. Then Cindy left. As the evening continued, the walls started closing in. She paced around the room, rapidly flipped through the magazines, but she couldn't sit still and her mind was racing. Finally, she threw down the magazine she had been holding and went to the closet for her suitcases. They weren't there. She slammed the closet door and stomped to the bed where she flipped on the nurse's light. After a few minutes, Cindy opened Suzanne's door. "Yes, Suzanne?"

"Where are my suitcases?" she demanded.

"They're in your room in Cottage A where you'll be staying," Cindy replied.

"I want them here." Suzanne stood with her hands on her hips.

"You can't have them here," Cindy answered as she began to leave the room.

"Why not?" Suzanne's voice was becoming obstinate.

"Because it's the rules."

"Screw the rules." Suzanne glared at the woman. "I'm paying a fortune to stay here, and I want my suitcases."

"You can't have them now." Cindy's voice was low and matter-of-fact. "You can't have the bottles you've hidden in them, Suzanne."

"What right have you got to go through my luggage?" she seethed.

"I didn't personally go through them."

"Then how do you know I have a bottle?"

"It's simple," Cindy replied. "I'm an alcoholic and I've worked here for three years. We all come in with our stash—just in case we need it."

"You don't understand," Suzanne pleaded. "I just need a tiny sip to help me relax. I'm not going to drink. Honest. I'm here to help me stop from drinking so much that I get drunk. But I just need a little sip to settle my nerves."

Cindy sat down in the chair and smiled at her. "No, Suzanne. You won't stop with one drink."

"Of course I will. I can't stand this." She furiously rubbed her temples. "I can't stand this."

"Let's talk." Cindy was gentle.

"I don't want to talk." Suzanne's anger was escalating. "I need one small drink, damn it. Just give me a drink."

"Suzanne, this is where the rough part starts. Try to lie down. It's not going to be easy."

"Go to hell!" Suzanne screamed. "Just give me a drink." She fell back onto the bed as if all energy was drained from her. She covered her face and began to cry. Then she bolted upright. "I'm out of here. Do you hear me? I don't need this." Her hands shook, and chills ran through her body.

Cindy walked over and sat on the edge of the bed. "Don't fight it so hard, Suzanne. Let me cover you up. The chills are going to get so bad nothing can warm you. Don't fight it. Try not to be afraid."

Suzanne's mind rested on Cindy's soft, soothing voice and the gentle hands that pulled the covers up over her shaking body. The shaking got so bad that her teeth chattered and she hurt from the movement. The minutes seemed like hours as her body revolted against the absence of alcohol.

Then the chills ceased, and her body began to relax. She believed the worst part was over. Then the fever came. She kicked the covers from the bed and thrashed around from the discomfort. As the hours passed, Suzanne was vaguely aware of Cindy who was trying to make her comfortable. The cool hands checked her pulse and gently pressed against her face to calm her.

Suzanne was calm for a few moments then the thrashing began again. She felt as though she was in the depths of the fires of hell. She struggled free of her hospital gown and lay naked beneath the sheet. Comfort slowly started to return. Then chills rampaged through her body again. By this time, Suzanne's mind was dazed and she was infuriated, terrified, and distressed, all at the same time. She was not sure where she was or who the gentle hands belonged to. Then the nausea came, and she clung to the side of the bed and emptied her stomach into a metal pan. She was too weak and sick to argue about anything. She just wanted to die, and she was certain she was going to get her wish.

Sunshine peeked through the mini blinds as Suzanne awoke from an exhausted sleep. Her thoughts were muddled as her eyes opened and her mind searched for memories and clues as to where she was.

"Hi," a voice said from the doorway.

"Hi," she faintly replied. There had been several nurses over the last several days, but Suzanne didn't think she had seen her before. Her long, dark hair and fair skin reminded Suzanne of Sarah.

"You've had a rough few days," the nurse said.

Suzanne's mouth was dry and scratchy. She noticed the pitcher of water and reached for a drink. After drinking one full glass, she drank another. The nurse walked over to the bed to take her blood pressure.

"Boy, am I thirsty."

"That's pretty typical. Between the fevers and chills, your body fluids need to be replenished."

"Am I done with it now?" Suzanne asked.

"With detoxification, yes. With the cravings and emotional upheaval that accompany alcoholism, no. That part has just begun."

"God," Suzanne sighed, "I don't know if I can do it."

"You can." The young woman put her hand on Suzanne's shoulder. "You're the only one who can do it, so don't give up on yourself. You're worth it."

Cottage A was a large one-story building. The room assigned to Suzanne had two beds, two nightstands, two dressers, and two closets. She stood in the middle of the room looking at her suitcases on the bed as she clutched her schedule in her hand. She had time to unpack and settle in, then she was scheduled for an individual counseling session.

"Don't look so sad. It's not that bad. In fact, it's a pretty good place to get yourself together."

Suzanne turned. A small woman with white hair smiled at her.

"Hi," Suzanne said. "You must be the counselor."

"No, I'm Annette, your roommate. You must be Suzanne."

Suzanne's eyes widened in surprise. "But, you don't . . . I mean . . ."

"You mean I don't look like an alcoholic?" Annette's smile turned mischievous. "Tell me, what do alcoholics look like anyway?"

"Well . . . I . . ."

"The answer is easy, honey," Annette said in a grandmotherly voice. "They look like you and me. Come on, I'll help you get settled in. For one whole month, this will be your home."

Annette stood up and held out her hand. "Now, let me take you on a tour of Cottage A and the dining hall which we fondly call 'The Mess,' then over to your counselor's office."

Suzanne had gone on a tour of the facilities before she checked in, but it didn't look the same. She was now on the inside looking out. Cottage A was filled with rooms identical to Suzanne's. Each room was painted in soft pastels, and the halls connecting the rooms were lined with artwork, needlepoint, and positive sayings done in calligraphy.

"A lot of this has been done by the patients. I'm working on one myself. I look forward to hanging it on the wall and leaving a happy memory somewhere."

"I'm sure you've left a lot of happy memories," Suzanne responded.

Annette stopped walking. "Suzanne, I'm learning to be honest with myself.

I've hurt a lot of people and have left very few happy memories along the way. You can't follow the path to addiction and not have hurt anybody."

"I haven't." Suzanne was defensive. "I'm sure I haven't. Besides, I don't have a husband or children. I couldn't have hurt anyone."

"Couldn't you?" Annette softly uttered.

In the small kitchen of Cottage A, a group of women were chatting. Suzanne was nervous. She had never been very good around other women. She never knew what to talk about.

"I couldn't even face the morning without whiskey-laced coffee," one woman said. "And I hid bottles all over the house so I'd never be far from a drink."

"I kept mine in my briefcase in a mouthwash bottle. A little green food coloring and people thought it was mouthwash. No problem." The women joined together in laughter.

Annette introduced Suzanne, and the women all reached out to her with friendly handshakes and smiles.

"It's time to take Suzanne to meet Liz," Annette told the group.

"Oh, you'll love her and hate her," one woman responded. "You'll hate her because she makes you deal with your problems. Then you'll love her for it."

Annette led Suzanne outside, and they walked along a tree-lined path to another of the one-story buildings that dotted the landscape. The lake glistened in the sunshine. Male laughter sounded through the quiet afternoon.

"Are there men here?" Suzanne asked alarmed.

"Sure. They're in other cottages. Addicts come in both sexes." Annette watched Suzanne. "Why, does that scare you?"

"No." Suzanne consciously slowed her breathing. "I was just wondering."

They entered a building filled with offices and Annette guided Suzanne down a hall and to a door with a nameplate that read "Liz Jackson."

"Liz does one of the group meetings for Cottage A. You'd never think she was a therapist to look at her. She's just a tiny thing with red hair and freckles. Her energy is boundless. Sometimes she really catches me off guard."

"What do you mean?"

"Oh, I don't know. The way she seems to be able to see into me."

Annette tapped on the door and it was opened by a woman fitting Annette's description. Liz Jackson's smile was wide and bright. She looked like she belonged on a beach playing volleyball or in the middle of a softball game instead of in an office at an alcohol and drug addiction center.

"Hi, Annette. And you must be Suzanne." Suzanne shook the hand offered to her. "It's nice to meet you. Thanks, Annette. See you later in group."

Annette gave Liz a wave and walked away.

Leading Suzanne into her office, Liz motioned to a chair close to the door and sat down across from her. "How are you doing, Suzanne?"

"Fine," she replied as she sunk into the comfortable, overstuffed chair.

Liz watched her. "You had a rough seventy-two hours."

"It was a little tough." Suzanne avoided making eye contact as she spoke.

Liz sat back in her chair with her elbows on the armrests. "Tell me what brought you to the center, Suzanne."

"Drinking," Suzanne stated, and when Liz didn't say anything in return, Suzanne started to fidget. "I mean, I drank a lot."

"Did you lose your job because of drinking?"

"No." Suzanne fidgeted.

"You just decided to come?" Liz tilted her head slightly.

"Yes." Suzanne quickly glanced at the counselor, then scanned the room for something to focus on so she wouldn't have to gaze into those kind, inquisitive eyes.

"That's great," Liz responded. "I had three suicide attempts before I finally went for treatment."

Suzanne's eyes widened in surprise. She knew the pamphlet had said that the counselors were former addicts, but at this moment, that wasn't registering. "You're . . . ?"

"Sure," Liz acknowledged. "Most of the counselors here are. We understand what you're going through because we've been there."

Suzanne leaned forward in her chair. "Well, my mother got sick."

"Are you close to your mother?"

"No," Suzanne reluctantly responded.

"Why don't you tell me about yourself and your family?" Liz settled back in her chair with a notepad on her lap.

Realizing that the questions weren't about to stop, Suzanne settled back in the chair. "There's not a lot to tell. I have two sisters. I grew up on a farm in northern Minnesota. My dad died many years ago. My mother is hospitalized in a diabetic coma. I'm a sales manager for a big company and live in Dallas, Texas." She paused. "That's all there is to tell."

"What was it like for you growing up?" Liz made a few notes on the pad.

"Like?" Suzanne squirmed in her chair, once again avoiding eye contact. "What do you mean?"

"Was it fun?" Liz asked.

"Fun?" Suzanne was confused. "Was what fun?"

"Being a kid."

"Fun?" The word seemed to stick in Suzanne's throat. "No, I wouldn't say it was fun."

Shifting the subject, Liz asked, "What did you like to do?"

"Oh, I don't know." Suzanne drummed her fingers on her leg. "What does that have to do with my drinking? Let's just fix my drinking."

Liz placed her pen on the table and leaned toward Suzanne. "And how do we do that?"

"I don't know." Suzanne peered around the room at the desk, the bookshelves that were filled with a myriad of books and titles, and finally to the diplomas on the wall before answering. "That's why I'm paying money to be here."

"So, since you're paying money, we should just make everything better for you?"

"Well . . . yes." Suzanne's eyes briefly met the counselor's.

"Can money do that?" Liz softly inquired as she sat back in her chair. "Just get everything fixed?"

"Well, no." Suzanne took a quick, deep breath and audibly let it out, showing frustration in every part of her body. "What's the purpose of this anyway?"

"Suzanne." Liz's voice became firm. "Why are you here?"

"Because you were on my schedule." Suzanne glanced at the woman as though she didn't understand the question.

"Why are you at the center?"

"To stop drinking, of course." Suzanne's fingers curled and uncurled as her hands stretched out on her legs. "Why else would I be here?"

"Why do you want to stop drinking? Everybody has to hit their own crisis. What's yours?"

Suzanne averted her gaze. "I don't know what you mean."

"Well," Liz smiled, "you can think about it and we'll talk more tomorrow."

"We're done?" Suzanne asked, completely baffled.

"No, Suzanne, we've just gotten started."

Chapter 27

Atlanta, Georgia

"I just thought it would be easier." Helene slumped back in the upholstered chair in Raymond Welsh's office. "Bill and I seemed to grow so close when I was away. He even told me he loved me a couple of times. But now that I'm home, it's harder than ever. Now, it's like playing a game where nobody knows the rules. At least we each knew what our roles were before."

"Would you want to go back to the old way?" Raymond softly inquired.

"No. I just want the new way to be easier. I mean, it's better than it was. Bill is home for dinner more often and we spend time together as a family. But it often feels awkward, as if we don't know how to relate to each other."

"Nothing's easy when you first learn how to do it," Raymond said as he leaned forward in his chair. "And that includes marriage. It takes a lot of hard work."

"But we're not new at marriage," Helene protested. "We've been married for over twenty years. It should be getting easier now."

Raymond settled back in his chair. "Why?"

She squirmed under his gaze. "Because we should know each other better than we do."

"People constantly change. You and Bill haven't been open and honest about your feelings, so how could you get to know each other under those circumstances?"

"It's just not what I expected." She looked around the room. "I mean, after coming face-to-face with all these feelings about my childhood, I felt like nothing would ever be the same and that I'd now have a handle on life. But nothing's changed that much. Bill still gets angry at Thomas, and Thomas sulks off to his room. I want them to talk, to get along. Why haven't they changed in that regard?"

Raymond gently touched one of her hands to bring her focus back to him and their conversation. "They didn't deal with their childhood, Helene. You did. Why should they have changed?"

"Because I have." Her eyes begged him to help her understand, to help her make things better. *It's got to be me. I must be doing something wrong.*

Raymond sat back in his chair. "Helene, you are not the controller and motivator of their lives. They don't respond to things you experience, but they do respond to you. They have their own lives, their own feelings, their own pasts." He gently smiled. "Not yours, Helene, theirs."

Helene scanned the diplomas on his wall. "But you told me that if one member of a family changes, that family unit can't be the same as it was." *Maybe I haven't changed. Maybe I just think I have.*

"It can't," he said. "You don't have control of what will change, and you can't decide when it will change."

"Well, what can I do?" She frantically flourished out her hands in front of her.

"You can do the things you've been learning to do. Continue to get healthier, set your boundaries, and talk about what's going on with you. The only thing you have control of, Helene, is the way you respond to situations and people—nothing else."

"But I never know what's the right way to respond to a situation. I never have."

Raymond's voice was soft as he responded. "There is no right way or wrong way. All you can do is be yourself. Respond in a way that feels good for you while respecting others and their boundaries. Just be Helene."

"I don't know who Helene is," she admitted.

"Maybe it's time you found out," he suggested.

Helene's eyes dropped to her hands. "I don't know how."

"That's why you're here . . . you're trying to learn."

"But I'm not learning very fast."

"Is there a time schedule?"

Helene sighed. "I feel like I've wasted half my life and I don't have all that much time anymore. I have to catch up."

"Helene, if you race through trying to make up for lost time, you won't enjoy this time either." Raymond lightly patted her hand. "Enjoy the process, Helene. Enjoy the process."

She glanced at him, confused. "What process?"

"Living."

"Mr. Foster." Lily's knock sounded on their bedroom door. "Mr. Thomas says he's not going to class today. He says he's sick."

Helene, who was curled up on the bed, leaning against the pillows that were propped up behind her, stayed quiet.

"Damn that boy." Bill quickly sat up on the edge of the bed and punched the mattress. "Nobody can be sick that much. He's a little over a month into his senior year and already he's missed three days. At this rate, he won't even graduate high school, let alone get into college. He's not getting away with it. He's not staying home." Bill angrily got out of bed and grabbed his robe. Turning toward Helene, he said, "Did you hear what I said?"

"Yes," Helene softly replied.

"Well, don't you have something to say?" He forcefully pulled his robe around him and tied it.

"No," she calmly answered.

"Well, what do you think about him staying home?" Bill said angrily.

Helene consciously kept her breathing even as she replied, "I think you have some strong feelings about it, and you and Thomas need to work it out."

He stared at her as if she had just grown three heads. Then he once again slammed his fist against the mattress. "Damn it, Helene. Don't you care? Do you care about anything anymore except yourself?"

Keep your cool, Helene. Take care of yourself. Don't get sucked in. He wants to fight with you instead of dealing with Thomas. Stay cool. Stay cool.

"Did you hear me, Helene?" Bill demanded.

"I did." She steadily met his gaze.

"Well, say something, damn it!"

Continuing to meet his gaze, Helene kept her voice soft. "I'm not going to fight with you Bill, so you can get mad at me instead of dealing with Thomas. I refuse to do that anymore."

"Oh, excuse me, Miss High and Mighty," he fumed. "I forget, you've got everything all figured out now. You're all healthy. Pardon me for having feelings you can't handle."

"This isn't new, Bill." Even though Helene wanted to pounce out of bed and leave the room, she stayed propped up on her pillows, looking directly at him as she spoke. "I've handled your anger for years."

"You want to see anger? I'll show you anger!" He picked up a shoe and hurled it at the large mirror on her dresser. The mirror cracked and glass perfume and makeup bottles scattered, some falling to the floor and shattering into pieces.

Helene's heart pounded so hard it hurt. She wanted to fight or run, yet she knew she shouldn't do either. Those would be her old ways of responding. Raymond had helped her understand the healthy thing to do was to remain quiet and let Bill deal with his own thoughts and feelings. So she silently watched Bill.

After a few moments of waiting for a reaction from her and not getting one, Bill sat back down on the bed. "I can't take this. This family is driving me nuts." Then he got up and headed for the shower.

"Mrs. Helene? Mr. Bill? Are you all right?" Lily called.

Helene stayed calm. "I'm fine. Bill just threw a shoe and broke the mirror. Nothing serious. Nothing that can't be fixed."

Bill stomped back in the bedroom. "Nothing serious? Three months ago, you would have had a fit."

"That was three months ago," she calmly replied.

Bill obviously didn't know how to react to this, so he resorted to old tactics. "I can't take this. Don't wait up for me tonight, Helene. I'll be late."

She didn't respond.

"Don't you have anything to say?" he urged.

Anger and fear were tumbling through Helene. *Stay calm and set your boundaries. That's what Raymond Welsh says. Set your boundaries, Helene. Set them.* "Yes, Bill, I do have something to say."

He glared at her. "What?"

"If you go to be with another woman, don't come home. Ever." Her voice was calm and strong. Her face was serious.

"I've never . . ." Bill stopped in mid-sentence. It was obvious that he had never seen her so serious. At her words, the anger seemed to drain out of him. "I'm sorry, honey. I'm trying to deal with Thomas, with us, with myself, and sometimes it's more than I can handle."

"I know," she whispered as she wrapped her arms around him.

They all sat in Raymond Welsh's office. It was Bill's idea. Helene was surprised when he had called and made the appointment. Now, he appeared to be very nervous.

"We've got to do something about Thomas." Bill began the conversation as soon as they were all seated and before anyone else could comment. "I can't stand it," he said. "The kid's not going to amount to a hill of beans. He's got potential. His IQ is high, his SAT scores were good, but his grades are lousy." Bill was inflamed. "If he keeps this up, he won't get into any good college. He'll end up starting at some two-year school."

"I'm not going to college," Thomas said, interrupting his father's tirade.

"You're what?" Bill glared at his son.

"I'm not going to college," Thomas said defiantly.

Helene glanced from Bill to Thomas to Raymond Welsh. She could sense that Bill and Thomas were going to have it out, and she was scared.

"Yes, you are." Bill slammed his fist against his leg.

"I'm not. It's my life, not yours. I'm not going to live it according to your dreams anymore." Thomas's voice was strong, but his eyes reflected fear.

"Well, then, you're not going to live off my bank account either."

"Fine. I'll move out," Thomas rebelliously replied.

Panic and fear filled Helene's chest, but she willed herself to stay silent. She surveyed Raymond's calm face and took a deep breath.

"What do you want to do, Thomas?" Raymond leaned forward.

"I'm not sure, but I don't want to be a lawyer."

"Fine, you'll be a good-for-nothing that can't support your wife when you get one," Bill sneered.

"At least I won't cheat on her." Thomas's eyes were dark, angry pools, glaring at Bill. "Maybe money isn't everything. Maybe a wife would rather have a husband who comes home instead of sleeping with anything in a skirt." Thomas whipped around to Helene. "Why did you put up with it? Don't you care about yourself? About him? About me?"

"I . . ." Helene was speechless.

"And you," Thomas turned back to Bill, "I'm tired of you trying to tell me what to do with my life when you've made such a mess of yours. You want me to follow in your footsteps. Why? What have you done that I should want to follow in your path? I don't even respect you, let alone want to be like you." His body shook. "You disgust me."

Bill's shoulders sagged as the energy seemed to drain from him. Helene stayed quiet for the rest of the session as Raymond worked with Thomas and Bill. She had no idea how angry Thomas had been with his father. *And who was I kidding when I thought Thomas didn't know about the dysfunction in our marriage?*

Helene felt as though a heavy curtain of denial was slowly being lifted off her life. They were finally all talking about their feelings, sometimes letting them explode into the air. At first she had been uncomfortable with the conflict, but now she knew that she would rather deal with confrontations than live with stiff politeness and silence.

Chapter 28

Minneapolis, Minnesota

Books were spread all over the kitchen table. Sarah was helping Alice with algebra. Sam was sitting by the coffee table in the living room, practicing his writing. Small red and blue plastic blocks were scattered all around him.

The three of them had settled nicely into an apartment in Minneapolis. The kids seemed to like their new schools, and Alice was attending classes at a junior college. Between educational grants, help from Helene, and part-time work at a local coffee shop, Alice was able to rent this small but nice apartment and financially take care of the three of them. It was much easier being a single parent than living with Jake and all the issues he caused. She hadn't filed divorce papers yet, because she could just handle so much at a time. That would be a priority next year. She was enjoying her new life, but everything was so different from the life she had before that she became overwhelmed at times. And tonight was one of those times.

"I can't get it." Alice dropped her pencil and put her head on her hands.

"Yes, you can, Mom," Sarah replied patiently. "Let's go over it again."

Alice bit at her fingernails. "School is hard. I didn't know it would be so hard. I'm surrounded by slim, beautiful, smart people and I feel dumb and fat. There's older people in my classes, so that's not so bad, but I feel stupid." She laid her head on the table.

Sarah threw her hands into the air. "Quit copping out! So you feel fat and stupid, then do something about it. That's what the counselors keep telling us. You ain't—I mean—you're not going to learn algebra if you just give up."

"Yeah, Mom," Sam chimed in. "I gotta keep practicing my handwriting. Things are hard for kids, too, you know."

Sam had been a calm oasis in a chaotic storm. Of the three of them, Sam seemed to have most easily adjusted to the changes. His teacher said he was doing well in school and he had friends he played with. "Have things been hard, Sam?"

"Yeah," he answered as he put down his pencil and started playing with the blocks.

"What's been the hardest?" Alice asked.

"Trying to be so different."

Alice glanced quizzically at her son. "Different, how?"

"Lotsa ways." Sam sat back on his knees. "We live clean now, and our apartment's nice. You're not so sloppy no more, and you don't go in your bedroom so much like you used to. And I don't gotta be afraid of Dad. He ain't here to yell and scream at you or make you and Sarah cry in the night."

Sam picked up a building block, seeming to study it. "Did you know some dads are nice? In our old neighborhood, my friends didn't have dads or else their dads were pretty much like mine. But here, it's different." He added the block to his growing structure. "My friend Tommy's dad throws a baseball with us. And he don't yell. When I had supper over there yesterday, I knocked over my glass, and my milk spilled. Nobody yelled, not even his dad. I got so scared, Mom. I figured he was gonna hit me, but he didn't. He even helped me clean up the mess. Then Tommy's mom poured me another glass, and we just went back to supper. That was so weird, but it was nice too—really nice."

"You got yelled at a lot, didn't you?"

"Yeah." Sam grimaced then went back to placing blocks, one by one.

"Mom," Sarah insisted, "let's work on your algebra. I don't want to be here all night."

"You're not going out, are you?" Alice panicked. Sarah hadn't been wild since their move to Minneapolis, but Alice was scared for her. She was scared whenever Sarah asked to go to a movie or out with a friend. Alice was afraid she was out having sex. How could somebody go through what Sarah went through and then go back to being fifteen? Alice knew that fifteen was no longer an age of innocence, but Sarah had gone through a lot more than most.

"No, Mom. You still don't trust me, do you?" The hurt was evident in Sarah's eyes.

"I didn't . . ." Alice stammered. "I mean . . ."

"I'm trying so hard, Mom. I'm even trying to talk different, so I don't sound so dumb. I'm buying nicer clothes with the money Auntie Suzanne gave me." Desperation radiated from her face. "I'm trying to be like other girls my age—girls who come from normal families—but I don't know how. So, I watch them, and then I imitate them. You're trying to do better for us. I see you struggling with school, and I know you get lonely down here where we don't know nobody except Grandma and she can't talk with you. And I know you're scared Dad might find us and hurt us. I know all that, so I'm trying to be better too. But it's hard."

Sarah's voice rose. "I have all these feelings I don't know what to do with. The counselor helps, but she's not there when some girl whispers about me when I walk into class. Or when we have to team up for a class activity and nobody wants me. It's hard when I see kids drugging or when kids are going out drinking. I'm tempted to do all those things, Mom, just so I can have some friends. But I can't." She drew a deep breath. "I can't because I feel so guilty already about all the problems I caused. If I hadn't told you about Dad, all of this wouldn't have happened. I could have just handled it and not messed you and Sam up, too, or I could have just run away—"

"Sarah, stop it!" Alice said sharply. "This isn't because of you. We needed to get away from your dad. Can't you see that? He's sick, Sarah, and we were sick right with him. If there's a fault, it's mine. I'm the one who's supposed to take care of you guys, and I wasn't. I don't know how either, Sarah, but I'm not as smart as you. I'm not strong like you, Sarah; I'm a quitter. I always take the easy way out—like staying married to Jake or stuffing my face with chocolate. I'm just a quitter."

"No, you're not," Sarah said gently.

"Sarah, I'm beginning to know about me, and I know I'm a quitter." She lifted her chin in the air and her voice grew firm. "But I don't have to stay no quitter." She pulled the textbook closer to her. "Now, about this algebra."

Chapter 29

Anoka, Minnesota

The large auditorium was packed. Suzanne curiously scanned the crowd. She wasn't sure what she expected to see, but she didn't expect them to appear so normal. Annette's words whispered in her mind, "What do alcoholics look like?" Suzanne's dad was typically dirty, unshaven, angry, and distant. Her mind connected the vision of him with alcoholism. Her misconception of alcoholics was one of the reasons it had taken her so long to acknowledge that she was one.

Three times a day the patients at the clinic gathered together. Suzanne was sitting between Annette and a tall red-haired woman whose name was Patrice. "I was named and christened Patricia, but I'm making my own choices now and I've decided I like Patrice. It fits me and the way I want to feel about myself. Patricia is for the way I was; Patrice is for the way I want to be."

Can people really do that? Make changes because they want to? What would that feel like?

"These gatherings and group sessions are the best for me," Annette whispered to Suzanne as the first speaker stepped up to the microphone. "I find out I'm not really weird after all. Other people feel like I do."

The first speaker was a man. Suzanne figured he was one of the doctors or hospital administrators. He was tall, dark haired, and attractive. He was dressed in a suit and looked like he had just stepped from the pages of a men's fashion magazine.

"Hi, my name is Evan, and I'm a recovering alcoholic and drug addict."

"Hi, Evan," the audience responded.

"I'm also a doctor." He shifted his position, and Suzanne got the impression that he was nervous. "I used to think that being a doctor kept me immune from the problems of the lower class. You know, problems like alcoholism. Only skid-row bums or guys who did manual labor are alcoholics. Guys in suits are too smart and above all that. And, of course, it's a given that doctors are above it all." Laughter trickled through the crowd.

Evan's voice grew stronger. "I pushed for achievement all my life, never taking care of myself or stopping to smell the roses. And the harder I pushed, the more I needed help dealing with the stress. Alcohol and prescription drugs were my answers. I could diagnose everyone else's problems, but I couldn't see my own. So, I kept getting worse and worse. I wouldn't listen to anyone. I was a doctor; I gave help. I didn't need it.

"So I lost everything. My wife, my family, my job. I hit bottom." Despair filled his voice. "But I'm coming back. It's been a year now. A year that I've taken one day at a time. Some days I cling to God, my higher power, with desperation, and some days I don't have to clutch quite so hard. But I'm making it and beginning to love myself in the process. That's what counts." Evan stepped away from the platform and applause sounded throughout the room.

"Why is he in the program if he hasn't had a drink for a year?" Suzanne asked Annette.

"He probably just comes in for the meetings. These meetings are open to the public. They're like AA meetings, only a little different."

"Different, how?"

"AA meetings are basically sharing stories of day-by-day life as an alcoholic. Here they also give us information about alcoholism. So, it's the same, but different."

Suzanne sat back. "Does everybody have to get up and speak? Do they make you?"

Annette smiled. "Suzanne, nobody forces you to do anything. Your recovery is your responsibility."

A woman stepped up to the microphone. She was tall and slender with waist-length black hair. She appeared to be in her mid-twenties. "Hi. My name is Sherry, and I'm an alcoholic."

"Hi, Sherry." Suzanne sat back as those around her participated in the greeting.

"Because of alcohol," Sherry continued, "I almost killed my baby." She wiped at her cheeks as though tears were running down them, but Suzanne was too far away to tell. "I was so excited when I was pregnant, and I tried not to drink too much. I didn't want to hurt the baby. So, I only drank at night—a nightcap to help me sleep. My daughter was small when she was born, and her immune system was very weak. By drinking through my pregnancy, I didn't give her a very good start. Well, she cried a lot. The first six months it seemed as though I never got a moment's peace. As the demands of motherhood grew, so did my drinking. It got to the point that I'd start drinking as soon as my husband left for work. By the time he came home, I was bombed. I'd plead fatigue, and he seemed to believe me."

Sherry was openly crying now. "One day I was bathing Penny. She was in her baby bath inside the tub. Penny had cried throughout her whole bath. I was exhausted, so I left her there to go to the bedroom and get a drink." The tears were now streaming down her face.

"She was in her baby bath. I thought she'd be okay." Sherry took a deep breath. "When I came back, Penny was lying facedown in the water with the baby bath on top of her. Somehow she had turned it over."

Annette was crying, and Patrice was sniffling as Suzanne fought to keep her emotions under control.

"She wasn't breathing. I threw a towel around her and stumbled to my neighbors. My neighbor started mouth-to-mouth, and her sister called the ambulance. Thank God. They saved my daughter, but the doctors say she'll have some brain damage. They just don't know how much." Sherry sobbed into a tissue. "My daughter has paid an enormous price for my addiction, and it almost cost her life. That was my bottom. Day by day, I struggle to get my life back so I can give my daughter the life she deserves." She took another huge breath. "I've lost her for a while. My husband left me and got custody of Penny. But we're working our way back together. I've hurt a lot of people, not the least of whom is myself."

Not the least of whom is myself . . . not the least of whom is myself . . . The words echoed through Suzanne's mind followed by the memory of Annette's words, "Haven't you hurt anyone? Haven't you?"

Chapter 30

Atlanta, Georgia

"Helene? Hi, it's Laura. I've missed you at our tennis groups."

"Oh, hi, Laura," Helene spoke into the phone as she sunk back into the leather loveseat in the den. "I don't think I'll be coming to the girl sessions anymore."

"Why not?" Laura's voice revealed disappointment.

Be honest, Helene.

Helene sunk deeper into the chair. "Laura, I grew up in an alcoholic home," she confessed. "I just can't enable or tolerate Stephanie and Catherine's drinking problems anymore. And what did we have beyond that?" She paused for a brief second. "We don't really know anything about each other. I mean, we didn't get to be friends. I'm not sure I know how to have real friendships, but I know that our tennis group wasn't a good example."

Laura was quiet for several moments. Helene's mind raced. *Well, your first try at honesty might just have backfired in your face.* Taking a deep breath, she tried to make amends for her honesty. "I'm sorry, Laura. I didn't mean to say anything to upset you."

"No, you didn't." Laura paused again. "You've changed, Helene. I can hear it in your voice. There's a strength I haven't heard before. Something's changed you. What is it?"

"It's a long story."

"I have a lot of time," Laura replied.

Suddenly, Helene's need for a friend rushed to the surface. "What are you doing now?"

"Nothing right now. It's my turn in the carpool today, so I pick up the kids at three, but until then, I'm free."

"Do you feel like grabbing your suit and coming over for a swim, a glass of iced tea, and some talk?" The invitation flowed smoothly from her lips, and Helene felt excited.

Surprise registered in Laura's voice. "I'd love to, but I'm not sure if I can find you in the daylight." They'd known each other for several years, but this was the first time Helene invited Laura to her home other than for dinner parties that she had hosted for Bill.

Helene laughed. "I know. My invitations haven't been proffered very often in the past."

"Are you turning over a new leaf?" Laura laughed.

"I'm trying to. I'm really trying to."

The water glistened off their wet bodies as the two women lay on lounge chairs in the warm September sunshine next to the kidney-shaped pool. "I saw Bill in the grocery store when you were away. I was surprised to see him. I thought Lily does all the shopping."

"She does." Helene smiled as birds chirped in the distance, and the sounds of Lily's music and her attempt to sing along floated out to the pool. "It must have been her night off. I guess they got tired of ordering pizza."

Laura adjusted herself on the chair and put on her sunglasses. "Bill said your mother was ill and that you and your sisters were back in Minnesota."

Helene nodded as she glanced around the beautifully landscaped backyard, feeling appreciation for the life she had.

"I didn't know your mother was still alive or that you had sisters."

"See?" Helene said with a smile. "I told you we don't know anything about each other."

Laura turned on her side and leaned against her elbow. "So, tell me. I'm curious. I'm especially curious about what's made the big changes in you. You seem like a totally different person."

Helene was quiet for several moments, then she rolled onto her side to face Laura. "What was your childhood like?"

Laura removed her sunglasses. "Like? I'm not sure I know what you mean?"

"Was it happy?" Helene paused. "Were you all close?"

Laura glanced at the water in the pool, then she answered, "Yes, it was happy but lonely. I'm an only child. My parents both had careers, but they spent as much time with me as possible. I didn't do a lot of things that children typically do, however. So, my people skills aren't very good. I don't have a lot of friends."

Helene heard Laura's words, but they didn't penetrate because she was already lost in her own thoughts. When Laura finished speaking, Helene hesitantly began talking. "My dad was an alcoholic. He yelled and screamed a lot, and my mother complained about everything. We weren't very close. In fact, I shut my family away from me for years. Then Mom got sick."

"Is she . . . okay?" Laura reached over and gently touched Helene's arm.

"She has diabetes," Helene responded. "We didn't know." Helene paused and glanced at Laura. "She didn't take care of herself, didn't eat right, and the doctor said she must not have taken her shots, because she went into a diabetic coma. And there's been no change. We finally had to put her in a critical care nursing home. She's in limbo, and that's sort of how my life has felt. It's like I was hanging between the past and the future, never touching the present."

Helene removed her sunglasses and ran her hand along the cushion of the lounge chair, avoiding Laura's eyes as she asked, "How do you feel about me now that you know my father was an alcoholic?"

"Why would I feel any differently?" Laura sat up. "I still want you to be my friend."

"Do you like me less because my background wasn't a normal one?"

"What's normal?" Laura sadly smiled. "I certainly wouldn't consider my background normal. Besides, look at you. You certainly didn't stay stuck in your background. You should be proud of yourself."

"Proud? Why?" Helene was startled by the response.

"Look at your life—how good it is."

Helene silently drew wet circles on the tile beside her lounger as they sat quietly for several minutes.

"Laura, do you and James have a good relationship?"

During the years Helene had known Laura, she had never before asked questions or even taken an interest in her personal life, as she didn't want anyone asking questions of her.

"Yes," Laura said. "We have a good relationship, but we both work really hard at it. I have to make him a priority, and he has to do the same with me. It took us many years to discover that, and we just about didn't make it through those years."

"You mean divorce?" Helene's eyes searched Laura's face as if to make sure she was telling the truth.

"I mean divorce with a capital 'D.' Work seemed more important than I was. I even accused him of having an affair," Laura replied in a matter-of-fact tone.

"Was he?" Helene gulped the question.

"He says he wasn't, but it took me a long time to believe him. The marriage was so bad that I tried to find something to blame it on. Then I decided to take all the guilt onto myself. That somehow I must be failing or we'd get along better. Then I'd fluctuate and blame the fighting all on him. Finally, I decided I was going to be happy and ask for what I wanted." She smiled. "Believe it or not, he listened, and it worked."

"You make it sound really easy."

"It wasn't." Laura sank back onto the cushion and stretched out. The breeze gently blew the leaves of the weeping willow tree at the far edge of the backyard. "We finally decided that we wanted the marriage to work and went to counseling as a last effort to save it."

"It apparently worked," Helene answered softly.

"Sure, the counseling worked, but so have we. And very hard too."

Thoughts tumbled through Helene's mind. *But James didn't actually have an affair; that makes it easier, doesn't it? Was Bill's cheating just an excuse for neither of us to have to work on the marriage?* She squirmed in her chair. She didn't know anymore. Maybe there was hope, but did she even want there to be hope? He wasn't cheating anymore, at least not from what she could tell. *Can it really be better?* Helene glanced toward Laura, who was lying face up soaking in the sun, her sunglasses covering her eyes.

"What did James say when you accused him of cheating?"

"He said that me even thinking he had an affair made him feel like he had. He called his work 'his mistress' and that it helped build up his ego instead of turning to me and our marriage to feel good about himself." Laura picked up her glass of iced tea. "Somehow we had forgotten to turn to each other to feel good about ourselves. In marriage, we forget to do that. We focus on everything else—the kids, money, jobs."

"Did you really believe him, Laura?" Helene stretched out on her chair with her sunglasses in place and stared at the fluffy white clouds floating in the blue sky.

"It took me a long time, but then I realized it was my own insecurities." Laura sipped her iced tea. "I had even thought of hiring a private detective. But then," she paused as if remembering, "we went to one of his company parties that was filled with beautiful, young women, and I finally realized that the only woman my husband had eyes for was me." She sighed. "A couple of years after James and I married, my mother told me that my father had cheated on her. I was so paranoid the same would happen to me, and those demons just about ripped apart my future."

Silence spread over the women as Helene dealt with the desire to want to ask more questions. She wanted and needed Laura as a friend—after today, she knew that more than ever. So, she didn't want to push too deep, too fast.

"Helene? Has Bill had an affair?"

The question jarred Helene's nerves like an electrical shock. "No, of course not. Not really."

As Helene stammered, Laura raised her eyebrows and said, "I'm sorry."

Helene shook her head, trying to dislodge the vice that was pushing at her temples. "I can't lie about this anymore, Laura. Especially not to myself." She took a deep breath as if to give herself strength. "He's had so many affairs I've lost count."

"Why don't you leave?" Laura asked as she reached out her hand.

The two women sat quietly for a moment, their fingers touching, before Helene answered. "I don't know. Besides, I don't think he's having them anymore. He knows that if he does now, I will leave."

"But you can't let go of what he's done?" Laura brought her hand back to her lap, and then after a few moments, she took another sip of tea.

"No, I can't. It haunts me . . . but I do love him."

"Do you talk about it?" Laura's voice was soft.

"Not really."

"Are you getting counseling?"

Helene quickly sat on the edge of the chair. "We're all getting individual counseling right now. And we've done some family counseling, but not just Bill and me. I wasn't ready to deal with those issues."

"Maybe you are now."

"Yes, maybe I am." Calm settled over Helene. "Other than my sisters and my counselor, you're the first person I've talked to about this." Helene smiled weakly. "It's nice not to have that horrible secret hanging over me."

Chapter 31

Anoka, Minnesota

"Okay, I've had it." The woman leaned forward with anger blazing in her eyes as she pointed at Suzanne. "How long have you been in these group sessions now?"

Suzanne sat there speechless. She had no idea what she had done to make Joan so angry with her. She had been attending group as she was supposed to and listening when others talked. What else did they want from her? Suzanne was in over her head. Life had been confusing enough without adding all of these counseling sessions and groups to the mix. She came here to stop drinking, not deal with other people's anger and their garbage. She had enough of her own.

The woman jabbed her finger at Suzanne. "I'm talking to you."

Suzanne squirmed. "I don't know. Over a couple of weeks, I guess." *What is her problem?* Suzanne scanned the room, looking for an ally or a way to politely leave and take herself away from Joan's anger.

"You guess?" Joan stood up with her hands on her hips until Liz, the group counselor, motioned her back into her chair. "You're damn right it's been over a couple of weeks!" She placed her hands on her knees, leaned forward into them, and raised her voice while glancing sideways at the counselor. "Two weeks of you sitting there judging us, not participating." She sat back against her chair so strongly that it skidded a few inches on the floor.

"Well, who the hell do you think you are?" Joan yelled. "I want to hear from you!" She crossed her arms in anger. "It's like you sit there listening to the rest of us spill our guts and you say nothing. Just like you're some kind of princess or something." Her words were coming fast now. "Well, you're in here, aren't you? So, you've got to be either an addict or an alcoholic. What's your story? You've had a free ride on us long enough."

The man sitting across from Suzanne joined in. "I think Joan's right." His voice was soft, but his gaze was direct. "I'm tired of it too. I got silent judgment all my life. I sure as hell don't need it in here."

Suzanne was being attacked and she didn't know why. Her arms curled around her chest. Her "fight or flight" responses were kicking into gear. "I'm sorry—"

"I don't want to hear sorry," Joan cut her off. "I want to hear about you, Suzanne."

Suzanne glanced at Liz, sitting quietly watching the interactions, then she looked back at the man and woman who were furious with her and she had no idea why. "Well . . . uh . . . I had a drinking problem, and things got pretty rough."

"Pretty rough? What does 'pretty rough' mean?" another member of the group joined in.

"Well, I drank every night," Suzanne stuttered. She was trapped and defenseless, like an animal in a cage that was being poked and prodded with nowhere to go. Grabbing the side of the chair, Suzanne gritted her teeth.

"So? We all drank every day, every night, all the time." Joan was still in attack mode. "It destroyed me. It destroyed my life!"

Suzanne leaned forward, eyes blazing, and her breath coming quickly. She was tired of being the victim. Tired of being bullied. "Well, it got rough at work, okay? Besides, leave me alone!" Her eyes narrowed at Joan then spanned the rest of the group. "Maybe I don't want to sit here and whine the way you all do. I don't have to dwell in the past; I just have to look to the future."

"The past is what put you here, Suzanne," Joe, another group member added. His voice was soft and his eyes were kind. "I know it's not easy." He turned toward the group. "Hey, go easy on her. You guys have been here almost a month. Give her some space."

"No, damn it, I won't give her space," Joan stormed. "I'm going to keep right in her face."

Suzanne started to heave a sigh of relief when Liz turned to Joan. "What is it about Suzanne that makes you so angry?"

Joan swung her whole body toward Liz. "She's smug! She quietly sits there like her world is intact, and I can't stand it."

"Why not?" Liz questioned tenderly.

"Because it's not." Joan's temper was beginning to defuse. "I know it's not. Nobody with a perfect world ends up here."

"Joan," John reminded her, "you thought your world was perfect, remember?"

Joan sat up straight in her chair and her voice once again gained some volume. "Yes, I remember. Maybe that's why she ticks me off. She reminds me of me, and that pisses me off."

Suzanne's hands had started to shake as the group interchange took place. She lowered her eyes to the floor to try to gain control of the hostility that was building up inside of her. The voices continued on. They were talking about her as if she wasn't there and she couldn't hear them. *I can't stand this. I can't! I can't!*

"Maybe she's just scared," John commented.

"And maybe she's not," Joan spat back at him. "Maybe she's sitting there making fun of all of us."

"Maybe," John began.

"Stop it! Stop it! Stop it!" Suzanne nearly screamed as she stood up with her fists clenched at her sides. "Quit talking about me as if I don't exist."

"Well, you don't exist," Joan countered. "To this group, you're inanimate. Dead." She stood up, glaring at Suzanne. "You don't participate," Joan fumed. "You don't share. We don't know anything about you."

"I'll tell you, damn it! All right? But just quit all this." Suzanne clenched and unclenched her fists. "I can't stand it. It's the same way my family was. They'd talk about me as though I wasn't even there. 'Suzanne is not very good at being with people. Suzanne is very shy. No, she's not shy, Suzanne thinks she's better.' The voices would go on and on, and no one would even look in my direction to see if I had a comment or was even alive."

Anger danced within her. "Well, I am alive! I was alive then, and I'm alive now. Maybe I don't know how to participate. Maybe I don't know how to talk to you without sounding like a whiner, and I detest whiners." She sank back into her chair as Joan carefully sat down in her own. "My mother was a whiner," Suzanne continued. "And I'm not going to be one—do you understand? I'd rather not say anything at all."

The heat of rage flushed up Suzanne's body. All control and logic had left her mind. She was not thinking about what she was saying. *These people want to know who I am. I'll tell them, damn it. They'll find out how awful I am and then they'll leave me alone.*

She leaned forward in her chair, daring anyone to say anything, to interrupt. "I'm a drunk, okay? I drank every night. I'd get as intoxicated as I could—even sloppy drunk. Then I'd pick up men. It didn't matter who or even where. I've slept with more men than I care to count, and I don't remember their faces let alone their names." She glared at Joan. "I'm a slut. You got that? A loose woman, a piece of garbage." Suzanne's voice was strong and angry. She stared at the group, ready to confront their hostility. She didn't see any, but her rage was in full swing now.

"Well, I got really drunk one night and ran into the wrong man. He's one of my salesmen. He took pictures. He's blackmailing me." She turned to Joan. "I've got to pay his price to keep it a secret or I'll lose my job. But he doesn't want just money." Her voice ended on a sob, and that angered her some more. Once again grabbing on to her rage, Suzanne turned to Liz. "You wanted to know my crisis? Well, now you've got it. Now you know I'm a drunk and a slut. Now you can all really shut me out."

Suddenly, Suzanne stood and screamed, "Now just leave me alone. Get the fuck out of my life and leave me alone." She headed toward the door, knocking her chair over as she went.

"Suzanne!" Joan called, but Suzanne kept marching away.

The sobs seemed to be coming from the very depths of Suzanne's soul as she buried her head in her pillow and clung to her bed. She was awash in a sea of pain; nothing made sense. Her whole world was tumbling around her. She felt alone and isolated as the sobs racked her body.

After what seemed like hours, the sobs started to ease and fatigue settled in. Gentle hands pulled a blanket up over her. Suzanne turned her head away from the wall. Joan was sitting quietly by her bed. Suzanne stared at her and whispered, "Go away."

"No, I'm not going away." Joan's voice was soft. "You think you're awful and all alone. Well, you're not either. You have to convince yourself you're not awful, but I can let you know that you're not alone." Joan reached out to put her hand on Suzanne's forehead, but Suzanne flinched and pulled away.

"I used to get hit a lot too," Joan said. "It seemed like nobody loved me. So, when I got older, I found love the only way I knew how. I went to bed with guys. By the time I was fourteen, I had slept with every guy in my class. It's a good thing my class wasn't really big." She sadly smiled.

"I really wrecked my body with all the sex I had at such a young age. But by the time my old man got done with me, it was probably already a mess."

Suzanne's eyes grew large and she held her breath.

"Yeah," Joan sneered. "My *father*," she spit the word as though it was something vile and foul-tasting, "started messing with me when I was a kid." She paused for a moment. "I've talked about all of this in group. Weren't you there?" Then she answered her own question. "If you're like me, you've probably been blocking everything out anyway."

Joan touched Suzanne's arm. "That's why you made me so mad. You remind me of me. And the way I handle things isn't good—shutting everything up inside, and feeling like I'm awful and weird and strange. And I'm not, Suzanne, and neither are you. Everybody's got something. I'm discovering that. Nobody is pain-free." She pulled the covers up around Suzanne's shoulders and quietly left the room.

Laughter circled around Suzanne's ears. It was play day, food was abundant, and so were the opportunities for fun and relaxation. But Suzanne didn't know how to do either without alcohol, so she sat on a chair, watching as the sun glistened through the large windows off the water of the pool. The laughter of the splashing adults seemed to bounce off the walls.

"Suzanne, hi." Water dripped from Patrice as she ran up to Suzanne. She had a huge grin on her face as she held out her hand. "Come swimming with me."

"No, I . . ." Suzanne squirmed, trying to avoid the cold drops of water bouncing onto her skin. Irritation was flooding over her, and impatience was pricking at her nerves. Why in the world were a bunch of adults having a "play day," as the treatment program called it? She hadn't played since she was a kid, and she frankly found it a waste of time. If they took this nonsense out of the schedule, maybe she'd be able to get out of here sooner.

Not taking no for an answer, Patrice shook her head to create an onslaught of water, giggled, and grabbed Suzanne's hand. "Come on."

Suzanne had no intention of being pulled into the antics, but Patrice's playfulness was contagious, and the little girl in Suzanne started to awaken. Playfulness hadn't been a part of Suzanne's life for decades, and the child inside of her was hungry for it. But the adult Suzanne had built a strong façade of seriousness and responsibility, and it wasn't going to come down easily.

Finally, Suzanne allowed herself to be pulled off the chair and toward the groups of laughing, splashing, swimming adults. Once she was sure Suzanne was following, Patrice let go of her hand and ran to the edge of the pool and jumped in.

Suzanne stood at the edge of the pool feeling abandoned. Now what did she do? Where did she go from here? She hadn't played much when she was a kid. How in the world was she supposed to learn as an adult? Besides, responsible adults didn't play. Did they?

Joe, one of the men from her group therapy, waved. "Suzanne, come on in, the water is great!"

The child in Suzanne surfaced and the water and fun was impossible to resist, so she cautiously dipped her foot into the water. Someone in the pool splashed her. The water was cold on her skin, and Suzanne's anger charged to the surface. "Stop it."

"No," a woman answered. "If you don't want to play, get out of the water."

Rage, her frequent companion the last couple of days, overtook Suzanne. "Fine, you want to play, we'll play!" Suzanne jumped into the pool, scooped her hands into the water, and splashed handful after handful at the woman.

Her intention was to douse the woman so thoroughly that she would get out of Suzanne's space and leave her alone.

After the first shock of cold water hit her, the woman reacted and started splashing back. Energies and emotions splashed back and forth as abundantly as the water. Soon they were both drenched. The woman observed Suzanne and started to laugh. "You look so funny." She fell back into the water in gales of laughter.

"You don't look so great either." At first, Suzanne was enraged, but as she watched the woman laugh in pure delight, laughter started up in tiny, little giggles. Unsure of the terrain, it peeked its head out of the hiding place of her soul. Then, little by little, the child in Suzanne gained strength, and delighted laughter pealed forth from between her lips as she playfully splashed her companion. When the laughter had finally eased itself back to a tiny giggle, Suzanne experienced a relief that was new to her.

"I'm Suzanne."

"I'm Louise." The woman danced in circles as she answered.

Suzanne stood on her toes in the water and joined the playful dance. "I can't remember laughing like that before," she admitted as she giggled and danced.

"I know. It's new to me, too, but it gets easier," Louise assured her as she suddenly slipped into the water and swam away. Suzanne watched her graceful strokes.

Wait. That was fun. Don't leave yet.

"Suzanne, can you swim?" Joe asked as he came up beside her.

Still bubbling with the delight of playing in the water with Louise, she answered, "Yes, but not too well. It's been a long time."

"I'll race you to the other end."

"Okay." Suzanne slid into the water and swam away. The exercise felt good as her muscles responded to the demands. The water flowed smoothly under the pull of her arms, and her breathing was strong and even.

Even though Suzanne had taken a head start, Joe was a stronger swimmer and reached their destination first, leaning over to help Suzanne up onto the sun-warmed surface. Several people were lying in the sun, some were dangling their feet in the water, and others were diving into the pool, climbing back out, and diving in again.

"Boy, that felt good." Suzanne removed some hair clips and shook her hair so it became free to fall around her face.

"Why do you always wear your hair pulled back?" Joe asked.

Suzanne had never thought about it before. "I don't know. I always have except—"

"Except?" Joe sat down at the edge of the pool and Suzanne joined him.

For a moment, the sun escaped her view as darkness threatened her. "Except sometimes toward the end when I was drinking and picking up men." Her voice became very soft. "Somebody told me I was pretty, and I actually believed it for a while."

"Actually," Joe smiled, "you're gorgeous."

Suzanne furrowed her brow, and Joe seemingly recognized her wariness. "I don't want to go to bed with you, Suzanne, so relax." He grabbed a handful of water and splashed it at her, causing her to gasp and then grin when she realized that she had gotten too serious for the playful afternoon.

Joe made a face at her as she kicked her feet in the water, sloshing it at him. "I want to be your friend." Letting his voice become serious for just a moment, he confessed, "I don't know how to be just friends with women, but I'm trying." Then his eyes sparkled and he grinned. "I can tell you that you're pretty without wanting something from you, can't I?"

"Well, sure . . . I guess so." Suzanne began to make small circles with her toes.

"Good." He smiled. "Now, let's just talk."

"About what?" She turned her head toward him as her feet continued to play in the water.

"I don't know." He shrugged. "I'm not good at small talk, but I want to learn. So, let's try it, okay?"

"Sure." Suzanne agreed. "I'd like that."

Chapter 32

Atlanta, Georgia

"Lily, I've decided to make a candlelight dinner for Bill and me tonight, so take the afternoon and night off." Helene hadn't done much of the cooking in the Foster household since Lily had started working for them when Thomas was five. Sure, she would prepare something to eat for her, Bill, and Thomas on Lily's nights off, but it was usually something simple. Tonight was different. She intended to try to bring some romance into her relationship, and a candlelight dinner was a good way to start.

Lily was in the dining room, polishing the table. "Why, Mrs. Helene, that's so nice. What can I do?" She put down her polishing cloth.

"Nothing. Thanks though. I'm going to do this myself." Helene started to leave the room and turned back. "Lily?"

"Yes, Mrs. Helene?"

"I feel so funny about this. Almost like I'm embarrassed." A pink glow formed on her cheeks. She surprised herself by admitting that to Lily. *You'd think I was sixteen getting ready for a first date.*

Lily walked over and laid her hand on Helene's shoulder. "Mrs. Helene, it's always awkward when folks try to get close when they're not used to it. I used to feel silly when I tried with my Jed."

"You did?" Helene knew Lily had been married, but her husband had died several years before she had come to work for them. *Lily, romantic?* A delighted giggle pulled at the corner of her lips.

"Why, Mrs. Helene, I'm a woman too. I don't think we're all that different no matter what color, or age, or how rich or poor we are. We all struggle, and we all feel strange or silly when we try to do things. We all doubt ourselves as women, wives, and mothers. We just do it at different times and in different ways."

Helene's arm slipped affectionately around Lily's waist. "You are a wise old soul, my friend."

Lily smiled. "Maybe not so wise, just a lot more miles on the old buggy."

Helene rested her head on Lily's. "I'm glad you're here, Lily. I need you now more than ever." And she did. Her life was changing daily, most of it positively, but the changes often left her feeling unhinged, needing someone solid to hold on to. Lily was her anchor.

"I'm glad to be here now more than ever."

"You are?"

"Mmmhmmm," the older woman murmured.

"Why?"

Lily pinched Helene's cheek and winked at her. "It's like you're waking up from a long sleep and discovering things." She touched her finger to the tip of Helene's nose. "Sort of like a little girl growing up. I just figure you need my caring now more than ever. Besides, now I don't have to be such a quiet friend. You're just not as blind as you was."

"I was pretty blind about a lot of things," Helene admitted.

"Honey, when you look in the mirror, you see more black than I do." Lily grinned.

"What do you mean?" Lily's homespun logic and analogies often confused and puzzled her.

"Well, when I look in the mirror, I see black because I am black. When you look in the mirror, you see black because you aren't looking at what's there," Lily stated matter-of-factly.

Helene shook her head. "Lily, sometimes you talk in riddles."

"Life is a riddle, Mrs. Helene. Just one great big one." Lily picked up the polishing cloth and began to shine the table using small, circular motions.

"You mean a puzzle, don't you?" Helene asked.

"That too." Lily smiled. "That too."

The table was set with china and crystal; shadows from the candlelight danced on the walls as soft music played in the background. Helene heard Bill's car pull into the garage and she glanced at the mirror for about the twentieth time in the last half hour.

Many times during the last two hours of preparation, she had almost stopped the whole process. She felt juvenile, stupid, anxious, and vulnerable. If it hadn't been for Laura's encouragement, Helene wouldn't have gotten this far. After their in-depth conversation last week, Helene and Laura had talked every day. Laura had made James a candlelight dinner a few nights ago.

"A candlelight dinner? Why?" Helene had asked.

"For romance," Laura had responded. "It's important to keep the romance alive in a relationship. And candlelight dinners really help."

"Oh." Helene had been sitting in the sunroom curled up on one of the chairs that faced the pool and the large backyard. Romance felt like a foreign word to her. She knew it existed, and commercials constantly encouraged purchases as a part of being romantic. Sure, she and Bill had courted in the beginning, but that was so long ago that Helene wasn't sure where to start or how Bill would respond if she did.

"You know," Laura had continued, "several years back, I wanted so desperately for James to treat me as a lover, but I didn't know how to get him to do that. And I certainly couldn't ask anybody. So I got my answers the way I always do—through books." Laura had laughed. "Every suggestion you can think of is in books, and I was going to try them all."

"Like what?" Helene was curious.

"Well, one woman author wrapped herself in plastic wrap and met her husband at the door." Laura giggled.

"Plastic wrap? Just plastic wrap? Tell me you didn't do that."

Gales of laughter had erupted from Laura's end of the phone. "I did. I mean . . . I tried. And failed."

"Failed?" Helene chuckled. "What do you mean failed?"

"Helene, it was the funniest thing you've ever seen. I left the kids with a neighbor to spend the night. Then I went to the store and got all these rolls of plastic wrap . . . you know, the real sticky kind. I hauled them up to the bedroom and took off all my clothes. I started winding the plastic around my legs, but I wasn't thinking too clearly, because instead of wrapping each individual leg, I wrapped them both—mummy-style."

Fresh laughter erupted. *Where in the world do people come up with these ideas?*

"I was concentrating so hard I didn't realize what I had done. I wrapped up all the way to my chest and crisscrossed it over my shoulders like a gown before I tried to walk. I couldn't. I had wound it so snugly around my legs."

The women were laughing so hard that they needed a moment to control themselves.

"Then I decided to unwrap myself and begin again, but the darn stuff was so sticky, it kept clinging, and when I did get it pulled off, I couldn't get it back onto the roll without sticking to itself. I was so frustrated that I hopped over to the dresser, got a pair of scissors, and started cutting the stuff off. Then the worst part happened."

"What? Did you cut yourself?"

"No. James surprised me and came home early." Laura giggled.

"Oh no." Helene held her stomach to try to control the laughter as she envisioned her friend wrapped in sticky, clear plastic, crying and trying to cut the blasted stuff off.

"At first, he was scared to death. He had no idea what was going on. I was crying uncontrollably, cutting the plastic wrap, and angrily pulling it off my body." Laura's laughter had settled into soft memories.

"Finally, James calmed me down and gently removed the plastic as I cried and told him what I was trying to do. He wiped the tears from my eyes. Then, as I sat naked on the edge of the bed, he gathered all the plastic wrap into one huge ball and put it on the chair by the window. He told me it was to remind him how much his wife loved him. He said he didn't know that."

Laura's voice became very soft. "He was very angry at himself for all the hurt he had caused me and was sure he had lost me. He was so touched at my plastic wrap efforts and his gentleness touched me. It was a beginning for us."

Her voice perked up. "Now all we have to do is see a box of plastic wrap, and we just start laughing."

Helene had remained quiet.

"Helene? You're quiet all of a sudden." Laura said.

"Do you think I could put romance and love back into my marriage?" Helene asked very softly.

"Not by yourself—it will take both of you," Laura answered. "But somebody's got to take the first step. But I don't recommend plastic wrap." They fell into another fit of giggles.

"Thanks," Helene said. "I think I'll try something easier.

And now, Helene was standing by the door when Bill came in. She was dressed in a simple black dress with a low-scoop neck. Diamond earrings, Bill's Christmas gift to her many years ago, glittered in her ears. Her hands nervously fidgeted as she smiled at her husband.

"Hi." He glanced toward the dining room and the flickering candlelight. "Did I forget something? Are we having guests tonight?"

"No, just us."

"Oh my God—did I forget our anniversary or a birthday or something?"

"No, nothing special." Gentle laughter surfaced in Helene as she watched her husband's discomfort. Placing her hand on his arm, she led him toward the living room. "Come in and relax a few minutes. I made some hors d'oeuvres and poured us each a glass of wine."

Confusion was apparent on his face. "Helene, are you okay? Do you have bad news and you're trying to soften the blow?"

Helene became serious. "Isn't it sad, sweetheart, that our life is so void of romance that we become uneasy or suspicious when it occurs?"

Bill's face softened. "All of this is just for us?" His eyes moved around the room, taking in the china, crystal, and candlelight.

"It is," she whispered as she watched the confusion in his eyes turn to joy.

He took her hand. "It's nice. Thank you." Then he glanced about. "Where's Thomas?"

"Staying the night at a friend's."

"Lily?" he asked as his fingers lightly traced the palm of her hand.

"I gave her the night off."

"You planned all of this just to be alone with me?"

"Yes, honey."

"You still love me, Helene?"

"I do."

"How can you after all I've done?" Bill said shakily.

"I just do, Bill." She softly stroked his face. "I can't explain it. Besides, I haven't been perfect either."

As panic rose in Bill's face, sadness gripped at Helene's heart, but she refused to give way to it. Laura had told her how hard it had been for her parents to get beyond the pain of infidelity—to get past the betrayal. "I didn't have affairs, Bill. I just haven't made you a very big priority. I think I took you for granted."

They stood awkwardly in the middle of the room as soft music played in the background. Helene knew they were standing on the edge of a chasm. The pain from their past could pull them into the darkness, or they could turn and walk toward the sun—the choice was theirs. As Bill slipped his arm around her waist, the stereo sent out the sounds of Elvis singing "Love Me Tender."

"May I have this dance?" His voice was soft, romantic.

"Here? Now?" Helene's heart bubbled with giddiness. When they were dating, Bill would often take her dancing, and she had loved the closeness of their bodies moving together and the smell of his aftershave tickling her nose.

"Sure." Pulling her close, Bill gently guided Helene around the room.

After all these years, she was still pulled in by his scent and his strong arms. Helene snuggled closer. Her head rested gently against him, and his lips softly touched the bare skin on her shoulders. Shivers ran through Helene.

"Are you cold, darling?" Bill asked as he gathered her closer.

Helene's arms slipped up and around Bill's neck as she pressed herself closer to him. She could feel his desire, and her heart melted. Years seemed to disappear as they danced together. She was once more a young woman very much in love with a man who made her heart jump and her dreams leap into possibility.

"I love you so much," he whispered in her ear. "Can you forgive me, sweetheart? I know I don't deserve it, but can you forgive me?"

"Shh . . ." She gently placed her finger on his lips. "Let's get lost in what is and forget about what was." Tonight she wanted to explore what was possible for the two of them and forget everything else. If they could find romance and intimacy the way Laura and James had, then everything else would be much easier.

"I can do that." Bill kissed Helene's earlobe, and his tongue softly traced the inner circle. Helene turned toward him and her lips sought his. Gently, tentatively, their lips touched.

Their eyes met as he kissed her mouth, her nose, her eyes.

Softness enveloped her as she enjoyed his lips against her skin. He found a favorite spot on her neck and his tongue followed a path down her chest and to the crevice between her breasts. Helene's knees grew weak.

His hands explored her body, playfully squeezing her waist, then softly floating over her breasts. In response, her nipples strained against the cloth of her dress. Bill pulled Helene into his arms and smoothly waltzed her around the room. She pushed into him as her arms wrapped around his neck. Minutes passed as they danced a courtship ritual.

His hands circled around her and Helene felt him tug at the zipper of her dress, then slowly pushed the dress down to her waist. She was only wearing a black garter and black hose. She watched his eyes open in surprise and his body respond in delight.

It had been a long time since he had made love to her like this. Over the last ten years, when they did have sex it was typically hurried as though he had other things on his mind. Tonight she could feel that she was all that mattered. His hands caressed her as she imagined a diamond cutter caressed a priceless gem, softly and carefully working his way over each curve, each line, each facet of the stone.

Helene responded as Bill slipped one arm around her back and the other under her legs and lifted her up against him. Their lips danced with each other as he carried her upstairs. Helene unbuttoned his shirt and played with the hair on his chest. Bill sat her on the edge of the bed as Helene traced the hairline that disappeared behind his waistband. Slowly unbuttoning his slacks, her fingers traced the bulging cloth.

"My God, Helene," Bill gasped. "You're driving me crazy."

She slid back on the bed and reached out to him. Bill crawled onto the bed and paused over her. His fingers explored her, searching for the moistness and swelling that would tell him she was ready. Their eyes locked as their bodies joined, and Helene gave into the wonder of their love.

A few hours later, the burned-out candles had been replaced with new ones. Helene and Bill were in their robes, quietly eating dinner. A soft aura floated around them.

"Bill?"

"Yes, honey?" His eyes locked on hers.

"I love you." She did love him. Tonight reminded her how he could make her knees go weak, her heart melt, and her entire body surrender. Those were the feelings and experiences she intended to focus on.

Bill laid his fork down and reached out and touched her face. "Forgive me. Please forgive me."

"I have. With Raymond's guidance and God's help, I have. Now I want to forget, but maybe I have to understand before I can."

"Understand what?"

"Why you did it. What I did wrong." There had to be something that she had done in their earlier years that had caused him to turn to other women. Her stomach was turning in knots, fearful that she would do it again and once more push him away.

"Wrong? You did wrong?" Bill wiped away a tear that slid down her cheek. "It wasn't you, Helene. It was me."

"Why?" Her lips quivered.

Bill pushed back his plate and stood. "Maybe it's time we really talked." He reached for her and led her toward the den.

Helene softly protested, "Our dinner will get cold."

"I like leftovers," he stated as he continued to walk toward the den.

"No, you don't," she protested. Internally she was struggling—part of her wanted to hear what he had to say, but part of her was terrified of it.

"I do now." Bill settled in his huge armchair and pulled Helene down on his lap. "Did you know that my dad had a lot of affairs?"

"No. Your parents seem to get along so well. I wouldn't have guessed."

What does that have to do with us? Think about it, Helene. Your parents' actions impacted you. Why would Bill be any different?

"They do get along well, if that makes any sense. They're very compatible, very career-minded people with brilliant minds." He paused. "When I was in my early teens, I began to notice that my dad was gone a lot at night and my parents didn't hold hands, hug, or kiss the way my friends' parents did. One day I asked him about it." Bill touched her chin. "I remember how uncomfortable he seemed, but he said he wasn't going to lie to me."

Sadness covered Bill's face. "He said that shortly after they were married, my mother had told him that wives just have sex to have babies. Once I was born, as far as she was concerned, that obligation was fulfilled. She told him that if he wanted to go elsewhere and take care of his male needs, that was fine with her. So he did. And that worked out fine for them, and they got along great."

His eyes searched Helene's. "I was young. I thought all wives felt that way. As I grew older and listened to guy banter, it sounded as though most men had affairs, even though now I know that's untrue. But at the time, it's what I believed, so that's what I did. But our marriage didn't work like my parents' marriage, and you pulled away from me. So I figured you didn't love me."

Bill pulled her closer. "Then I had to prove to myself I was loveable, and it just got crazy. As the years went on, I felt caught in this trap. I didn't know what put me there in the first place or how to get out of it. Then I couldn't do anything right as a husband, so I tried to be a father—the way my father was—and that didn't work because you aren't like my mother. It got out of control and I didn't know how to stop the cycle."

Helene kissed his forehead.

"Raymond told me to talk to you. But how could I? I wasn't going to risk losing you. And we've been so busy in counseling for ourselves and for Thomas that it didn't seem to be the right time to deal with us."

His words were circling in Helene's head as she tried to make sense of what he was saying. *What a terrible experience for him. A teenage boy has no idea how to handle information like that. What in the world was his father thinking? And why didn't he tell me? Why didn't I ask questions?*

Bill's eyes were wide as he waited for her response, and as she returned his gaze, tenderness flooded Helene's chest. *I'm not the only one who let a bad moment or experience in my childhood negatively impact my life.* As she sat in her husband's lap, Helene once again knew that she loved all the goodness that was a part of him. She knew they would not recover from past mistakes in just one night, but they were definitely on the right path, and if they both put time and attention into the relationship, they could create the type of marriage they both seemed to want.

Helene placed her cheek against his. "Maybe now's the right time."

"Maybe it is." Bill kissed her cheek, gathered her in his arms, and pulled her snugly to him.

Chapter 33

Anoka, Minnesota

The auditorium was packed again. Suzanne felt sad. Some of the people she had gotten close to were leaving the program to go to halfway houses or continued hospitalization.

"Hi, I'm Annette, and I'm an alcoholic." Suzanne's roommate smiled down at the audience. "I look like everybody's grandmother, don't I?" She grinned. "Well, I hope you don't have a grandmother like me." The audience responded with laughter.

Annette told her story, but Suzanne was dealing with a mixture of sadness, joy, and anxiety. So much had happened to her in the last weeks. She had been here almost three weeks and couldn't imagine leaving. She had finally found security and friendship. Since that day in group when they'd pounded through her shell, Suzanne had opened up and talked about her drinking, her past, her childhood, and her father. And the more she talked, the more acceptance she found; she was realizing she was not alone in her pain. She was not the only woman who drank and slept around, she was not the only woman who was scared of men, and she was not the only woman who was raped by her father.

Suzanne had heard the saying that there was safety in numbers, but the number of women she had met here who were molested as children scared her. *It's a frightening world if that's what's happening to our children,* she internally shuddered.

Annette slipped back into the seat as Suzanne smiled at her and reached out to touch her hand. "I'm going to miss you," Annette said.

"I'm going to miss you too, Granny," Suzanne affectionately answered. "I'm going to miss lying in bed talking to you through the darkness of night. The nights have been bearable because your voice would float over to me from the other bed. And even if we weren't talking, I could listen to you snore."

"I don't snore." Annette laughed.

"Do too." Suzanne smiled as they turned their attention to the next speaker.

Later that afternoon, Suzanne sat in Liz's office for her regular session.

"Well, Suzanne, we've been successful. One of the halfway houses in the Minneapolis-St. Paul area will have an opening at the end of next week, and that's when you're scheduled to leave here. I'd recommend that you continue your individual counseling with me for a couple more weeks as you slowly get integrated into the groups and counseling at the house." She paused and smiled. "You've come a long way, Suzanne, but you've only won some battles, not the war."

I don't want to leave. I've found security and friendship for the first time in my life. I have things in common with these people. It's not that way in the real world. I don't want to leave.

Liz was still talking. "Have you decided what type of employment you'd like to find while you're at the halfway house? Would you like to stay in sales?"

"No!" Suzanne slapped her hands against her knees for emphasis.

"Why not?" Liz asked, surprised. She placed her pen on the paper in her lap and leaned back in the upholstered chair.

"Because I don't." Suzanne glanced around the room, avoiding Liz's eyes.

"Suzanne, you're going to have to eventually deal with Jeff. He's not going to just go away. Don't run from something you really like to do just because of him."

"It's not just him." Suzanne quickly stood and began pacing in the small space between the chairs. "It's the whole world I had. I don't want it again." She stopped and stared out of the window. "Maybe I'll go back to school and go into psychology."

Liz's eyes twinkled as she responded, "I wouldn't rush into anything. That's a frequent response. The field already has too many people who are in it to try to straighten themselves out. Give yourself time and figure out what you'd really like to do. During the stay at the halfway house, I usually recommend that people work at a job, not a career. The purpose of the next few months is to learn how to stay sober in the everyday world. It's easier in here because it's such a structured, controlled environment. The real world isn't like that."

Sadness washed over Suzanne. "I wish it could be."

"You feel that now because your life has been so chaotic," Liz continued. "You can change that, Suzanne. Remember, your life has to do with your choices and how you respond to the world around you."

"That's what's so tough. The world scares the hell out of me, and I just want to run and hide. And I've done my hiding in a bottle up to now."

"But no more, right?" Liz gently tapped Suzanne's knee.

"No more," Suzanne agreed, but she didn't feel completely convinced.

The auditorium was crowded. A sea of faces stared up at her. The last five weeks had turned her world upside down and inside out. She felt like a different person, except she wasn't sure how she was different. Stepping up to the microphone, Suzanne placed her hand around it to steady herself.

"Hello. My name is Suzanne, and I'm an alcoholic."

"Hi, Suzanne," the voices chorused back.

Chapter 34

Minneapolis, Minnesota

"Geez, Helene. I just can't deal with all this stuff," Alice complained as she stood in the kitchen talking to her sister on the phone. "I mean, most days I don't know why the hell I'm trying to go to college. I mean, I barely made it through high school." She ran her fingers through her hair and blankly stared out of the kitchen window toward a row of nicely kept apartments. "And I'm scared to death for my kids because of what they've gone through. I feel guilty about marrying Jake in the first place. Now I just want to forget I did and get on with life. I don't want to have to deal with this."

"You have to deal with it, Alice," Helene said. "Nobody else can do it for you." She sighed. "I think you should press charges. As far as I'm concerned, he belongs behind bars."

"Yeah, okay, so he does." Alice turned from the window and started to pace. "But what about Sarah? Kids have this bonding kind of love for parents. It's like no matter what they do, their kids can't totally hate them. What if Jake went to prison? What would that do to Sarah?" She plopped down on a kitchen chair and stared absently at a small picture on the wall.

"But what if you don't press charges? What if he hurts another young girl? What if he marries again? What about some young stepdaughter?" Anger was seeping into Helene's voice. "When are we going to stop this sickness, Alice?

When?" Her voice was climbing. "We've got to stop it. Do you hear me? If we don't stop it, the cycle will continue for our kids, our grandkids, and on and on." Helene paused, her breathing fast and shallow. "Sorry, I guess we hit a hot button. I can't tell you what to do. I don't have to live with it either way. I just hope you don't take the easy way out just because it is the easy way."

Alice sat silently at her kitchen table, not knowing what to say. She just wanted to hide in the closet and eat a dozen chocolate candy bars. She wanted the crazy, fast world to stop so she could sit out a turn or two. She didn't want to make a decision that would affect Sarah forever. Too many of her decisions had already done that. She just couldn't handle her kids being hurt anymore.

She sighed deeply and made circles on the table with her fingers. "Helene, I just want somebody to tell me what to do. That's all. Just tell me what to do. You're the oldest; you know what's best. I guess I should press charges if you think I should."

"Oh, no, you don't," Helene said. "No way are you going to place the burden of that decision on me. I can barely make my own choices. I'm not doing yours."

Confusion, vulnerability, and despair were whirling through Alice. "I gotta go now, Helene. I can't talk about this no more."

"So what are you going to do?" Helene pressed.

"I said I can't talk about it no more. I'm gonna hang up now, okay?" She pushed the chair away from the table and once more began to pace.

"Okay, but . . ."

"I'll call you another time, and we'll talk more. Bye." Alice hung up the phone. Her nerves were on edge. She felt as if everything was pressing in on her, that her world was choking her to death. Thoughts of her mom haunted her. The vision of her lying there in a coma was more than Alice could bear. Angry thoughts raged through her mind. *Why can't Mom just die? Why can't Jake just die? Why won't everybody just go away and leave me alone?*

When Alice and the kids had gone to see her mom the previous weekend, Alice hadn't wanted to go but felt she had to. She tried to go once a week, but with school, work, and the kids, there wasn't much time left. She couldn't just ignore her mother, lying in limbo as she was. Maybe she didn't love her mom the way she wanted Sarah and Sam to feel about her, but there were some deep feelings that Alice couldn't explain. And that was what scared her about Sarah and Jake.

Alice was scared to death of Jake. Even though she had filed a restraining order, she was still scared that he would find them and kill her like he said he would. And if she pressed charges, what was it going to be like for Sarah? What would they put her through in court? What would it feel like for Sarah to have to tell strangers about what her father did to her? Alice didn't know anything about how incest cases were handled—she just knew what she had seen on television regarding rape cases—and she didn't want Sarah to go through anything like that. Instead of finding out about how incest cases are handled, Alice retreated into her childhood-taught tendency of not asking questions.

And she was trying to fight the urge to stuff herself with food. The counselor had told her about an Overeater's Anonymous group, and Alice was thinking about going, but she was too embarrassed. She could do this by herself. She knew she could. She just needed willpower. Two voices in her mind kept arguing.

"You don't need to eat," the good voice encouraged.

"But I want to," the rebellious voice countered.

"You don't need to," the gentle voice tried again.

"But I'm going to," the defiant part of her responded.

The voices argued back and forth as Alice paced the full length of the apartment, wanting to scream in frustration. Finally, she couldn't take it anymore and headed back to the kitchen. She no longer kept chocolate candy bars in the house, but she needed chocolate—now! She frantically searched the pantry for something chocolate. She pulled out some chocolate chips, marshmallows, and nuts. Shoving a handful of the chocolate chips into her mouth, she carried her find to the stove and pulled out a pan. She melted the chips and added the nuts and marshmallows. Then she spread it into a pan to make one large candy bar.

She was carrying the pan to the refrigerator to let the chocolate concoction set when she changed her mind. Sitting down at the table, Alice grabbed a handful of the gooey mess and shoved it into her mouth. Handful after handful followed until the pan was empty. Her actions were robotic as she compulsively consumed the sweet, gooey mess.

Her hands and mouth were smeared with melted chocolate, and a headache began at the back of her neck. Her mind was dazed, but calm slowly returned. Chocolate did that for her. She hated herself for needing the chocolate, and she hated herself even more for giving in to that need.

As she sat at the table, Alice became conscious of her chocolate-covered hands and how she must look. Picking up the pan, she hurried to the sink to clean up her mess before the kids came home.

Alice felt sick to her stomach. *It's all that sugar, stupid. Your body needs decent food.* Going to the refrigerator, she searched for healthy food and hurriedly ate quantities of baked chicken and steamed broccoli, left over from last night's dinner, that would take away the effects of the chocolate concoction.

Sarah's face was white as she and Sam came in the door. It was a Friday in late October, and the last few weeks had been good for Alice. She had talked with Sarah, and they had decided to press charges against Jake.

"He's sick, Mom," Sarah had said. So their social worker had set up an appointment with an attorney and they had started the ball rolling. And everything had been okay. Until today.

"Mom, we saw Dad." Sam smiled, but then he looked at Sarah and his smile disappeared. "He scared Sarah and made her cry."

"You saw your dad?" Panic gripped Alice's throat. "Where? How did he know where you were?"

"He was on the corner by Sam's school when I walked to pick him up."

"But how did he know?" Alice's panic was growing into fear. Jake hadn't contacted them or bothered them since they had been in Minneapolis. They were safe. He couldn't find them. That was why she had felt safe enough to press charges. It had never occurred to her that he hadn't tried to find them before now.

"What did he do?" Alice was trying to keep the fear and panic out of her voice. "Did he try to hurt you?"

Sarah's eyes were huge moons in her pale face. Sam was oblivious to the trauma encircling him. "He didn't do nothing, Mom. He gave me some money—five dollars!" Sam's freckled face beamed with amazement.

Alice drew him to her and stroked his cheek. "That's a lot of money, Sam." *How do I explain to you that your father didn't give you that money to be good to you or to make you happy? How do I tell you that your father is a bastard?*

As these thoughts ran through Alice's mind, she kept her eyes on Sarah, who was standing very still. The color had still not returned to her face.

"Sam, have you got homework?" Alice's attention turned to her young son and how to get him out of the room so she could talk with Sarah.

"Yeah." Disappointment filled his face. "Do I have to do it now? I wanna call Jimmy and tell him about my five dollars."

Alice didn't have the strength to enforce the homework rule right now. "Okay, Sam, call Jimmy, but don't talk too long. Then get right to your homework, okay?"

"Sure, Mom." He grinned as he walked away.

Alice gently placed her hands on Sarah's shoulders. "What did he say, Sarah? What did your dad say that's got you so scared?"

"He's gonna hurt us, Mom," Sarah whispered.

"I won't let him do that." Alice stepped close to her daughter, determination flaring in her eyes. "I won't."

Sarah shook her head and her shoulders fell as though the burden of the world rested on them. Her lips trembled and chills shook her body. "He grabbed my breast, Mom, and said I wasn't going to get rid of him. He said we'd better drop those charges and that he could do whatever he wanted with us whenever he wanted."

Fury mounted in Alice. "The courts will protect us, Sarah. The courts and the law."

Sarah shook her head. "That isn't true, Mom; they can't. Remember what that policeman said when he took us to the house?" Sobs of fear escaped her. "We'll never get away from him. Never."

Alice put her arms around Sarah as she tried to bring her voice down to a soothing tone. "I won't let him hurt you ever again. I promise."

Sarah quickly pulled away. "He said he'd kill you. Do you hear me? He said he'd kill you if we didn't drop the charges. And he will too. We know him. We can't win, Mom. He's got us; we can't win!" Sarah turned and ran to her room.

Alice stood helplessly in the middle of her kitchen. She reached into a drawer and pulled out a huge knife, holding it in her hand as if she was going to plunge it into someone or something. "I'll kill him before he can hurt us again. I swear I will."

"Sarah?" Alice tapped gently on her daughter's bedroom door. Sarah had been in her room all night. Alice had often listened at the door to make sure she was okay. For several hours, all Alice had heard was sobbing. She wanted to go to her, but Alice couldn't—not until she didn't feel so scared. She couldn't let her kids see her fear. For too long she hadn't taken care of them. She would now take care of them, somehow. Over the last months, Alice and her sisters had learned they could do something about their problems. They didn't have to be victims. They didn't have to stay helpless.

Alice's first instinct was to call Helene. She always seemed to have ideas or answers. But Alice wasn't going to do that this time. And she wasn't going to call the social worker either. She was going to fix this one herself—somehow.

"Sarah?" she called again.

"What?" a weak, small voice answered.

"I want to come in, okay?" Sarah didn't answer, but she didn't protest as Alice opened the door and walked toward the bed. The room was lit only from the streetlight shining in through the window.

The bedspring groaned as Alice sat down beside Sarah. Disgust at her weight and herself folded over Alice. *I'm fat, but I'm okay.* She grabbed at an affirmation the counselor had given her to say. *I'm okay, I'm okay, I'm okay. I can take care of us. I can, I can, I can.*

Alice gently stroked Sarah's face. "I know I haven't done very good in the past at being a mom. I feel so bad about that." Her voice was low and soothing. "But I'm gonna take care of us now, Sarah. I promise."

"But how?" Sarah's voice was filled with despair.

"I don't know yet. I haven't figured it out, but I will." Alice had no idea what she was going to do. Jake had controlled her life for so long. How could she get him to go away and leave them alone?

"Are we gonna press charges?"

Alice took a deep breath. "I don't know. I just don't know."

"I'm just so scared, Mom. I don't want him to hurt me no more. Yet I want him to love me like a daughter. And he doesn't. Today I saw that. He doesn't. It's like he thinks I belong to him, like I owe him instead of him being responsible for taking care of me. I need a father, but mine just wants to hurt me."

Fresh sobs quaked through Sarah as pain swept across Alice's chest. "I know, baby. I know, and I'm so sorry." Alice laid her cheek against Sarah's as their tears pooled together.

When Sarah finally fell asleep, Alice retreated to her own room and crawled into bed, but sleep wouldn't come. Her mind had been circling. The television had been playing in the background without her paying any attention to what was on. But she suddenly tuned in to the movie on TV. A woman with a hat pulled down over her face was having coffee with a rough-looking man. As Alice became absorbed in the scene, she realized that the woman was hiring a hit man to kill her rich, abusive husband. Sirens went off in her head. *That's it!* They could get rid of Jake. She didn't have to kill Jake; somebody else could! Excitement pulsed through her body before common sense and reality took over. *No, that won't work. What if I get caught? What would happen to the kids?* The dumb woman in the movie kept a journal. Dumb! You never put something in writing you didn't want somebody else to see!

She turned away from the television set, disgusted with herself. *Now you sound like Jake . . . mean and stupid, and you're not, but . . .* Suddenly a flash of brilliance flickered through her mind as a smile played on her lips. *He'll never believe it. Yes, he will. He's sick enough to understand being crazy.*

Alice grabbed a sheet of paper from her notebook and started to write out her plan. It was three in the morning by the time her plan was firmly set in her mind.

She planned to call Jake first thing in the morning, and she tried getting some sleep during the few remaining hours of the night, but sleep wouldn't come.

Finally, daylight arrived. Taking a deep breath, Alice reached for the phone and dialed Jake's number.

Alice expected to be scared when she heard his voice, but she wasn't. He had pushed her too far. *He's not going to hurt my kids. Not ever again.*

"Jake, it's Alice."

Silence, and then, "What do you want, bitch? Did you get my message?"

"I did, Jake." Alice's voice was calm and firm. "I'm dropping the charges."

"Now you've come to your senses."

"I'm also hiring someone to kill you." *There, I said it. I can do this.* She had never taken an acting lesson in her life, but at that moment Alice felt like she deserved the Academy Award for her performance.

"You what?" Silence. "You crazy bitch. Do you know who you're dealing with? If anybody's going to kill anyone, it will be me killing your fat ass."

Alice took a deep breath to keep herself from shaking and keep her voice calm. *Breathe. Just breathe. You can do this. Don't be his victim any longer.* A wicked grin flashed over her face as she remembered the scenario she had written out last night. "Oh, he's not going to kill you right away, Jake." Alice paused to let the silence work for her. "But if you ever come near the kids or me again, he'll kill you right away. He'll be watching you and protecting us. He's a mean man, Jake. You understand mean, don't you?" *Bravo, Alice! That was really good.*

She held her breath for a moment and then her voice sped up. "He's been in prison, and he told me about things they do in prison to men who rape their daughters. That's what he said he'd do to you, Jake. He said he'd cut off a certain part of your body and shove it in your mouth, then he'll slice your body with long deep slits and watch you bleed to death."

Jake was breathing very hard and Alice could hear him gulp. "You're crazy. You can't get away with that. You don't know anybody like that."

She couldn't press charges and fight Jake through the system. She couldn't protect any other woman or girls he might hurt, but she could protect her kids. And she was going to do it her way.

Alice's voice was still calm. "If you don't think I know anyone like that, just come near the kids or me again."

Jake was quiet.

Alice was beginning to enjoy having power over Jake. "And, oh, Jake, if anything happens to me, and I mean anything, you're dead." Her voice dropped to a low, strong tone. "So, you'd better hope I live a long, healthy life."

Alarm was edging into Jake's voice. "You can't do that. I'll kill you. I'll kill the kids. I'll hurt them, Alice, I will."

Fear for her children pushed Alice back against the wall, but the fierce need to protect them was raging within her and shoved her back into the path of her enemy. "Do that, Jake, and you'll die too. I don't think you're hearing me, Jake." She slowly enunciated every word. "You've messed with me and my kids long enough. I'm protecting us the only way I can—I've hired a killer. You're gonna die, Jake. How soon depends on how close you come to me or either of my kids."

"Alice, you're bluffing."

Alice was silent.

"Alice?"

"If you think I'm bluffing, Jake, then test me." Slowly Alice placed the phone back in its cradle. After slipping on her robe, Alice padded down the hall to fix breakfast for her kids.

Chapter 35

Atlanta, Georgia

Helene was sitting in the breakfast nook planning their Thanksgiving menu when Thomas came home from school. He had been coming right home after classes and spending more time with her, the way he used to. The counseling sessions were definitely helping all of them and life was pleasant.

"What are you doing?" Thomas asked as he grabbed a glass of milk and a cookie, then pulled out a chair near her.

"Putting together our Thanksgiving menu. Is there anything particular you want besides turkey, and a lot of it?" Helene always enjoyed putting together the menu for their Thanksgiving dinner. She and Lily always made the meal together and Bill's parents joined them each year. His parents now lived in Arizona and didn't travel back to Georgia much, but Thanksgiving was always an exception.

"Make sure we have lots of pumpkin pie as well, and that pretty much takes care of it for me."

Thomas had always loved pumpkin pie. Even as a small child. "Remember when you were about six and you took one of the pies from the kitchen when Lily and I weren't looking, and you ate the whole thing in your room? I found you sitting on your bed, pumpkin pie all over your face, and the empty pie tin in front of you." They both chuckled at the memory. "I thought you would be sick, but when Thanksgiving dinner was ready, you ate your fill of turkey and all the trimmings, plus another piece of pumpkin pie."

"Guess I've always had a good appetite."

"That you have."

"Mom?" Thomas said in a serious tone. "Would you tell me about my grandmother? We've talked a little bit about her in counseling, but I'd like to know more."

Helene put her pen down. "Sure. What would you like to know?" She wasn't sure what she could tell him. It had been so many years since she had interacted with her mother that she really didn't know much about her. Except that she was lying in a coma until her body finally shut down and she died.

"Where is she now, and how is she doing?"

These questions she could answer. "She's in a full-care nursing home in Minneapolis, not too far from where Alice and the kids now live." Sorrow tugged at her heart. "At this stage, she won't recover from the coma. The doctor says her heart will one day just stop beating. Until then, we'll keep her as comfortable as we can."

"Was she a good mother?"

Helene scanned the memories of her childhood. True, when she was at her childhood home, she had remembered the cookies and fry bread, and those were good memories. But her son was asking if Anna had been a good mother. Helene sadly shook her head. "She wasn't the type of mother that I wanted or needed, but now I understand that she did the best she could. Her life was very different than mine, and it was very hard. She was just a girl when she was forced to marry my father, and he wasn't a kind man."

"Did he yell a lot?"

She didn't have to think much to reply to that question. Her recollections of her dad were filled with visions of him yelling, screaming, or ranting. "Yes, he did. And he was often physically mean to all of us."

"You mean he hit you?"

"He did." Helene's mind flashed back to the many times she, Alice, and Suzanne had suffered the lash of his belt or a brutal slap from his large hand, but she wasn't about to share those specific memories with Thomas.

Thomas munched on his second cookie. "Did you love him?"

Helene paused for several minutes as her mind formulated her answer. "It's hard to love someone like that. We feared him, but I don't remember having any other feelings associated with my father, especially not love or affection.

"I'm really lucky," Thomas said. "I get mad at you and Dad, especially Dad, but I certainly know I love both of you very much."

"That's good to hear." Helene reached over and took a piece of his cookie, and he offered her a sip of his milk.

"Why do you think Grandpa was so mean?"

"I really don't know." Helene walked over to the counter and grabbed each of them another cookie. "He was an alcoholic, and that probably exacerbated the issue, but I don't know where all the anger came from. I don't know a lot about his life or his childhood. His parents died when I was very young and Mom wouldn't talk about them."

"What about Grandma's parents?"

"I don't know much about them either. My Mom was pretty closed-mouthed about anything that had to do with my grandparents. Her dad died when I was about four, and her mom died when I was six. One day I'll show you pictures of my family."

"You have pictures?"

"A box of them."

"Why haven't I ever seen them?"

"I've kept them hidden," she said as she tousled his hair.

"Don't mess with my hair," he teased. Becoming serious again, he asked, "Why would you hide pictures?"

"Why do we do any of the things we do? I surely don't know." And she didn't know. Why had she hidden the photos away in the attic for over twenty years? Whatever negative power they once had no longer existed.

"Then, it all makes sense," Thomas said.

"What makes sense?"

"Why you didn't stay in touch with your family."

"How does that make sense?"

"Well, from what I've learned in school, kids pretty much learn what they've lived and you learned that family wasn't special, and for that matter, wasn't even supposed to be talked about."

Helene leaned back against her chair and gazed at her son. "When did you get to be so smart?" Sometimes her son had a homegrown logic that was beyond his years of earthly experience.

"It's in my DNA," he grinned.

Helene got up, stood behind him, and wrapped her arms around her son. "You, my precious son, teach me so much."

"Thanks, Mom," he hugged her back, untangled himself from the embrace, and took his glass to the sink.

Helene walked to the window, gazed out at the blue sky, and said a prayer of gratitude.

Chapter 36

Anoka, Minnesota

It was the first week of December of 1990, and the Christmas tree stood in the corner of the main room of the halfway house. Its branches were bare and ready to hold the decorations. Six adults sat on the floor in a semicircle in front of the tree, quietly talking.

"Christmas has never been a good time for me." Frank frowned as memories seemed to surround him. "If there wasn't some kind of crises going on around me, I made one. I feel really bad about the awful memories I gave my kids."

Frank was almost thirty-five and had two children, but Suzanne knew he hadn't seen them for a while. She had gotten to know the stories of all the people in the halfway house. In fact, several others had already left. Six months was the maximum time that anyone could stay here. Most people stayed two to four months, but Suzanne had been here seven weeks and planned to stay as long as she could. She didn't want to think of leaving. She didn't want to go back and face her old life, but she knew she had to. But not until her maximum time here had been used up. In the meantime, she would take it one day at a time and continue to find her balance and try to figure out her life. First, she would enjoy a special Christmas surrounded by the people here in the house. Her first Christmas of sobriety. She was excited and scared.

"It's the Christmas season," Rosanne, a forty-five-year-old lawyer, added. "Let's talk of hope and what we want from the future. I'm so tired of the past.

I've been dealing with my past for months now." A childish gleam appeared in her eyes. "Let's make Christmas wishes. I used to make birthday wishes, so let's start a new tradition—Christmas wishes."

"Okay," Eric, an ex-professional football star whose addiction ruined his career, joined in. "We'll take turns putting ornaments on the tree, and for every ornament, we'll make a Christmas wish."

"Aloud or in private?" Frank asked.

"Aloud," Rosanne insisted. "Who wants to go first?"

They all hung back. No one wanted to go first. She knew she didn't. She wasn't about to take a chance of feeling stupid.

"I will." Sherice stepped forward. She was twenty-five years old and had been on drugs since she was fifteen. From the talks they'd had, Suzanne knew that Sherice had done everything imaginable to support her drug use. She had been trying to kick the habit for close to five years. She had never made it very far. This time she'd been drug-free for four months. Suzanne admired the girl. She had no college education, no job skills—she had to start from scratch. Yet her strength and determination seemed to often surpass everyone else in the house.

Sherice stood over the box of decorations and contemplated the collection of handmade ornaments that were created by previous "guests," as they laughingly called themselves. Reaching into the box, she gently pulled out a tissue-paper dove whose wings flapped precariously. "This dove reminds me of me. He has the appearance of a misfit, like he could never fly, but his ability and strength go way beyond the surface of his looks." She placed the bird on the tree. "I wish for love—the unconditional kind."

Eric went next. He selected a star. "I want another chance to play football, and I want to be a star again. But this time, I want to use my fame productively."

"God, this is getting sappy." Stella, the hard-nose of the bunch, stood. She grabbed an ornament. "I just want to get on with life. I've wasted so damn much of mine that I just want to get out of this place and start living."

"What do you think living is?" Frank asked. "It's day by day, remember? This, kiddo, is part of living."

"Yes," Suzanne reflected, "enjoy the process. That's what my older sister keeps saying—enjoy the process."

"So what's your wish, Suzanne?" Frank turned toward her.

"I don't know." Suzanne gazed bewilderedly at him. "I don't think I ever learned to wish."

"You must have wished as a kid."

"Sure, I used to wish my father would leave me alone or die. But I don't think I did happy wishing."

"Well, think happy," Rosanne urged. "If you could have anything, what would you want?"

Suzanne thought for several moments. "Another chance at my marriage."

The room became quiet. Suzanne had talked about everything else in their group sessions, but never about her marriage except to say that she had been married.

"Why?" Sherice broke the silence.

"Because I was so happy for a short time."

"Couldn't you be happy again in another situation?" Rosanne inquired.

"I don't know, and I'm not sure I'm willing to try. I think I had a chance at the very best and blew it. How could anyone ever compete with Stephen?"

"Why should they have to?" Frank asked. "You can't go back, Suzanne, but you can go forward. And you're not the same person now. Are you sure you're not living in a fairytale land of memories and have Stephen on a pedestal where he doesn't belong?"

Suzanne turned angry. "I didn't pick your wishes apart, so leave mine alone." An awkward silence settled in the room.

"Okay, my turn," Rosanne chimed in, breaking the tension. "My wish has already come true. I'm going to be able to practice law again. And I can't think of anything I want more." She paused. "Yet, I'm scared. It's a stressful career. Before I handled the stress by drinking. What will I do now? I don't know."

The phone rang in the hall off the kitchen. Frank rose to get it. "Suzanne. For you."

Suzanne was glad for a reason to leave the group. She just wanted to decorate the tree. She couldn't handle making wishes and putting all this heavy feeling into Christmas. She was dealing with too many feelings right now as it was. She'd just blurted out her deepest feelings, and they betrayed her by picking her wish to pieces. She didn't do that to theirs, and she was hurt at their response.

"Hello?" Suzanne said into the phone.

"Hi, boss. A very early Merry Christmas."

"Hi, Melanie!" Suzanne was delighted to hear her secretary's voice. Melanie had called Suzanne every other week since Suzanne had been gone. Their boss–employee relationship had grown into a deep friendship and Melanie was Suzanne's advocate in the world to which she would return, unless she figured out another option.

"How are you?" Melanie asked.

"Oh, Melanie, it's so good to hear your voice." The caring in Melanie's voice cut into the hurt and dejection that Suzanne had carried over from the wishing scene and and she blurted out, "I'm so scared, lonely, and bewildered."

"I thought everything was going okay," Melanie said hesitantly.

"It was, I mean, it is. But this isn't where I need to be, and I realized that when I heard your voice. Yet, I'm too scared to come back to where I was. I'm in limbo. I've outgrown the treatment process here. I need to take what I've learned and go on, but I'm scared to death."

This was a new realization for Suzanne. Just hours ago, she was content to be right where she was. Now it was not okay. Over the weeks of working her twelve-step program, Suzanne had learned to trust her higher power. She still couldn't think of her higher power as the God she felt deserted her in her childhood, but she had learned to trust in a power greater than herself. Over the months, her higher power had gently led her through steps of growth, and tonight she had gone through another one.

"It will be okay, Suzanne," Melanie soothed. "I'll help you. Everybody here is supportive. Believe it or not, the rumors have been kept to a minimum." She tried to insert some humor into a heavy moment.

"Do they all still think I'm handling family matters?"

"That excuse is wearing thin." Melanie paused. "But since Mr. Warren and I know the truth, and we're both supportive, what does it matter? He's your boss. I'm your secretary and friend. What else do you need?"

Suzanne smiled. "You are my friend, Melanie. And I'm glad, but I'm worried about that too."

"Why?"

"Will we still be able to work together so well now that you know I'm an alcoholic? Will you still respect me? I mean, it's been great to share with you about treatment and all I've been going through, but now that I'm going to be coming back, I don't know if it's such a good idea."

Melanie's voice was soft and caring. "I respect you even more now that you've gone through treatment, and I understand you better. Besides, I've been reading about recovering alcoholics."

"You have? Why?"

"Because I care about you, and I want to help."

"I've never had anybody care enough about me that they'd actually do research." Suzanne grinned. "So, what do you know about me?"

"I know you need support people in every phase of your life. We nonalcoholics call those people friends. I was one before, I'm still one, and I'll continue to be one. Maybe it takes special people to work together and be friends, but we're special—so it's a cinch."

"I'm so glad you're part of my life."

"Me too, boss," Melanie said. "What are you doing for Christmas?"

"I'm not sure. In fact, my plans of ten minutes ago have changed. It's time to get out of treatment. My counselor told me I was ready three weeks ago. I just couldn't face it at the time. I need to think about it, but right now I'll finish up the things I need to do here and leave the week before Christmas. Then I'll spend Christmas with Alice and her kids, if they'll have me. And then I think I need to come back to Dallas. It's time to face my problems and put my life in order."

"Richard's been asking about you." Melanie's voice was tentative as she brought up the subject.

Suzanne took a deep breath as she placed her hand on her chest. "What did you tell him?"

"Only that your mother is very sick and you've taken a leave of absence," Melanie responded.

"What did he say?" Suzanne began to pace as much as the phone cord would allow.

"The same thing he keeps saying—to tell you he hopes everything is okay and that he misses your company."

Suzanne stopped pacing for a moment as she clutched the phone close to her ear. Her voice rose a bit. "Why didn't you ever mention him before?"

"I didn't think you were ready," Melanie softly replied.

"And I am now?"

"I think so."

Moments of silence passed.

"Melanie?" Suzanne peered out at the snow-covered landscape. "Why don't you ever mention Jeff?"

"Why should I?" An edge crept into Melanie's words.

"I think you're smarter than that." The barren trees were covered with snow, and snowflakes were lightly falling from the sky. "I think you know he's tied into why I ran back home."

"I'm not going to ask. If you want me to know, you'll tell me."

"What have you told him?" Suzanne touched the windowpane as shivers ran through her. Bile formed in her throat at the mere mention of Jeff's name.

"That what you do is none of his business," Melanie firmly stated.

Turmoil circled through Suzanne as she stared straight ahead, no longer seeing the scene in front of her. It was time to take a step, a risk, and she believed Melanie was a safe person to do it with. "Has he tried to find out where I am?"

"He has," Melanie confirmed. "Can you believe he even tried to use his good looks and lady-killer ploys on me to find out?"

A smile passed over Suzanne's face at the inflection in Melanie's voice. "What did you do?"

"I told him if he didn't back off, my husband would pound his pretty-boy face into an ugly, unrecognizable lump."

Suzanne gleefully laughed. "Such harshness from such a normally gentle woman." At last Suzanne had a protector, someone who cared enough about her to fight the dragons that lurked in the darkness of her life.

"*Steel Magnolias* is not just the title of a movie. Believe me, Jeff doesn't want to push me too far."

Suzanne made a decision, took a deep breath, and decided to take the risk. "He was blackmailing me, Melanie."

Melanie's voice was sharp. "Who? Jeff? Why?"

She took another deep breath as her fingers pressed harder against the window. "He has pictures." Two more breaths. "I got drunk and slept with him. He took ugly pictures." Bile surged into her throat at the memory. Now she held her breath waiting to hear Melanie's reaction. As she waited, a headache pulsed at her temples.

"God, another good reason to give up drinking. It gives you crummy judgment in men! But what's the big deal? How could he use that against you?"

Suzanne sat down in a nearby chair and tenderly placed her hand on her chest. "He was going to show them to Mr. Warren and pass them around to my other sales reps."

"Suzanne!" Melanie sounded angry. "You let him blackmail you with that? It might have been embarrassing to have it come out, and the rumors would have flown for a while, but that wouldn't have been the first sexual indiscretion this company has seen!"

"They would have fired me, Melanie." *And what would I have done without my career? It was all I had.*

"You're crazy to think that. Don't you know the kind of reputation Jeff has? Haven't you heard him bragging about getting women drunk because it makes them easy? Don't you know this company has been waiting for a good excuse to get rid of him? Attempted blackmail can land his butt in jail. And don't you know the credibility you've built? Sure, you don't have a reputation for being a very warm person, but people know you're fair and you'll get the job done right. I can't believe this! I'm so angry I'd like to punch the crap out of Jeff Davidson, and then lovingly box your ears."

Suzanne wasn't sure she had heard correctly. "You don't think I'm garbage?"

"No, but I think you're very smart to stop drinking if that's the kind of situation it gets you into. In fact, I don't get it." Suzanne could hear Melanie's frustration clearly coming through the phone. "You're afraid to have coffee with Richard when you're sober, but you get drunk and end up sleeping with Jeff?"

"It's called being an alcoholic," Suzanne replied as she once again paced within the distance the phone cord would allow. "The drinks change my personality and I'm able to try to get my needs met when I'm drunk." Her voice softened. "I'm beginning to learn how to care for myself, but I'm just beginning. The tough thing about treatment is that we dig through garbage and unearth a lot of memories and feelings that we're not fully prepared to deal with. It's a catch-22. I feel like I've stepped from one merry-go-round to another. This one might be healthier than the last one, but it's still confusing and it still moves too fast."

"I wish I understood it better," Melanie softly stated. "I'd like to be able to help you, but I really don't totally understand what you're going through. I know about the theories of alcoholism and what the twelve-step program is, but I don't understand the pain, the confusion, or the thinking that seems to be so impossible to comprehend."

"Do you think I'm crazy?"

"Heavens no. I think you're one strong woman. Alcoholism seems to be a tough battle to fight. I can't believe you kept as much order in your life as you did."

A comfortable silence permeated the air as the women relaxed in the atmosphere of friendship.

"Suzanne, would you like to spend New Year's Eve with us?"

While Suzanne was touched by Melanie's offer, her heart sped up at the thought. "I don't know," she said, "I haven't thought that far ahead."

"We're having a small party."

"I don't think I need to be around alcohol or parties right now."

"Oh, stupid me. I just won't serve liquor. It's a good idea not to serve it anyway. The more I read about alcoholism, the more it makes me want to never touch a drink."

Suzanne teased, "Are you compulsive and over-reactive?"

"Well," Melanie laughed, "we all have something to deal with, don't we, boss?"

"Yes, I guess so." Suzanne smiled as she moved back toward the phone base on the wall.

"Will you call me when you're coming back to Dallas? I'll pick you up at the airport."

"Would you? I'd like that. We'll talk again before Christmas. And thanks for calling. Your timing was a huge, great blessing."

"My higher power directs me too." Melanie's smile came through the phone. "Remember, I'm your friend."

"I know."

After she finished talking with Melanie, Suzanne had dialed the number of her counselor and made an appointment for later that day. Now she sat in his office. She had just told him that she was ready to go home.

"Have you thought about this a lot?" Pete asked.

"I have, and I know it's time to leave as soon as I tie up loose ends."

"How do you plan to do that?"

"I'll give my notice at the department store where I've been working and I'll work there through Christmas Eve. Then I'm going to spend a couple of days with Alice and the kids. I'll check on Mom, then I'll fly back to Dallas. But before I do that, I've got an appointment with the minister of the church I've been attending. I need to do my fifth step."

"What about your sponsor?" Pete was making notes. "Will you keep this one?"

"Until I get established in an AA group in Dallas." Suzanne squirmed in the hard chair.

"And what about Jeff?"

"I finally told my secretary about him, and she was extremely understanding and supportive. So, that gives me strength to meet with my boss and hopefully with his support I can face Jeff. You know our motto . . . one day at a time."

"Well, Suzanne," Pete put down his pen and sat back in his chair, "I'll get your release papers ready. You've come a long way."

She smiled. "But my journey's just beginning, and that's the scary part."

Chapter 37

Atlanta, Georgia

Helene and Bill were curled up on the sofa, chatting, and enjoying the quiet evening, the twinkling lights on the beautifully decorated Christmas tree, and a mug of hot cocoa when Thomas came downstairs.

"Hi," Bill called out. "Want to join us?"

"Sure. What are you doing?"

"Enjoying the lights and talking about things you'd probably call 'corny.'"

"Try me," Thomas replied. "Sometimes I can be sentimental."

Bill chuckled. "At eighteen, what can you get sentimental about?"

Helene saw the expression on Thomas's face turn to one of irritation. "Why do you do that?"

"Do what?"

"Always put me down?" Thomas crossed his arms over his chest.

Helene was mentally preparing herself for another battle between the two of them. Lately, the confrontations didn't happen often, but they still happened, and she had learned to stay out of them.

"I don't always put you down." Agitation crept into Bill's voice and he sat up straighter. "Your mom and I were sitting here having some quiet moments and sharing fun memories when you came in. Apparently I didn't answer the way you wanted me to."

Bill leaned forward, grasping his cup in his hands. "Why are you always so angry at me? I thought you had forgiven me. I thought some of our past was out of the way, but I can't seem to get through to you. I feel nervous around my own son. Like I'm always being judged, and I never come out on the winning end."

Helene didn't move a muscle as she watched the scene playing out before her.

"And I always feel like I'm not good enough," Thomas moved his weight from his left foot to his right foot, "that anything I do is not good enough, that I can never live up to your expectations, no matter what I do."

"That's not true. Why don't you know how much I care about you?" Bill pleaded.

"Because you don't tell me." Thomas's shoulders sagged with the weight of his words.

"But I show you," Bill gently protested.

"I don't see it." Thomas shrugged.

"I earn a good living for you. I give you opportunities a lot of young people don't have." Bill set his cocoa cup on the coffee table and was listing off things on his fingers.

Thomas shrugged again. "I've always had them." His arms spread out in front of him in a questioning gesture. "How would I know what it's like not to? And that's material stuff." He wrapped his arms around himself. "What about how you feel?"

Bill leaned back into the sofa, smiling softly. "What happened to the days when men didn't get caught up in feelings?"

"Remember that time in therapy when you said you had used affairs to run away from your feelings about us and your fears of losing us?" Thomas stared at Bill, and Helene was amused at how alike they were. That was probably one of the reasons they butted heads. "It doesn't sound to me as though you didn't get caught up in feelings," Thomas retorted.

Bill's tone was soft. "We were talking about when you were small. I was remembering those Christmas mornings when you would burst into our room and pull us downstairs to the Christmas tree. Remember the red tricycle Santa Claus brought you? The roller skates? The train set?"

Thomas nodded and sat on the floor in front of them.

"Where did all those good times go?" Bill gently touched his son's knee. "We had them. I helped you ride the tricycle, stand on the wobbly skates, and set up the train set."

Helene smiled at the memories, then pain filled her heart when she heard Thomas's reply. "Yes, you did. Even then, I remember feeling that I didn't do it right, especially with the roller skates. I fell and skinned my knee. I started to cry, and you called me a sissy. And you got mad when I broke one of the train tracks when I was putting it together."

Her hand was on Bill's back and Helene felt the breath go out of him like he had been kicked in the stomach. His words came slow. "Do you only remember the bad things? Don't you remember anything good?"

Helene was ready to jump in to the conversation to try to make it right. *Stay out of it. They have to create their own relationship with each other. It's not up to you to make it right.*

Thomas stared at the floor. "I'm working on it, Dad, but I need to get the bad memories out of the way. And you won't ever talk to me about them. Sure, I work with Mr. Welsh," he glanced up at Bill, "but I want to talk with you. I need to know why I don't measure up. I need to know what I can do so you'll love me."

Helene gently rubbed Bill's back to let him know she was there.

"I've thought about it a lot," Thomas said, "but I don't know why you don't love me. I have a lot of friends, the teachers at school like me. Mom loves me, but I can never get through to you. I don't know what I'm doing wrong."

Helene was about to say something when Thomas said, "Aren't you going to answer me? Even now when I'm making a fool of myself, you just sit there staring, and I feel dumb for even opening my mouth." He turned toward Helene. "Mom, won't you say something?"

Before Helene could utter a word, Bill said, "You've grown into a man."

"Dad," Thomas replied, "have you heard anything I just said?"

Bill sighed. "I've been dealing with you like you're still a child. It's always been my responsibility to make the decisions for your future. My choices always affected you, and that was frightening. I was responsible for this tiny human being who couldn't take care of himself or make his own choices. Somehow my mind was still caught on little Thomas. How could I not see that you have grown into a man?"

"I don't feel like a man."

"Why not?"

Helene relaxed against the sofa, fascinated with the conversation and the way her husband and son were beginning to actually talk and connect with each other. *Now this is some Christmas gift.* She inwardly glowed.

"Because I feel so scared of the choices I have to make." Thomas stood and walked to the window. "Even though I want to make them for myself, I'm scared of going out on my own, yet I need to so I can survive and not be a shadow of you. I'm scared of everything, Dad." He turned to Bill. "You were right. I am a sissy, and I hate it that you were right."

Thomas leaned against the windowpane. "That's one of the reasons I drank, you know. When I drank, I felt strong enough to be whatever I wanted and say whatever I felt. Yet, when I was drunk, I didn't know what I really felt because I was drunk. I feel so screwed up."

"You're not a sissy, Thomas. I feel scared a lot too. I don't show it, and I don't talk about it because I was taught that a real man handles his own problems. Well, some 'real man' I've been." Bill glanced toward Helene. "I've cheated on my wife, and I've let my son down. The two most important people in my life have experienced irreparable damage because of me."

Bill reached for a tissue to wipe his eyes. "I've been really proud of you, but I pushed you so you'd succeed. That's the way my father has always been with me. He never talked soft to me, and I always thought I turned out fine. Except now. Now I'm beginning to know how much I've hurt you and your mother. But I can't go back. I can't take it away." He drew in a deep breath. "What can I do to mend this gap between us?"

"Telling me you're sorry would help."

Bill quickly got up, walked over to Thomas, and wrapped his arms around him. "I'm sorry, Thomas. God knows I'm sorry. Can we start again? Can I have another chance?"

Helene was crying. As if remembering that she was in the room, Bill and Thomas slid down on either side of her and surrounded her with their arms.

As Helene snuggled between the men she loved, she heard her son reply, "We can try, Dad. We can certainly try."

With a newfound hope, Helene went to the kitchen to make more hot cocoa. As she waited for the water to boil, her mind bounced back to the day she had received the phone call about her mother. Helene's life had been a mess. Her marriage had been a sham, and her son had been close to failing school and slipping into an alcohol addiction. That was in the beginning of July. Now it was mid-December, a short five months later, and her life was totally different. She was falling back in love with her husband—more each day—and he was doing the same with her. Their lovemaking was tender and often, and they were discovering a level of intimacy they hadn't previously known. Helene was happier than she ever thought she could be.

The whistle on the tea kettle brought her back to the present. She fixed three fresh mugs of hot cocoa, placed them on the tray, and left the kitchen.

The flames in the fireplace gently danced among the logs, and Christmas music softly floated through the air. Thomas was stretched out on the floor lying on his stomach, his chin resting on his folded arms. Bill was relaxed in his chair. Helene handed them each a mug of cocoa and curled up on the sofa. "We are really lucky," she murmured.

Bill grinned at Thomas. "Is this where she'll tell us about all the little kids who don't get much for Christmas?"

Thomas smiled. "Probably, it's about that time."

Helene tossed a pillow at her son. "You two are spoiled rotten." Then she became serious. "Actually, I was thinking about Christmas when I was a child."

"What was it like, Mom? You've never talked about it."

"It really wasn't very special. Mom tried hard, but she hardly ever had money. And Dad was usually drunk."

Helene sighed as memories continued to flow into her mind. "In spite of it all, though, my sisters and I managed to have some good memories. One year, Alice and I made Suzanne a doll out of Dad's white socks that we stuffed with rags. Then we took yarn and made the hair, and thread to create the eyes, nose, and mouth."

Helene chuckled at the memory. "It was such a gangly doll. One sock was the body, two socks formed the arms, two for the legs, and half a sock for the head. We sewed it together with these long, crude stitches. As I think about it, it was the ugliest doll I've ever seen," she burst out laughing, "but Suzanne loved it. She played with it for a long time. But she always kept it hidden from Dad because if he found out that we had taken his socks, he would have beaten us."

"Did he hit you a lot?" Thomas's face was serious and his eyes were dark with concern.

"When I was young, yes." Helene pulled her knees up close to her chest and wrapped her arms around them. "As I grew older, he seemed to become afraid of me." She remembered that Alice had mentioned that, and as Helene thought about it, she knew it was true. She wasn't sure why, but as she got older, her father stayed away from her.

"Do you hate him?" Thomas asked.

"Hate?" She thought for a moment and gently laid her hand on her son's arm. "No, I don't think so." *Was it hate?* Over the last months, Helene had been trying to figure out exactly what she had felt for her father. She still didn't know. The word that came to her mind when she thought about him was "indifference."

"Did you love him?" Thomas asked.

"No. There's some feeling I don't know how to explain. He's part of me. I'm not sure I like that, but he is."

"Well, one thing I know for sure," Thomas responded, "is that I'm very glad you both are a part of me."

Those words from her son were like a symphony of beautiful music exploding in Helene's world. She turned toward her husband who was grinning from ear to ear.

Chapter 38

Anoka, Minnesota

Suzanne was nervous as she sat down across from Pastor Andrews. They both knew she was there for her fifth step. It sounded so easy on paper to admit her wrongs to God and another human being.

It wasn't easy to talk about all the things she had done, but AA believed it was necessary. *As long as we hold blackness in our hearts, it will keep our lives black. Bringing our secrets to light takes away their power.*

"Suzanne, you know God forgives our sins if we ask Him." Pastor Andrew's eyes were kind as he sat back in his chair with his hands folded on his desk.

Suzanne was quiet.

"Do you believe in God, Suzanne?" he asked.

Suzanne peered into his soft eyes for several seconds as the palms of her hands pressed against her lap. "I believe in a higher power, or God as I understand Him." She paused for a moment. "But that doesn't mean it's going to fit your understanding of Him."

He smiled. "I don't think it's important to fit my understanding. Do you?"

"Well, no." Her hands rubbed the top of her legs as she squirmed in her chair.

"Are you nervous?"

"Of course I am," she answered. "I don't know if this is a good idea. I know

I have to go through this. It's part of my treatment's release requirements, but maybe it's not a good idea to talk to a minister about all my sins."

"Why not?" His hands stayed folded on the desk.

"I can't take your judgment." Suzanne paused. "I've given myself too much already."

"Why would I judge you?" The pastor sat back in his chair in a relaxed manner.

"Because you're a pastor and have never done the things I've done."

He smiled again and replied, "The things that trouble our souls are probably dissimilar, but I am human just like you." Pastor Andrews placed his elbows on the desk. "That humanness keeps me humble, believe me. I can't judge you, Suzanne, because I haven't walked in your shoes. I am simply here to listen. That's it. I am someone with whom you can talk and hopefully unburden some of the shame and guilt you've been carrying around for years."

Suzanne watched the man as he talked. She guessed he was in his late fifties, and from the pictures on his desk, he had a wife, children, and grandchildren.

"My father raped me when I was very young," she blurted out. "Does that shock you?"

"It saddens me, but it doesn't shock me. Unfortunately, many women have experienced such a traumatic thing."

"And God allows it," Suzanne fumed. "Why?"

"Do you think God allows it?"

"If He has power over everything, He had to allow it. In other words, He deserted me. We talk about God the Father; I've had my fill of fathers. They use their power to hurt, harm, and abandon. I don't see God as a father, I can't."

"Okay."

"Okay? You're not going to try to convert me or convince me that I'm wrong?" She was prepared for him to tell her that her thoughts or ideas about God were wrong. And she was ready to stand up for herself and her beliefs. They were hers. She got to choose.

"No."

Quietness settled in the room. *No? You're not going to try to tell me I'm wrong?*

Pastor Andrews interrupted her thoughts with a question. "Who is God as you understand Him?"

Suzanne stared at the pastor for a few moments as if she wasn't seeing him. "A friend. One who helps me take one day at a time. One who gently encourages me. Someone who is always there. Someone I can talk to at any time."

Pastor Andrews sat in silence, listening intently.

Taking a deep breath, she continued, "I've done a lot of things I'm not proud of. Some things I'd rather not talk about, and other things I don't ever want repeated." She feebly smiled. "That's why I chose to talk to a pastor. You're used to keeping confidences."

She inhaled deeply. "Because of what my father did, when I see men, even when I'm sober, I have sexual thoughts. My mind is so dirty, so sexual. I've done things that are so bad I can't bear to think about them. And now I'm told that in order to get healthy, I have to not only think about them, but I have to tell somebody else."

Suzanne's voice became matter-of-fact as she started to recite a checklist of her sins. "I've slept with so many men I can't remember. I've had sex in hotel rooms and cars. I've been drunk out of my mind every time I did it, but that doesn't make it right. I shoplifted when I was young. It makes me sick to my stomach when I reflect on what I've done. I had sex with my father when I was so young I didn't know what it was and that other kids didn't do it. And sometimes it felt good—that's what's so awful about it all. Even when I look back at all the sex I had when I was drunk, it wasn't always bad, and that's what makes me so bad."

Suzanne continued to pull memories from behind the closed door of her past. Then something changed, and a switch was thrown. She was no longer distanced from the words she was speaking. Now she was soiled, seared, and marred by them. Her countenance changed, her shoulders sagged, her head bowed, and great wrenching sobs tumbled out of her. She covered her face, trying to hide her humiliation and shame. She tried to shove her self-disgust back inside of her the way she had done all her life, but this time she couldn't. This time, a large volume of feelings had gathered into a fierce strength that demanded release.

Suzanne's struggle resembled the process of having a baby. The action of getting the child through the birth canal could be long and arduous as the mother strained under immense pains and pressure. But she couldn't quit, because there was no way to go back, no way to ignore the pressure of the child inside of her. Nor could Suzanne ignore the pressure of the pain, torment, fear, and distrust that had built up through the years. They couldn't go back and dissolve into nothingness. They had too much substance to them.

The sobs continued and grew in depth as the sounds reached into her very core and unveiled the tormented heart of a young child. They continued to grow in fierceness as they tapped into the confusion and hatred she'd carried since her teenage years, finally erupting as they reached the source of the contemptuous bitterness she'd become one with as a grown woman.

As her humiliation, torment, and anguish were pushed through the dark perceptions of her innermost shame and guilt, space was opened up inside of her for feelings never before felt. A light giddiness settled over her. It was such a new experience for Suzanne that she pushed it away and fought its existence.

But the good feelings wouldn't go away this time. She couldn't push them back and hide them with her shaming tactics. They seemed to have a mind of their own as they took over. A smile pushed at the corners of her mouth. She felt good! It couldn't be ignored. She wanted to get up and dance around the room. It was silly to even think of it, but her feet jiggled in rebellion of her chosen inaction.

"Are you okay, Suzanne?" the pastor asked.

"Yes, thank you," she replied.

"You seem happy. Your eyes are dancing."

"Mine? They are?" A giggle escaped from her smiling lips. "I do feel good." *In fact, I feel really good. I wonder why?* Suzanne had become used to confusion, anger, fear, and anxiety. Joy, happiness, and hope were new to her. She didn't recognize them when they surfaced.

"That's not unusual," Pastor Andrews said.

"It's not?" *Is it really okay to feel this? Am I really going to be okay?*

"Do you need to talk more, Suzanne?"

"No." She had been required to talk so much lately that she was ready to stop talking for a while.

"Would you like me to say a prayer, Suzanne?"

"Well, yes, I guess so. In fact, the seventh step is asking God to remove all my shortcomings. This might be an appropriate time, don't you think?"

I don't want to mess up in AA. Please don't let me mess up in my recovery. Help me to know what to do and when to do it. Please God, help me.

She bowed her head and closed her eyes. Then she felt the touch of his hand and her eyes flew open, her hand abruptly pulled away from his, and fear washed through her.

Concern crossed the pastor's face, and he quickly said, "I didn't mean to frighten you. I won't hurt you."

"Oh, I know." Suzanne was embarrassed by her reaction. "I guess I'm just jumpy."

"Suzanne, would you start the prayer and then I'll finish?"

"Oh, well, yes. I guess." She hesitantly bowed her head. "God, help me to remove my shortcomings and to be a better person." She didn't know what else to say. She didn't know how to pray with a minister listening. She knew how she had learned to talk to God, but that was her way, and she was sure it wasn't the right way.

Moments of silence passed and the pastor didn't pray. Suzanne didn't want to say "amen," because that would end the prayer and he hadn't had his turn yet. Slowly, opening just one eye, she peeked at him. His eyes were closed and his head was bowed. Closing her eyes, Suzanne whispered, "You can pray now, Pastor Andrews."

Clearing his throat, he began, "Heavenly Father, we know your power and your love, and we know that you can take all of the pain in this world and turn it into something good and powerful. Lord Jesus, please take the pain this child of yours has experienced and let it blossom inside her and grow into a blessing. Hear her, Lord, as she asks for your help, and give her guidance and wisdom, Lord, to continue on the path of sobriety. In your glorious name, we pray. Amen."

The pastor's eyes glistened with tears. She didn't understand that he was feeling compassion for her. She was uncomfortable. "Are we done now?"

He smiled. "We're done whenever you feel like you want to be done."

"Oh. Okay. We're done." Suzanne stood and awkwardly held out her hand. "Thank you."

"Thank you, young lady, and may God bless you."

"Thanks." Suzanne smiled as she hurried outside. She was feeling happy and she intended to relish in the euphoria and make it last as long as she could. *What makes me happy?* Images of Sarah and Sam popped into her head. The last time she had visited, Sam had convinced her that she had to help him build a house with blocks, and she had. With Sam she could be a child, and that was exactly what she needed right now.

Chapter 39

Atlanta, Georgia

Helene was slowly surfacing from a restful sleep when she heard the gentle tap on her bedroom door. She turned to Bill's side of the bed only to find it empty. "Yes?" she called.

Bill's head peeked in and Thomas was right behind him. "Morning, Mom," he said with a smile.

Bill came in with a tray. "We made you breakfast."

"Breakfast? You two made breakfast?" Helene sat up in bed as they moved toward her. She wasn't sure what this was all about, but she welcomed the thought of having breakfast in bed. The old Helene would have worried about crumbs or spills, but this new Helene relished the thought of being pampered.

"Scrambled eggs, toast, fruit, and coffee." Thomas rattled off the menu.

"I'm impressed." She smiled at Bill, who had placed the tray on her lap and then turned to Thomas and placed an arm around his shoulder. She couldn't remember a time when Bill had ever brought her a cup of coffee in bed, let alone breakfast.

"We're quite a team in the kitchen." Bill's eyes twinkled.

Thomas's arm slipped up over his father's shoulder. "Unbeatable."

Helene had never seen them like this together. Their eyes sparkled with laughter, and their faces were gentle. "Well, what a nice surprise. Where are your breakfasts?"

"Downstairs," Bill informed her.

"Will you join me?" She patted the space on the bed next to her.

"I'll get them," Thomas volunteered on his way out of the room.

"I'll help." Bill followed his son.

In a few minutes, they returned and sat together on the huge bed enjoying breakfast. The eggs were a little salty, the toast was a bit burned, and the coffee was very strong, but it was the best breakfast Helene could ever remember having.

After they finished eating, they were curled up on the bed talking when Thomas asked, "Why haven't you taken me to meet your family and see your mom? I know you've gotten closer to your sisters because you talk about them a lot."

"I didn't think you'd want to go."

"Well, I do."

"Why didn't you say so?"

"I don't always know. But I've been thinking, and I'd like to see Grandma before she dies."

"She doesn't look like herself, Thomas. She is frail." One more time, she regretted keeping her son away from her family for all these years. Would he have liked his grandmother? Maybe her mom would have delighted in meeting her grandson. *Don't build fantasies, Helene. Mom didn't delight in Alice's kids. She was who she was.* Helene was still trying to figure out how to deal with who her mother was and love her as she was. She hadn't gotten there yet even though she now felt a bond with the woman she had stayed away from for two decades.

"I'd still like to see her."

Helene glanced toward Bill. "I'm not sure when we could go. Christmas is only three weeks away. Maybe after the first of the year."

"Will she still be alive?" Thomas asked.

"I'm not sure." A weight of sadness settled over Helene. She had mixed feelings about Thomas seeing her mother the way she now was. Heck, she had mixed feelings about Thomas meeting her mother, period. But she couldn't deny him the chance to see his grandmother and meet his aunts and cousins. In fact, why would she want to? She had spent her whole life keeping her past and present separate, and now that they were merging, she wasn't sure how to handle it. She recognized that it would take her a while to adjust to her new reality.

Bill's voice was just above a whisper when he asked, "Why don't we go now? Before Christmas?"

"Can we?" Feelings of surprise and gratitude gathered in Helene's chest.

"As soon as we can get plane reservations," he responded. Then he glanced at Helene and added, "I think it's time Thomas and I met your whole family."

"I didn't realize it was so cold up here." Thomas pulled his ski jacket collar up around his neck. "How did you ever play outside when you were a kid? I'd freeze to death." They had just stepped out of the Minneapolis-St. Paul airport and were walking toward their rental car.

"You get used to it," Helene wrapped her wool coat snugly around her, "but I must admit that my blood has thinned. It feels colder than it did when I was a kid."

It was about a thirty-minute ride to the nursing home where she, Suzanne, and Alice had transferred their mom before Helene had gone home. She hadn't been up to see her mom since, but she sent flowers every week to help keep the room cheerful, and Alice kept her updated on their mom's medical prognosis. Nothing had changed.

Snow covered the ground, and the windows of the nursing home were glazed with frost. Helene, Bill, and Thomas willingly stepped into the warmth of the lobby. A few elderly people were seated in the chairs scattered around the large room they passed as they headed down the hall.

Her mother's room was eerily quiet, as the only sounds they heard were the machines that monitored her vitals. The frail body was covered under a light blanket. Helene walked to the side of the bed as Bill and Thomas stood close to the door. Helene placed her hand against her mother's wrinkled cheek. "Mom," she whispered, "I brought some very special people to meet you."

Helene stroked the old woman's forehead. "This is Bill, my husband. He's what I wish you could have had. A good man makes such a difference." Helene's tone was hushed and soothing as she felt Bill come close to her. "And this is Thomas, your grandson. You'd really like him, Mom. He's such a nice young man."

Helene reached into her bag and pulled out a beautifully wrapped Christmas package. "See the colors, Mom? I remember you used to say you liked the colors of Christmas."

Helene continued talking to her mom as she unwrapped the gift. Thomas and Bill stood silently by her side. Pulling out a pair of colorful wool socks, she continued, "I hope you like them. I remember you used to complain that your feet were always cold. Mine are like that too. Did you know that? Well, these will keep your feet warm."

Helene pushed back the side of the blanket and reached for the frail blue-tinted feet. She felt Thomas back up a few steps. She carefully slipped on the socks. "You're so cold. Do you need more blankets? I'll have the nurse bring more blankets." She tucked the covers around her mother the way she used to do with Thomas when he was a child.

"She doesn't seem like she could be your mother," Thomas whispered. "I mean, you've always been so pretty."

"She was pretty once, but life drained it from her," Helene stated.

Bill rubbed her lower back and she felt calm. "I believe she hears us." She turned toward Thomas. "You can talk to her. She can hear you."

Then Helene sat down on the edge of the bed. "I'm sorry you didn't get to know Thomas before, Mom. So many mistakes in so many lives, for so many years, but we're doing better now. We're all doing better."

She rubbed her mother's arm. "I wish you were here to see it. Yet somehow, I feel you do know. I feel you in this room, Mom. And you've changed. At first, I could feel your hostility, but now I feel gentleness. I feel your love." She took a breath. "Is it you who's different? Is it me? Or have we both changed?"

As Helene's words trailed into quietness, Thomas slipped onto his knees by the bed. "Grandma . . . it's nice to meet you." His words were faltering and awkward. "I didn't really know I had another grandma. I mean, Mom never told me. I mean, the few times I asked, she said she wasn't close to her family." He was struggling and panic covered his face.

Helene smiled at her son. "She understands, Thomas. She understands."

They visited a little while longer, then piled in the car and headed down the road. They hadn't spoken since they left Helene's mother's room. The silence was a comfortable one, yet it was permeated with sadness. Helene turned around to make sure Thomas was okay. His eyes were closed and small snores were emanating from his mouth. She marveled at his ability to fall asleep so quickly.

Glancing at Bill, she said, "I've never really known my mom, but I'm really going to miss her."

"You talk as if she's dead." Bill took his eyes from the road for a moment.

"She certainly isn't living. I hope God mercifully takes her home," Helene whispered.

"To be with your dad?"

"No. Dad didn't go to be with God." Helene's words were monotone as she stared straight ahead.

"Helene, how can you say that?"

"I know my father, Bill," she said.

"Are you saying he went to Hell?"

"I am." Helene's glance flickered and resentment crept back into her voice. "And that's where he deserves to be."

"Honey," Bill reached for her, "tell me what I can do to help."

"Just be here," she replied. "Just let me know I'm okay with you, no matter how crazy or confused my past was, or my family may be."

"I can do that."

Helene sadly watched the road ahead. "How did we live together for so many years and not know about each other?"

"I was raised not to ask," Bill replied.

"And I was raised not to tell. That's what Mom always said, 'Don't talk about what goes on at home, Helene.' She would warn me if I was going to a birthday party or to stay overnight at somebody's house. But what else could I talk about? It was all I knew. Pretty soon I just kept to myself."

"What a match we are, my love." Bill touched her leg. "My mother used to stop my questions with, 'Other people's business is their own, William. If they want you to know something, they'll tell you.' And I believed her."

"How did we ever get to know each other?"

"We didn't," he answered.

They slipped into a comfortable silence. Finally, Bill cleared his throat, and said, "I don't know if my timing is appropriate, but I thought we'd go skiing."

Thomas was apparently now awake because Helene heard stirring from the backseat as a sleepy voice questioned, "Skiing? This is Minnesota, not Colorado. It's the land of frozen lakes, not mountains."

Helene turned toward him. "I'll have you know there are wonderful ski and winter sports not far from here."

"In Minnesota? Are you sure?"

Helene burst into laughter. "Bill, we can't let this young man continue to live such a sheltered life. I think it's time he experienced the fun of a Minnesota winter."

"I was hoping you'd say that," Bill smiled. "I made reservations at Buck Hill ski area, which is not far from Minneapolis. I thought we'd spend a few days enjoying winter before we flew back home."

"But we didn't bring appropriate clothing."

"I guess we'll have to buy some."

"That could get expensive."

"Well, I knew I had worked hard all these years to put money in the bank for some reason. Maybe it's time we got wild and crazy and spent it."

Helene wrapped herself with the love and camaraderie that was snuggling around them. She unbuckled her seatbelt and slid closer to Bill. "I think skiing sounds great, and I haven't been sledding in years."

Bill put his arm around her shoulder. "I've heard ice fishing is fun. Driving around on a frozen lake entices me."

Helene could see that Thomas was reluctant, but she and Bill's enthusiasm seemed to draw him into their plans. "Only if we also rent a snowmobile. I'd love to drive one."

Helene turned toward Thomas as worry surfaced in her eyes. "I don't know. You could get hurt on a snowmobile."

"Mom, I'm not a kid."

Bill drew her closer to him as he whispered, "He's right, Helene. He's a young man now. We have to let him grow up."

Helene glanced at the men in her life. "Okay, as we say in Minnesota, you betcha. But first, we do some shopping and then introduce you both to the rest of my family. After that, though, we ski, fish, and snowmobile!" She grinned at Bill. "Lead on!"

Chapter 40

Minneapolis, Minnesota

More than six weeks had passed since Alice's phone call to Jake, and they hadn't heard anything from him. The social worker had pushed hard about pressing charges, but Alice had dropped the case, refusing to even discuss it. So after a few weeks, the matter dropped into the background of their lives and peace seemed to return to the family.

It was December and Sam was getting into the holiday spirit. "How are we gonna decorate our tree, Mom?" he asked as he stared at the bare branches.

Alice hadn't thought they'd even have a tree, but the couple next door had gone out today and cut down their own tree, bringing an extra one for Alice, Sarah, and Sam. They'd even bought them a stand.

The neighbors had just left when Sam's questions began. "Our decorations are with Dad. What are we gonna put on the tree?"

Alice's mind searched for an answer. "We'll do like people many years ago. We'll string popcorn and cranberries and make paper decorations."

"Popcorn and cranberries? Oh, Mom," Sarah rolled her eyes, "that's corny."

Alice laughed. "Corny. Popcorn. Get it?" Her sense of humor had been emerging lately and she was enjoying those moments. Laughter hadn't been a very frequent visitor in her life, and she was beginning to discover that she had a sense a humor. She liked it.

"Mom!" Sarah gave her a stern look. "You're weird." Then she grinned.

"Okay," Sam persisted. "When are we gonna do the tree? Next week's Christmas, you know."

"Well, how about tonight? Auntie Suzanne is planning on coming over, so we could see if she wants to help."

"Sure. She's nice." Sam was matter-of-fact. "Just make sure she doesn't tell us how to do it. It's our tree, you know."

Alice smiled at her son. "Well, if she tells you how to do it and you want to do it your way, you could tell her."

"I could tell a grownup that?"

"Sure, Sam, as long as you say it respectfully. You talk to me, don't ya?"

"Sometimes."

"I think you could talk to Auntie Suzanne too."

"Oh, okay. She can come then."

A few hours later, Alice, Sarah, Sam, and Suzanne sat on the floor in the living room with bowls of popcorn and cranberries in front of them. They each had a large darning needle threaded with thick strings that were in various stages of becoming popcorn and cranberry garland. Christmas music played on the stereo Alice had picked up at a garage sale, and gentle chatter filled the room.

"Alice, this is such a neat idea. It feels so homey." Suzanne put another piece of popcorn on her string.

"Yeah, all we need is a fire glowing in the background."

"Some year you'll have that, Alice," Suzanne assured her as she stretched out her garland in front of her to see its length.

"Do you think so?" Alice threw a few pieces of popcorn into her mouth and made a face at Sam. She wasn't sure she could envision herself living in a house with a fireplace, but the idea tickled at her imagination. She was going to college now and hadn't ever thought she'd do that. So, who knew what possibilities were around the corner?

"Yeah, we will, Mom," Sam joined in. "I'm gonna buy you one when I get big and rich."

"See, Alice?" Suzanne responded. "Sam is going to be big and rich, and Sarah's going to be a top fashion model or a doctor, or both. Then you can sit back in the lap of luxury."

Sarah's eyes grew big. "Me, a model? Get real."

"Why not?" Suzanne glanced at her niece. "You're gorgeous."

"Mom says I look like you," Sarah said shyly as she squirmed in her spot on the carpet, trying to get comfortable.

"You do?" Suzanne peered at Alice who was just tying off her garland and reaching for a string to start another one.

"Uh-huh. So you can both be models."

Suzanne and Sarah quickly peeked at each other with mischievousness gleams in their eyes. They both grabbed a piece of popcorn, tossed it at Alice, and in unison declared, "Get real."

"Okay, you're in trouble if you do that again," Alice warned as she grabbed some popcorn.

"Let's have a popcorn fight," Sam declared.

"I don't think so." Alice dropped her popcorn as she stared at three raised hands each filled with popcorn. "I think I'm outnumbered."

Before the popcorn ammunition could be released in her direction, the doorbell rang and Alice shouted, "Saved by the bell!" She scampered up from the floor and hurried from the room.

"Ho, ho, ho," Helene laughed as Alice opened the door.

"Helene! What are you doing here?" Alice attempted to brush the scraps of popcorn off her slacks.

"Visiting." Helene smiled as she pulled Alice to her in a big hug.

"All the way from Atlanta?" Alice murmured against Helene's shoulder.

"Sure." Helene finished her hug, released Alice, and stood there smiling.

Alice was speechless and embarrassed. She didn't want Helene to see her apartment, which was small and plain compared to the pictures she had seen of where Helene lived. And she especially didn't want her to see them having to decorate their tree with popcorn.

Either Helene didn't notice Alice's hesitation or she chose to ignore it. "I brought somebody for you to meet." She smiled as she walked past Alice and let a tall, dark-haired man step into the doorway. "This package-ladened man is your brother-in-law, Bill." Then she turned toward the young man standing next to Bill. "And this good-looking young man is your nephew, Thomas." Helene then pointed at Alice. "And this is my sister, Alice."

"Hi," the men responded together.

Now Alice was really embarrassed. It was bad enough that Helene saw her apartment, but to bring her lawyer husband and the nephew Alice had never met without notice was too much! Alice couldn't take it. She wanted to run into her bedroom and eat something—anything.

"Auntie Helene!" Sam's freckled grin looked up from his task. Soon Sarah, Suzanne, and Sam all abandoned their garlands and were at the door joined in a hug with Helene. Alice stood there in a daze as Bill and Thomas waited awkwardly at the door still loaded with bags of gifts.

After all the introductions were complete, Helene turned to Alice and said, "Did we surprise you?" Her voice was filled with excitement.

"Well, sure, I mean . . ."

Helene stepped farther into the living room. "Oh, Alice, what a wonderful idea—popcorn garland! I've never done that. Can we help?" She slipped down onto the floor where the bowls were assembled.

"You want to string popcorn?" Alice asked.

"I'd love to," Helene said as she pulled off her gloves, stuck them in the pocket of her winter coat, and reached for a string. Soon Suzanne, Sarah, and Sam joined her.

Bill and Thomas left the packages by the front door, shed their winter coats next to the packages, followed Helene into the living room, and sat on the floor on either side of her, while Sam gave instructions as to how garlands were created.

Alice watched for a few moments, forgot about any embarrassment or concern she initially had, and sat down in the space she had vacated. She picked up her needle and thread and continued creating her garland.

With the innocence of a child, Sam looked at Helene and inquired, "How come I've never seen you before, and now I see you a lot in a not so long time?"

"Because I was a very silly lady." Helene smiled as she stopped stringing her garland and looked at her nephew.

"Didn't you like my mom before?" Sam asked.

Helene fluffed up his hair. "Actually, Sam, I didn't like myself."

"I feel that way about myself sometimes," Sam said as he munched on some popcorn.

"Me too." Suzanne grinned, and they all laughed.

They were all having such a good time that Alice had lost track of time until she heard Bill remind Helene that they had about a forty-minute drive.

"Where are you off to?" Suzanne asked.

"We're going to spend a couple of days showing Thomas what fun a Minnesota winter can be," Bill answered.

"Do you gotta go?" Sam protested. "Can't you just stay here till Christmas?"

"I'm afraid not, Sam, but we'll come up again, and then we'll stay longer. Does that sound okay with you?"

"Sure." Sam pointed at Bill and Thomas. "Will you bring them with you?"

"Do you think I should?" she teased.

"I think so."

"Then I will."

"I'll call you when we get back home early next week," Helene promised, then the three of them left.

When they were gone, Sam pointed to the bags of wrapped gifts by the door. "But they forgot their presents."

"I think those are for us," Sarah said.

"For us? Are you sure?" Sam's freckles seemed to dance with delight.

"I'm pretty sure," Alice assured him.

That was all it took for Sam. He dashed to the bags, started unloading them, and carried the gifts to the tree. Then he paused, turned to Alice, and with a serious face said, "I think I like having them for family."

Alice smiled. "I do, too, Sam. I do too."

Chapter 41

Minneapolis, Minnesota

Three days before Christmas, Sarah and Alice were in the kitchen making Christmas cookies. "Mom, is Auntie Helene very rich?"

"To us it seems so," Alice said as she rolled out the sugar cookie dough, "but to the world, probably not." She had no idea how much money her sister had even though she had occasionally contemplated what "rich" really meant.

"Can we be like that one day?" Sarah was carefully laying out the cookie cutters they were planning to use.

"You can, but probably not me." Alice tried to see herself living the type of life that Helene lived—having a housekeeper, being able to fly somewhere at the spur of the moment, going to a country club for dinner—and she couldn't. She knew her life would now be better than she had ever had before, but her aspirations weren't at the level of Helene's life. She'd be happy teaching grade school, supporting her kids, and owning a nice little house. Those were her dreams.

"Why me and not you?"

"You're young, smart, and pretty. I'm not." Alice stepped off to the side and motioned for Sarah to begin cutting out the cookies. "Besides, I don't see myself that way."

Sarah carefully pressed the cookie cutters into the dough. "Are you divorcing Dad?" She quickly glanced at Alice.

Alice looked up, startled. "Probably." She had been thinking about divorce, but at this point in time she just wanted to let sleeping dogs lie.

"Will you go out with guys?" Sarah had cut out several cookies in the shapes of a bell, a Santa face, a Christmas tree, and a Poinsettia, and she was placing them on a cookie sheet.

"Me?" Alice asked. "Who would want to go out with me?" Having a man in her life was the furthest thing from her mind. Someone to tell her what to do or get all angry and crabby when things didn't go their way? No thanks. She was getting used to being single and was entirely happy with things the way they were.

"Probably lots of guys," Sarah said.

"Honey, I'm fat and not very pretty. Men look for young, thin, pretty women."

"Not all guys." Sarah crumbed up a Santa cookie that had not turned out the way she'd wanted it to.

"Probably the good ones." Alice went over to the sink, put her hands in the soapy water, and began to wash the bowl.

Sarah quietly asked, "Why don't you go on a diet and lose weight?"

Alice played with the soapy water as she thought about Sarah's last question. She had been trying to be more conscious of what she ate, and she had been walking back and forth to the coffee shop on the mornings she worked. But she still had chocolate binges from time to time, and losing weight just wasn't a priority for her. She knew obesity caused all sorts of health problems, and she had to get serious about losing weight. But she could only tackle so many life changing issues in one year, and as far as she was concerned, she had handled her quota of "big stuff" this year.

In answer to Sarah's question, she simply replied, "It doesn't seem that easy for me, Sarah. I get nervous and I eat. It helps me calm down. It's like Auntie Suzanne says drinks used to do for her."

"Well, can't you go to treatment like she did?"

Alice dried her hands on a towel and turned toward Sarah. "I don't know, maybe."

"Do you want to be thin?"

I don't know. Do I? Alice had been heavy for most of her life. She had gotten used to it. "Hey, these are hard questions." Alice turned back to the sink. "I thought we were gonna make cookies and have fun, and here you are making me think. We've got a break from school, let my brain rest, okay?"

"Okay, Mom, that's fair." Sarah placed the cookie pan in the oven. "What do you think Auntie Helene and Uncle Bill got us for Christmas?"

"I can't even guess, but probably something nice."

"He's handsome, isn't he?" Sarah smiled.

"Who?" Alice's mind had been wandering as she dried the dishes and put them away.

"Uncle Bill!"

"Oh. Yeah, I guess he is."

Sarah grabbed a small piece of cookie dough and munched on it as she leaned against the counter. "I want to marry a rich, good-looking man some day."

"If you want to, you will." Alice was beginning to think that the world could be open for endless possibilities for her kids. And she was now determined that she was going to help them become whatever they wanted to become.

"Is it that easy?"

"No, but wanting is probably a good start." Alice placed her arm around Sarah's waist.

"What did you want when you were my age?" Sarah asked.

"Sarah, for goodness sake." Alice hugged her, then walked to the oven to check the cookies. "I've never heard you ask so many questions. What in the world are you trying to do, drive me bonkers?"

"No, Mom. I'm trying to talk to you. That's what mothers and daughters do."

Alice was quiet. They had come so far—she and Sarah. When they were with Jake, they had been adversaries. Back then, Sarah thought her mother was fat, lazy, and disgusting. Now she was trying hard to talk to her. As she pulled the cookie sheet from the oven, Alice thanked God for the way kids seemed to bounce back from a crisis.

Now that Jake was leaving them alone, Alice had almost forgotten what life with him was like, but a replay of the last beating he'd given her occasionally flashed in the back of her mind. She would never put up with that again. A part of her didn't understand why she put up with it then. The other part did.

Sam rushed in through the door with snow-covered mittens. "What day will it be Christmas?"

"Four days from now," Alice answered.

"Are we gonna have more presents under our tree than we have now?" Sam's cheeks were pink from the cold as he pulled off his mittens, snow pants, and jacket, dropping them in a pile by the door.

Alice pointed at the pile. "I don't think so."

He quietly turned, hung his jacket and snow pants on hooks in the laundry room off the kitchen, and put his mittens on the floor under the hooks. "But I only have a little one from you."

"Sam!" Sarah scolded him as she stirred the frosting for the cookies. "Mom doesn't have money, you know that!"

"I know . . ." His face fell as he reached for a cookie and Sarah smacked his hand. "I'm sorry, Mom."

"Me too." Alice looked at her son as pain pinched at her heart. Then Helene's words rang in her ears, "If I can ever help, all you have to do is ask." Alice wiped her hands and looked at Sarah. "Will you watch the cookies? I've got to go to my bedroom for a minute."

As Alice left the room, she heard Sarah scolding Sam. "Now you made her cry, you bozo."

Alice stopped in the hallway and peeked back into the kitchen to watch her children.

"Did not!" His hands on his hips, Sam made a face at his sister.

Sarah offered him a cookie. "You did too. Don't ask her about presents no more. Okay?"

"Oh, okay." Sam's chin dropped. "I wasn't trying to hurt her."

"I know, Sam. I know." Sarah put her arm around him. Alice smiled at the sight, then headed down the hallway.

Once in her room, she sat on the bed, reached for the phone, and dialed Helene's number.

The sisters chatted for a few minutes as Alice asked how the winter excursion had been for Thomas, and Helene's laughter and stories made Alice smile.

When Helene asked how they were doing, Alice got to the point of the call. "I need to ask a favor."

"Sure."

"Helene, it's really hard for me to ask you this, but the kids have been through so much, and this is the first Christmas I've seen Sam so full of hope." Alice took a deep breath. "Would you loan me two hundred dollars to buy the kids a few Christmas presents?"

"You didn't find it then?"

"Find what?" Alice asked. Was she supposed to have looked for something?

"The card," Helene answered.

"What card?"

"Bill and I left a card for you. I was going to give it to you when we were there, but we were all having so much fun, and I wanted to keep it just between us. I couldn't seem to get you alone for even a minute, so I just left it for you in the most obvious place I could think of without leaving it sitting out in the open. I figured you would have found it by now."

"You did? Where did you leave it?" Alice's eyes scanned the room as if she expected to find it sitting out in plain sight.

"In your kitchen cabinet with your plates," Helene answered.

"Oh, no, I didn't . . ." Alice's hand dropped to her lap. "You left me money?"

"Yes."

"Why? After everything you've done and all the presents you bought." *That's a dumb thing to say since you just called her and asked her to loan you money.*

"Because we love you, and I figured that with school and your other expenses, your budget might be tight." Helene's voice was soft. "Raising kids costs money."

"It sure does." Silence. "I feel a little dumb that I called."

"Why would you feel dumb?"

"Because I asked." Internally, she was scolding herself for calling. Here

Helene and Bill had already left her something and she didn't find it. *But wait a minute, why in the world would I ever think they would leave me something in my dish cupboard?* Sometimes Helene really mystified her.

"I don't. I feel good." Helene's voice sounded happy.

"Why?" *There are times this sister of mine seems to talk in riddles.*

"Because you asked," Helene replied.

"Oh." *Okay, that makes sense.* Happy chills danced down Alice's arms. She was getting used to being cared about and she liked it.

After she hung up, Alice felt so giddy she tried skipping toward the Christmas tree and almost fell. Shaking her head at herself, she walked the rest of the way and opened the kitchen cupboard as Sarah and Sam watched her. At first glance Alice didn't see an envelope—just dishes. Then she lifted the plates, and there it was. A square envelope. She turned her back to the counter and leaned against it, holding the card against her chest.

"What's that, Mom?" Sarah asked.

"A card." Alice allowed herself to feel the love that Helene must have for her to do something so nice.

"From who?" Sarah persisted.

"Auntie Helene and Uncle Bill."

"Why would they leave a card under our dishes?" Sarah put the finished cookie on a plate and picked up another one.

"They didn't. They left it on top. Somebody must have moved the plates," Alice explained as she continued to hug the card.

Alice didn't say anything as she took the card and walked to her bedroom. Sitting on the bed, her hands trembled as she opened the envelope. A cashier's check for $1,000 fell into her lap. The note in the card said, "Do something special for all of you."

The tree glowed with the newly purchased lights, and the new packages crowded around the tree. Suzanne had taken the kids ice skating so Alice could go shopping and surprise them. Tomorrow was Christmas Eve, and her kids were going have a good one thanks to Suzanne and Helene. For the first time in her life, Alice knew the special feeling of having sisters.

She put the last of the groceries in the cupboard and set the candle centerpiece on her dinette table as Suzanne, Sarah, and Sam returned. Their faces were flushed from winter's chill and the exercise of skating.

"It's time for some nice hot chocolate." Suzanne laughed. "These bones need something hot and soothing. And I don't think I'll ever be able to sit down again." She rubbed her backside.

"Auntie Suzanne was funny, Mom." Sarah giggled. "She kept falling down, but I think some of it was on purpose because a cute guy kept helping her up."

Suzanne pretended shock. "Why, Sarah! I'd never do that."

"Why not?" Sarah grinned mischievously. "I would! He was cute!"

"He was kinda cute, wasn't he?" Suzanne conceded.

"Mom!" Sam rushed into the kitchen. "Our tree's filled with presents!"

"It is?"

"Yeah! And they say they're from you!"

"Can you imagine?" Alice laughed.

Sarah looked curiously at her mother and walked to the living room. "Mom! How could you do all this? The tree even has lights!" Sarah returned to the kitchen. "Where did you get all this money?"

Alice pulled her daughter to her. "Honey, let's just say there are such things as Christmas miracles. They're called sisters."

It was Christmas morning, and Suzanne's arms were filled with packages. She had to ring the doorbell with her thumb.

Sam opened it and his freckled face broke into a grin. "More presents! Great!" Then in his excitement, he turned into the room and yelled, "Mom, its Auntie Suzanne with more presents. Isn't this a great Christmas?"

Alice came up behind Sam. "Suzanne! What did you do?"

"Went shopping." Suzanne's face flushed with happiness.

"I see that, but you're crazy. You're not working, and your therapy has cost you a lot of money. What if your job doesn't work out? You said you were worried about that." Alice helped her inside, as they both struggled with the shopping bags.

"I was." Suzanne set her bags down and placed her hands on her sister's shoulders. "I didn't spend more than I can afford, but I realized something today. I'm in charge of my life. Me and nobody else. I've been giving other people that power for too long. Sure, there's going to be problems, but I can find solutions. My life doesn't have to be a crisis. I need to take one day at a time, but that's not just so I won't drink again; that's also to enjoy what each day brings—a fresh beginning. And I'm starting here with you, the kids, and Christmas because you've helped me so much. Your home and your life is an anchor in my time of chaos. It's what helps me not to go nutty."

"Mine?" Alice's mouth dropped open.

"Yes! First we strung popcorn on the tree. Then you made cookies and sent me ice skating! I feel like a kid! I feel better than a kid. We never did things like this when we were young. You're constantly improving your life. You came from an oppressive situation, and you keep pulling yourself and us upward. It's like you keep reaching for something, but how do you know what to reach for?" Suzanne was talking a mile a minute.

Alice was sheepish. "It's nothing wonderful. I just read the ladies' magazines from the grocery store."

Suzanne smiled at her sister. Alice had come such a long way since summer. They all had. They all seemed to have climbed up out of holes of darkness. They certainly weren't on top of their mountains yet, but they were on upward paths.

"I love you, Suzanne," Alice said.

Suzanne started to cry. "I know."

"Mom, Auntie Suzanne, you're not getting sad are you? It's Christmas." Sam seemed anxious, as if he was afraid something would ruin this Christmas.

Suzanne knelt down and embraced her nephew. "No, Sam, I'm not getting sad. In fact, I feel so happy I could burst into many little pieces."

"Oh yuck," the boy rolled his eyes, "that would be gross."

Laughter bubbled in Suzanne's throat. *God, but I'm glad to be alive!*

Chapter 42

Dallas, Texas

It was the first Monday in January of 1991, and Suzanne was returning to work. She'd had a wonderful Christmas with Alice and the kids and had spent the time between Christmas and New Years to return to Dallas, her condo, and her life.

Before coming back home, she had asked Melanie to go to her condo and remove all the bottles she had stashed there. She'd been tempted to keep one or two a secret, but in the end, she'd revealed all of her hiding spots. Melanie had done a great job clearing them out.

She had spent a quiet New Year's Eve and Day thinking about the new year and the new life she was about to create. She'd called Alice and Helene on New Year's Eve, and as the new year slipped in, Suzanne uttered thankfulness for her family.

She adjusted her skirt and jacket before opening the door to her office. Melanie's smile brought warmth to Suzanne's chilly feeling. Her hands were so cold. She had been trying to warm them all morning.

Her boss, Mr. Warren, was meeting her in her office at nine, and then Jeff was due at eleven. *It's today or never. I'll either confront my past today, or it will devour me.*

"Hi, boss! You look terrific!" Melanie got up from behind her desk and embraced Suzanne in a hug.

Suzanne felt like a child entering kindergarten for the first time. "I am so nervous, Melanie. I feel so totally different from the woman who left here in July."

"Don't be." Melanie gazed at Suzanne for a moment before continuing. "You certainly look different. I love your hair down and full like that. You look so pretty, so soft."

"Thanks." Suzanne blushed.

"Graciously accepting a compliment, and you're blushing! I'm impressed. The old Suzanne would have brushed it off or made excuses. We have a totally new woman here."

Suzanne looked around the office and then down at her watch. "Let's hope I'm different enough and strong enough to deal with Jeff Davidson. I'm scared to death."

"You'll be okay. Go get reacquainted with your office, and I'll bring you some coffee."

Suzanne entered her office and sat at her desk. Her stomach curled in disgust as she remembered her last encounter with Jeff on this desk, but this time, the disgust was not pointed in her direction.

"I hope you still drink your coffee black." Melanie set the cup on her desk.

"Actually," Suzanne smiled, "I've started adding sugar. My sweet tooth has really kicked in since I quit drinking."

Melanie sat in the chair facing Suzanne. "Is it really hard? Not drinking, I mean."

"Very hard. I have to fight it every day, one day at a time. Sometimes I have to fight it one second at a time."

"I really admire you, Suzanne."

"Admire me? Why?"

"Because you're kicking an addiction, and from what I read, that's a big task."

"Good morning!" a voice called from the front office.

"Oh, hi, Robert," Melanie called.

When did she started calling him Robert? Suzanne stood, straightening her suit jacket nervously.

Robert Warren walked into the office with his hand outstretched. "Suzanne, it's good to have you back."

"Thank you, Mr. Warren. It's good to be back."

Melanie then excused herself and closed the door behind her.

"She is a terrific secretary and loyal friend." Robert gazed kindly at Suzanne.

"I'm very lucky to have her as both." *Let's get on with it. I can't think of small talk when I'm scared to death about my future.*

Robert sat down and sipped on his coffee, studying Suzanne. "You look different, Suzanne. And I like the change."

"Uh . . . thank you, Mr. Warren." Suzanne cleared her throat in an attempt to get rid of the lump that was settling there. "I have a lot to explain, don't I?" *Where do I begin? How do I do this?*

"Do you?" He smiled at her.

"Well, sir, my leave of absence was rather sudden and unexpected."

"I understand that your mother became very ill and that somehow triggered your need to deal with your alcoholism."

"It did. I mean, it was part of it, but there is more."

"Melanie led me to believe there might be."

Suzanne stood up and slowly paced the room. *Give me strength, Lord. Give me strength.*

"Well, sir, you see . . . when I was drinking, I would go to bars and get pretty drunk." Suzanne clenched her hands together. "I didn't know what I was doing half the time. I'd end up going home with different guys. I had a lot of one-night stands."

Sympathy filled Robert's eyes. "Suzanne, you don't have to tell me this. That was your personal life."

"I do have to tell you, sir, because it didn't stay with my personal life." She took a deep breath and hurried on before she lost her strength. "One night, I got very drunk, and I ended up in bed with Jeff Davidson."

"Oh."

"And he took pictures."

"He did what?"

"He took a lot of pictures. And he said if I didn't do what he wanted, he'd make sure everyone in the company saw them." Robert was silent, and Suzanne's heart sank. "I panicked, Mr. Warren. I was so embarrassed and so afraid of losing my job." She shakily took a deep breath. "Finally, his demands got to be so much that when my mother got sick, it was a good excuse to run. And that's what I did. I've been running since then."

"And now you've stopped?"

"Yes." *But I want to run again right now. To the nearest bar, preferably.*

"What demands did he make?"

"Businesswise, he wanted more money."

"So, the raises, the bonuses? He wasn't improving?"

"No."

"What about his improved numbers? His calls and productivity?"

"They were fixed, and I allowed them to slide, along with escalated expense reports." Suzanne's breath was shallow. She would never walk away from this with her job, but by God she was finally going to be rid of the secrets. All the dark, ugly secrets.

Robert ran his hand roughly through his hair, and his eyes were troubled. "These are some pretty serious offenses you're confessing to, Suzanne."

Suzanne didn't answer him. She didn't have to.

"I can't let these offenses slide without disciplinary action for both Mr. Davidson and yourself." He watched Suzanne for a few moments. "Are you in possession of any of these photographs?"

She nodded. "Jeff gave me copies because he wanted me to remember who was in charge."

"Do you have any of them here with you?"

Turbulence assaulted her face as waves of red washed over her pale cheeks, but she simply nodded again.

"I understand that Jeff has an appointment with us this morning." Suzanne nodded once more. Robert leaned forward in his seat. "Do you trust me, Suzanne?"

Silently Suzanne sat behind her desk and assessed the man across from her. Her mind ran over his treatment of her the last years, and her experience with him as a person in general. "If I didn't, I would have turned in my notice without coming back to work."

Robert seemed surprised but not offended by her frankness. "Suzanne, I'd like you to place your pictures in an envelope and hand them to me."

Suzanne ran her tongue over her dry lips, reached into her purse for the envelope that held the pictures, and slid it across the desk.

"Now, please pull out copies of Jeff's reports that were fudged."

Suzanne stiffly walked over to her file cabinet. She clumsily went through the files. *Take a deep breath. It's going to be okay, and if it's not, you can make it okay for yourself. This isn't the only job in the world. If you have to start from scratch, so be it. You've got yourself, and that's not a bad beginning. You're going to be okay.*

When she sat down again, Suzanne's boss moved closer to the desk and began reviewing the files. They spent the next hour going over reports, with Suzanne answering the questions Robert had about the reports and her division.

He closed the last file she had put in front of him and leaned back in the chair. "You have been very negligent in your responsibilities, Suzanne. You've cost the company undeserved bonuses, raises, and expenses. For these infractions, I'm going to put you on a ninety-day probationary period and reduce your salary by fifteen percent a year."

Robert leaned forward and gently put his hand on hers, which was fidgeting with a pen and slightly trembling. "Suzanne, if I let your infractions go unpunished, I'd be as guilty as you are of shirking my supervisory responsibilities."

"I know." Suzanne's voice was barely above a whisper as her mind circled and tried to find some balance in everything that was happening. Then Melanie's voice came over the intercom and Suzanne's breath caught in her chest.

"Jeff is here." Melanie's voice was filled with disdain.

"He's early." Panic rose in Suzanne's chest. Then taking a deep breath, she responded, "Thank you, Melanie."

"Do you need a few moments alone before we meet with him?" Robert asked.

Suzanne shook her head. "That would only give me time to feel, and then I'd fall apart."

He nodded. Reaching for the phone, he pressed the intercom button. "Melanie, send Mr. Davidson in."

When Jeff walked through the door, the cold wind of reality chilled Suzanne. She was face-to-face with a perpetrator and predator, and for once she was not going to act like a victim. *I'm not going to cave in. I'm not going to be frightened. I'm going to take what comes, but he's not going to use me. No more. No one is going to use me again. I won't be a victim anymore.*

Jeff nodded toward Robert and condescendingly smiled at Suzanne. "Suzanne, I've missed you. You're looking beautiful."

Scumbag.

Suzanne straightened her shoulders and held her head higher. "Have a seat, Mr. Davidson."

Jeff's eyes registered some confusion, but his ego seemed to take over as he smirked and sat down. Jeff was barely settled in his chair when Robert pushed the envelope across the desk to him. "I'd like you to explain these to me."

Jeff picked up the envelope, and as he felt the contents, his eyes flew to Suzanne. Momentary panic seemed to seize him as his eyes grew wide. Then he snickered toward Suzanne. "I think they speak for themselves."

"Do they? What do they say?" Robert said firmly.

Jeff glared at Robert. "That she got smashed and turned into a slut." Anger seared through Jeff's eyes.

"Have you ever been drunk?"

"Well, sure."

"Have you had sex when you're drunk?"

Jeff fidgeted in his chair but didn't answer the question.

Robert leaned toward Jeff. "What if Suzanne had been the one behind the camera that night? Would the pictures have been all that different?"

Jeff flew to his feet. "Wait a minute! She's the boss. She's the one who's in charge. Why am I suddenly on trial? She's a drunk and a slut. Is that the kind of woman this company wants in charge?"

"No, it's not."

"And do you agree she's the boss and should be in charge?"

"I do."

"Then what are you going to do about it?"

"I'm going to fire the person responsible for this entire mess."

Jeff settled back into his chair and straightened his tie.

Robert turned to Suzanne. "Suzanne, do you agree that I don't have a choice?"

Suzanne looked at him and meekly nodded.

Robert reached for the envelope of pictures and placed them in front of Suzanne. "Okay, I have no choice." He stood and turned toward Jeff. "You're fired."

Jeff stuttered in astonishment. "Me? I . . . I . . . Suzanne's the boss . . . she's responsible. Why me?"

Robert clicked off points with each finger. "For falsifying expense reports and activity reports, for unsatisfactory job performance, and also for blackmail."

Resembling a deflated balloon, Jeff sunk back into his chair.

"However," Robert continued, "I'll give you a choice."

Life returned to Jeff's eyes.

"You can resign, effective immediately with the realization that no recommendation will ever be forthcoming from this company, or I can terminate you here and now. Whatever option you choose, when you walk out of that door, you will no longer be employed by this company."

Stunned by the course of events, Suzanne just sat there lost in thought; she'd missed the rest of the conversation between the two men.

"Suzanne?" A voice broke her stupor.

"Yes, sir," she answered, shaking her head to clear it. Jeff was no longer in the room, and Robert was standing a few feet from her closed office door. *When did Jeff leave?*

At the end of her first day back at work, Suzanne gratefully slipped her shoes off and sunk into the cushions of her sofa. Even though she'd been home for a few days now, it was so good to be back. The day had taken its toll. Robert knew all about her problems, and he still believed in her. That was a new feeling for Suzanne.

At eight-thirty that evening, Suzanne went into the bathroom to run a hot bubble bath. She was just beginning to undress when the doorbell rang.

Re-buttoning her blouse, Suzanne looked through the peephole. It was Jeff! Her heart hammered violently in her chest. *God, no!* The doorbell rang again. Suzanne lifted her head, straightened her shoulders, and opened the door.

"Hi, baby." He was drunk.

"What do you want, Jeff? I'm not your baby."

"Oh, yes, you are," he snickered. "I'm not done with you yet. You're not getting off this easy. You may have Warren bamboozled, but if these pictures make it up to the big boys, you and Warren are both dead."

Suzanne's chest tightened. *Don't let him do it, Suzanne. Don't let him make you a victim. Call his bluff!*

Jeff pushed past her, but Suzanne kept her cool.

"Send the pictures to the top, Jeff. If I get fired, I'll handle it. But I think you're forgetting something. I was your boss. I can have you blackballed from the industry. I'm not without power here, and don't you forget it."

Jeff stumbled backward in surprise, and then he angrily advanced toward her. "Are you threatening me, bitch?"

Suzanne screamed inside as her fears pounded at the walls of her soul. *Stay cool, Suzanne. He's bluffing. Be careful, be smart, don't be a victim.* She casually stepped away from Jeff and headed toward the kitchen. *If I need a knife, I'll have one at hand.*

"No, Jeff, I'm not threatening you, but I'll no longer be used. If you want to send the pictures to the chairman of the board, that's your choice, and I'll just have to pay the price for my behavior. Just remember, we all eventually have to pay the price for our choices, and that goes for you too."

"It's not going to be that easy," Jeff threatened as he followed her into the kitchen.

"You're not welcome in here, Jeff. I think it's time you left." Suzanne stood with her back against the kitchen counter.

"I'll decide that," he swaggered, and catching Suzanne off guard, he grabbed a large handful of hair and roughly pulled her toward him.

Don't panic. Don't panic. Suzanne calmly looked at Jeff's face only inches away, and didn't say a word as she edged herself along the counter.

Jeff plunged his hand into her blouse and roughly kissed her. Suzanne used all the willpower she had to keep herself calm as she planned her defense.

Reaching behind her, she slowly opened the drawer where she kept her large knives. As Jeff's hands assaulted her body, she curled her fingers around a large knife. At the same time, using all the strength she had, brought her right knee up and into Jeff's groin. He doubled over and stepped backward, swearing profusely. Suzanne kicked him in the chest, knocking him flat onto the floor. She grabbed a wooden kitchen chair, laid it across his chest, pushed against it with her foot, and pointed the knife at his throat.

Her breathing was fast but her voice was steady and cold. "Hear me well, Jeff. This is over." She scratched his neck with the tip of the knife. "If you try to hurt me again, I'll kill you." She applied more pressure to the knife. "Quit now, Mr. Davidson, while you have a piece of your life left, because you're not dealing with the old Suzanne. And I don't think you want to push the new Suzanne to the point where you'll unleash her fury, because you won't live to tell about it."

Terror showed in his eyes as Jeff lay completely still.

"Do you hear me?" Suzanne shoved the chair into his chest.

Jeff nodded as he yelped from the pain.

Suzanne moved the chair from his body, and while holding it in front of her with one hand and the knife in the other, she hissed, "Now get the hell out of my home and my life before I decide to slice off a body part or two."

Jeff scrambled from the floor and hobbled to the door, clutching his groin.

Suzanne held her breath until she heard the sound of the door closing. Then she ran to it, turned the dead bolt, fell onto her knees, and sobbed.

Chapter 43

Dallas, Texas

"Well," Melanie smiled at Suzanne. "We made it to Friday afternoon. One week down and an eternity to go."

Suzanne returned the smile. "Melanie, you're wonderful. I was really worried that we wouldn't be able to work together now that you know so much about me, but you are as absolutely terrific as ever."

It was Melanie's turn to blush. "Thanks, boss. But changing the subject, what are you doing this evening?"

"I don't know, but I was thinking that I haven't seen Richard all week. Does he have a girlfriend or something?"

Melanie smiled softly at Suzanne. "I don't know, but I do know he asked about you every week you were gone."

"He did?" Suzanne placed her hands on the desk and looked at Melanie.

"Uh-huh." Melanie slipped into one of the chairs.

"What office does he work in?"

"You don't even know that?" Melanie's mouth dropped open. "What planet did you live on?"

"A very lonely one," Suzanne admitted.

"He works for the engineering company down on the fifth floor."

"I'll be right back, Melanie." With a smile, Suzanne got up from her desk and left her office.

Suzanne convinced Richard's secretary that she was an old friend, so she was permitted to walk down the hallway and stand in front of his open door unannounced. Suzanne leaned against the doorframe. "Hi. Working hard?"

Richard glanced up and seemed confused. Then he jumped to his feet. "Suzanne! Hi! When did you get back?"

"I've been here all week. I thought you've forgotten about me, so I thought I'd look you up."

"Forget about you? Never! It's been one of those weeks. How are you? Welcome back. You look beautiful!" he gushed.

Suzanne blushed. "Thanks." Then clearing her throat, she said, "I've turned down so many invitations from you that I was wondering if perhaps you were more gracious than I and would accept a last-minute dinner invitation from me."

Richard's eyes danced. "Dinner? Tonight?"

"Yes, if you're free."

"I'll make sure I am."

"Great! I can finish up by about six. Is that a good time for you?"

"Suzanne, I've been trying to take you out for over a year. Finally, you're willing!"

Suzanne stepped from one foot to another.

Richard smiled. "I've embarrassed you."

"Well, not really. Sort of. I guess I'm not used to someone being anxious to go out with me."

"I don't know why it should surprise you."

"Well . . . I . . ." she stuttered to a stop and then started again. "See you at six." She smiled as she turned and left.

When she returned to her office, Suzanne tried to work, but her thoughts kept wandering to her decision to meet Richard for dinner. *How can you go out with someone as nice as Richard if Stephen is still implanted in your brain?*

Since Christmas, she had been dreaming a lot about Stephen. The dreams were always the same. He was standing in the distance surrounded by fog and his arms were outstretched. Suzanne ran toward him, but no matter how fast she ran, she could never reach him.

Stephen had been on her mind so much that finally last night, Suzanne dug out an old address book. She'd put it in her purse and had brought it to work. About three years after their divorce, he had been transferred to Boston and had wanted her to have his number. She didn't know if he even worked for the same company, but she had to try. She closed her office door, sat down at her desk, pulled the number out of her purse, and with shaky hands, dialed it.

Suzanne had to talk to a receptionist, a secretary, and an assistant before she heard Stephen's voice. "Suzanne? Suzanne, is that you?"

"Stephen? I can't believe you're in the same company. But considering what I had to go through to talk with you, you must have advanced up the ladder."

"Well, I've got a plush office with a view."

"Impressive." She smiled.

Silence settled over both ends and finally Stephen broke it. "Why are you calling, Suzanne? After all these years?"

She leaned back in her chair and looked out the windows at the Dallas skyline as she softly answered. "To say I'm sorry."

"Sorry?" Stephen asked.

"Yes. For all the hurt I caused you because of all my childhood pain. You are a beautiful, caring man, Stephen, and I did love you very much. I wanted you to know that."

"Suzanne. I don't know what to say. All these years . . ."

"I know." She quickly got up from her chair. "I'm sorry if I'm upsetting you, but I've made a lot of changes in my life, and I'm trying to clear up all the loose pieces so I can move forward."

"You never remarried, Suzanne?"

"No." She leaned against the edge of her desk, once again gazing out the window.

"Will you ever?" His voice was soft.

"I don't know." She tugged at the collar of her blouse, which suddenly felt tight.

"I don't know if I'll ever remarry either," Stephen said.

"Oh," she paused, shocked. "Oh, I thought you had, or I wouldn't have called."

"Why not?" Stephen asked.

"I don't want you to think I'm . . . not . . . I mean . . ." *He never remarried!* The phone felt hot to her touch. "I've got to go, Stephen."

"Are you afraid, Suzanne? Since I'm not married, does that scare you?"

"No . . . yes . . . I still feel too much." Her eyes scanned the room as if she was a caged animal trying to escape.

"Is that bad?" he insisted.

"Yes . . . no . . . it didn't work then, so it wouldn't work now." She paced around her office.

"Maybe not. Maybe we wouldn't even like each other now," Stephen said quickly, "but I can't get rid of your ghost from my mind. You haunt me in my dreams. I couldn't help you all those years ago. I didn't understand, but now I would learn how to be there for you."

No! This isn't what I wanted. I wanted to close an old chapter with Stephen, not open a new one!

"Suzanne?"

"Yes?" Her eyes darted around the room again.

"Could we be friends?"

"I don't know." She let out a sigh, sat heavily into her chair, and placed her elbows on her desk.

"Could we try?"

She closed her eyes and took a large gulp of air before answering quietly, "Yes."

A brief sigh was heard before Stephen said, "Good. Is it okay if I call you from time to time? Besides, Boston is far away. I can't be a threat to you long distance, can I?"

Suzanne fought to regain her composure and softly laughed. "You're right. I'm being silly. I'd love to have you call me." Suzanne gave Stephen her number, wrote down his home number, and stared at the phone long after they'd said good-bye.

A few moments later, a tap sounded on her door, and she distractedly called, "Come in."

Richard peeked his head around the door. "I'm quitting early. Does that sound good to you? It's Friday, I'm hungry, and it's time for new beginnings." He held out his hand to her.

Suzanne looked into his gentle, smiling eyes. Standing up, she grabbed her purse and held out her hand to him. "You're right. It is time for new beginnings."

Chapter 44

Atlanta, Georgia

I can't believe he'd do this! I thought everything was going so well. Where is he? It was Friday night around eight and Bill wasn't home yet. He hadn't called, Helene had no idea where he was, and her stomach was tied in knots. Thomas was spending the night with a friend, and Lily had gone for the day. *Where is he?* Her mind bounced from concern that he had been in an accident to the nagging memories of his past infidelity.

Over the last several months, she had gotten used to Bill being home around six every night, and on Fridays he would often be home earlier because they had made Fridays their date night. It was "their" night to watch a movie together, enjoy a candlelight dinner, attend an event at the Fox Theatre, or go out to eat.

And now he wasn't here. The dinner she had made was cold, the candles burned down to stubs, and the apple pie she had made for dessert was waiting patiently on the counter.

She curled up on the sofa in the den and waited. Helene had become so excited about their life, their relationship, and what they were finally building together. Now she was terrified that something was wrong and it would all crumble down around her.

When she heard the garage open, Helene jumped off the sofa and walked briskly to the kitchen. As she passed a hall mirror, she glimpsed a face with red, swollen eyes, and mascara smeared on her cheeks. Had she really been crying that much or that long? Her vision in the mirror told her she had.

The door from the garage opened and Bill rushed in, almost running into her. "I'm so late. Honey, I'm so sorry I'm so late." Then he stopped and looked at her. "Helene? Honey, are you okay? What's wrong?"

"You didn't call. It's Friday night and our date night," sobs tumbled from her. "You were supposed to be home. I thought something was wrong. Why didn't you come home when you were supposed to?" A hiccup escaped between the blubbering. "I was worried—you could have been in an accident." She glanced away from him. "Or maybe you went back to old habits."

Surprise engulfed her as Bill's arms quickly wrapped around her. "I should have called. I'm so sorry I worried you." He stepped back and looked at her. "Old habits?"

Helene nodded.

Bill led her to the stools at the kitchen counter. "Honey, I promised you I would never cheat on you again. Ever. And I meant it."

"But," she hiccupped, "a leopard can't change its spots that easily."

"It's a good thing I'm not a leopard," he teased. "Because a man can change his habits. And this man has."

"But why are you so late?"

"I had something very important to do."

"What could have been that important on a Friday night?"

"I had some shopping to do."

"Shopping?" Helene stood up. "Are you serious? Shopping?"

Bill pulled a small square box from his jacket pocket and slipped down onto one knee as he opened the box. "Helene Miller Foster, will you marry me again?"

Helene's mouth dropped open and her eyes bulged with surprise as she looked at a diamond ring surrounded by emeralds in one of the prettiest settings she had ever seen. "What? I mean—we are already married." Helene fell back on the stool. "You're crazy."

"About you. Absolutely." Bill was still on one knee. "So, will you marry me again?"

"What?" Her mind was trying to comprehend what he was talking about.

"We can renew our vows."

"How? Where?"

Bill shifted to his other knee. "Will you say yes so I can get up off my knees?" His voice was playful. "We can talk about all the details then, but my knees are killing me. I'm not as young as I was the first time."

Joyous giggles emanated from Helene. "Yes. Yes, of course I will." As Bill stood up, Helene placed her finger on his lips. "You, Bill Foster, have become a very silly man."

"I know," he agreed.

They were now snuggled together on the sofa in the den as Bill explained his plan to her. If Helene agreed, in two weeks they would renew their vows in the chapel of the church they sometimes attended with just Helene, Bill, Thomas, and the pastor present.

"I want a chance to let you know how serious I am about being the husband you've always deserved. Will you let me do that?"

Helene quietly snuggled in his arms, her heart and mind reeling with excitement and delight. "I will." She snuggled closer, feeling very loved.

She now knew that nothing was ever perfect, but she relished in this new beginning with her husband and son, her newfound connection with her sisters, and the closure with her mother. Her childhood was a part of helping her get to this point in life. Things were what they were, and if she couldn't change it, she needed to learn to live with it in a positive way. Maybe her childhood and her past were like any other family inheritance. It all depended on what she did with it.

Chapter 45

Minneapolis, Minnesota

At first, Alice thought the doorbell was ringing in her dream, but slowly she fought through the fog of sleep to realize that the doorbell was really ringing. Clumsily getting out of bed, she groped for her robe, pulling it around her as she headed for the door.

Looking through the peephole, Alice saw two uniformed officers—a woman and a man. Her stomach dropped.

The kids—oh my God, the kids. No, they're both in bed. It's Mom. It must be Mom. She's dead. She's finally dead.

But why would the police come to the door?

The doorbell rang again.

Well, open the door and find out, dummy.

Alice opened the door but did not remove the chain lock. She peered out of the five-inch gap that the chain permitted. "Yes?"

"Mrs. Hudson? Mrs. Alice Hudson?" The female officer asked as they both showed Alice their badges.

"Yes?"

"May we come in?"

"Why? What's this about?"

"About your husband. Please, may we come in?"

Fear consumed her. If it involved Jake, it couldn't be good. "Okay," she whispered, "but my children are sleeping, and I don't want to wake them."

Alice closed the door, removed the chain lock, and opened the door to let the officers in. As the officers walked into her living room, fearful memories of Jake filled her mind. *He's turned me in. He told them I threatened to have him killed. They're going to arrest me. What's gonna happen to the kids? I was so stupid to think I could get away with it.*

Once they were inside, the female officer took Alice's hand and motioned her into a chair. "We're sorry to have to inform you, Mrs. Hudson, that your husband was killed tonight."

"Killed? What do you mean killed?"

The male officer looked directly at her and replied. "He was in an automobile accident. He had been drinking. He ran his car into a telephone pole at a very high speed."

"Oh my God," Alice slumped back against the chair.

"Mrs. Hudson," the male officer continued, "did your husband have any enemies?"

Alice's thoughts were jumbled. *Jake's dead. Did I do this?* She was trying to make sense of what they were saying. "Enemies? Jake? Well, I don't know. I mean, not everybody liked him because Jake could be a mean man. But I don't think he had no enemies."

"Do you know of anyone who would want to kill your husband?"

"Kill him?" Alice gulped and tried not to panic. "No, no. I don't know anyone who would kill him."

"Where were you tonight, Mrs. Hudson?" The officer looked at her.

"Have you been to Duluth lately?" the female officer fired another question at her.

"What are you talking about?" Alice raised her voice and stood up. "Tell me why you think that somebody wanted to kill Jake. Why are you asking me where I was tonight and when I was last in Duluth?" Her hands were shaking.

"When the men who were at the gas station across the road got to your husband, he was screaming about being chased. His words were, 'He's after me. He's gonna kill me. She did it. He's really gonna kill me.' But the guys who saw the accident said your husband's pickup was the only one on the road at that time, and it was a straight stretch, so he didn't lose control at a corner. It looks like he drove right into the pole. Why would your husband think someone was trying to kill him?"

"I don't know." Alice paused. "When Jake was drinking, he'd say funny things. It's like he'd go out of his head."

"You mean hallucinate," the male officer furnished her with the word.

"Yeah, hallucinate." Then reality slapped Alice hard in the face. Her mind continued to function, but her feelings shut down. "Jake's dead? I guess I'll have to have a funeral. How do I tell the kids? Does his mother know? Jake's dead?"

"Mrs. Hudson, are you okay?" Gentle female hands touched hers.

"Okay? Yeah, I'm okay. I gotta call my mother. No, I can't do that, she's not here. I'll call Helene. She'll know what to do. I'll call Helene."

"Mrs. Hudson, can we call someone for you?"

"No, I'm fine. I'm okay. Where is Jake? Who do I call?"

The officers gave Alice a piece of paper with phone numbers on it.

"Mom? Mom, what's wrong?" Sarah stood in hallway in her pajamas with her hair tousled about from sleep, looking at the two officers. "What's happened, Mom?"

"Sarah." Alice looked at the officers with a blank stare. "That's my daughter, Sarah. You can go now."

"We won't leave until we know you're okay, Mrs. Hudson."

"Mom! What's wrong?" Panic seemed to grip Sarah.

Alice walked over, put her arms around her daughter, and pulled her close. "It's your father, Sarah. He's dead."

"Dead? He's dead?" Hysterical laughter escaped from between Sarah's lips. "How can he be dead?"

The night became surreal for Alice as she went through all the motions. Once the police officers left, she woke Sam, and they all sat together, just holding each other. Then as morning came, Alice made the necessary phone calls and plans for Jake's funeral.

It was close to noon when Alice tucked an exhausted Sarah and Sam back into their beds. Then, going to her bedroom, she dropped to her knees and cried tears of relief.

Chapter 46

Minneapolis, Minnesota

The warm light that had been behind her for so long was starting to draw her away from the room in which her body lay. "Anna, it's time now," a strong, kind voice beckoned her.

She had floated above her humanly body for months, watching her daughters and loving them. She had been given a second chance. She had been able to see them change, grow, and begin to love her. They were special women, her daughters.

In the beginning, she thought they'd drive her mad. She was a dying woman, and they filled her sick room with their troubles and their angers. Such pettiness! But they worked it out. Anna thought they'd never talk to each other, but they changed. Each day they got closer to each other and to her. She was so proud of each one.

That Helene, she was always the strong one. She was so mad at Anna in the beginning, but then she softened. The warm socks at Christmas and the flowers every week—they were always so pretty. And that family of hers was wonderful! Anna was going to have handsome great-grandchildren that she could watch over, and she looked forward to it.

Anna's spiritual heart had been burdened as she had listened to what Suzanne and Sarah had gone through with their fathers. She didn't understand why people did things like that to innocent children. She certainly had a lot of questions she wanted to ask when she got to the other side.

The last time Suzanne was here she looked different. She had softened and just talked about her feelings. Anna's soul had cried and danced at the same time. Suzanne would be okay.

Alice had still worried Anna some up until today when she had come to Anna's room. She had lost weight over the weeks since she had visited and was holding her head higher than she ever had before.

Once Anna had seen all three of her daughters happy in their lives, she knew it was time for her to leave. She could now be released from the limbo of her coma. She could follow the warm light that was beckoning her.

As Anna's spirit left this world, she whispered through the gentle breeze, "I'll be with you, my daughters. I'll always be with you."

Acknowledgments

It takes a team of people to transform a manuscript into a book, and I've had an amazing team with me on my journey from writer to author. Eternal gratitude goes to my my editor, Allison Itterly, and my publisher, Katy Whipple, for their patience, knowledge, and talent as we tweaked and honed to get the story to where it needed to be. Helene, Alice, Suzanne, and I all thank you.

A big thank you to the rest of the team with BQB Publishing—Heidi Grauel, Dave Grauel, and Robin Krauss. Each one of them added their expertise and their hearts to help me bring this project to fruition.

Love and heartfelt thanks to Glenn Leidich, my wonderful husband and friend, for encouraging my passion to write, dealing with my frustrations and self-doubts during the process, and understanding when I stayed in my pajamas for an entire weekend, locked away with my computer and my manuscript.

My daughter Lori Lee has always been my biggest fan and read the manuscript so many times before I submitted it that she knows these characters as well as I do. Her love and support kept me moving forward.

Deep appreciation goes to my own mom who is no longer with us. From her, I learned strength, persistence, and determination. And a special recognition and thank you to my own siblings—Darlene, Beverly, Mike, Kathleen, Pamela, and Brian—for the memories, struggles, triumphs, and family inheritance that we all share.